Encore

To Vicky,

Love is a dance
between two hearts
dancing as one ♡♡

RUTH CLAMPETT

Ruth Clampett ♡

ISBN: 978-0-9966857-9-5

Cover Design:
Michele Catalano Creative

Cover Photograph/Graphics:
Fotolia

Content Editor:
Angela Borda

Copy Editor:
Melissa of There For You Editing

Interior Design & Formatting:
Christine Borgford of Type A Formatting

"Here's to the ones who dream,
foolish as they may seem.
Here's to the hearts that ache;
here's to the mess we make."

~ La La Land

Encore

1. The Prince of Awkward

"I'M NOT GOING TO A male strip club with our female co-workers! Are you nuts?" I say to my team partner, Billy, as I feel my face flush.

He slowly pulls my ergonomic chair away from my desk, and then swivels it so we're facing each other. "Oh yes you are," he replies with an arched brow and playful grin.

It's near quitting time at World Tech Solutions, a glass monolith in the mid-Wilshire corridor of Los Angeles devoted to the fine art of computer programing. WTS has made a concerted effort to hire more women than traditional tech programing companies do, and tonight you can really feel that fact since more than half of the cubicles surrounding us are empty. Most of the women on our floor snuck out early for the girls' night out in honor of our team leader, Brittany, getting married. Apparently, they're going to a male stripper revue.

Billy isn't the first one to push me to come along. In the break room earlier I overheard the girls talking about what to wear tonight before they dared Billy and I to join them. There was even mention of bringing extra panties so they can throw them onstage for the dancers. I had trouble restraining my look of horror. I could only imagine the skimpy outfits they're going to show up in and the debauchery that will ensue.

"You should come. They have girl strippers, too," Katie said in a teasing tone before winking at me.

I pushed my glasses up my nose and dragged my fingers through my hair. "Women strippers?" I asked, confused yet somewhat relieved that she didn't know I have no interest in disrobed females, especially since I'm not keen on my co-workers analyzing my personal life. "Isn't it a club focused on entertaining women?"

Katie nods her head, encouraging me on. "Yes, but I've also heard it's an *anything can happen* kind of place."

I was suddenly picturing demure Katie with ruffled hair and pink cheeks as a barely clad woman worked her over, and I stifled back a laugh and focused on the bigger issue.

"I don't understand why getting married gives you the license to put yourself in a dubious situation right before your big day. Isn't that counter-intuitive?"

"Oh, Charlie!" she said with a laugh before walking away.

Now back in the safety of my cubical, I search my mind for excuses to get out of going. I always feel like an outsider at these social events with my co-workers, which only makes me feel worse about myself. But Billy is the most stubborn, unrelenting person I know.

Plopping down uninvited to the chair on the edge of my cubicle, he leans forward with a conspiratorial look. He rubs the stubble on his chin and lowers his voice. "Do you know how horny they will get after those guys put on their show . . . rubbing against them? Touching them?" His eyes are wide with excitement.

Billy has sex on the brain. There isn't a day that goes by where it doesn't come up in conversation.

"Is Claire going?" I ask. He's had a thing for Claire ever since they worked on the Anderson Baker project last year. She had a steady boyfriend at the time and was off limits, but that didn't stop him from mooning over her. Recently word in the break room was that they broke up, and I suspect that's why Billy is so keen to go tonight.

He shrugs, trying to look casual. "I don't know. I texted her to see if she needed a ride but she never responded."

"You know, Billy, I'm not really up for this tonight. I'm tired."

"From playing video games all night?" he asks, with an exaggerated eye roll. I'm pretty sure that everyone at WTS knows I don't have any real friends outside my job, or a social life.

"Maybe," I respond sheepishly. He doesn't know that I actually spend more time online working the stock market than building dystopian worlds on my Xbox.

"Come on, you need to be my wingman. I can't show up alone for something like this . . . that's creepy!"

"And the two of us showing up isn't?" I ask with an arched brow.

He leans over closer to me. "I hear that the girl strippers also do a number with the girl customers on stage. I saw some video on their website and it was scorching. It gave me some *sexaaaay* feelings, if you know what I mean."

I try not to cringe at his intonation as he waggles his eyebrows.

"Is that so?" I imagine it in my head with a sexier encounter than the one I pictured with Katie, and I don't feel even slightly titillated. It's not the first time I've wondered why the idea of women touching each other has never turned me on at all. But then again, I always knew I was wired differently than everyone, not only by how I think, but in who I desire.

"Besides, you owe me." Billy folds his arms over his chest.

I think back to the week before last when he stayed late with me to find the glitch in my program that was due to our client the next day.

Releasing a long sigh, I shake my head. "All right. I would've been screwed if you hadn't have helped me out last week."

His grin grows wide. "So you'll go? I'll pick you up since parking is a bitch there."

I nod, a feeling of doom creeping up my spine. But seriously, a bunch of women screaming as built men seductively roll their hips, while women stuff money in their tiny briefs, doesn't sound like entertainment to me.

"I'll get you at 7:15." He dashes out of my cube before I can change my mind.

I'm still thinking of ways I can get out of going as I inch my Audi through the heavy traffic down Wilshire Blvd. toward our condo. World Tech wasn't my first choice in the programming jobs that I was offered out of Cal Tech, but it was ideal in that it was just over a mile to get home. Now I have the peace of mind knowing that if my sister, Sasha, is suddenly in crisis, I'm close. Of course the added bonus is my commute is nothing like most of my co-workers who travel in from the valley or even farther where they can afford the rents. L.A is a crazy expensive city.

I turn onto Robertson and stop-and-go-drive past the chic boutiques and restaurants lining the exclusive street. For a guy who grew up in Paso Robles, I never imagined living someplace like L.A., especially in such an upscale part of town. But life has a way of taking a sharp turn when you least expect it, and Sasha and I living parentless on the edge of Beverly Hills is proof of that.

There are areas in the City of Angels that I may have fit in better, or at least felt less conspicuous, but our condo is two short blocks away from Cedar Sinai Medical Center and that was the first item on our list of priories. Caregiver Estella, in particular, likes to walk Sasha to her appointments, which allows Sasha fresh air and sun, and they avoid the nightmare of the parking structures and getting Sasha in and out of the van. It's a win all the way around.

The final part of my drive this day is a cruise through the lavender tunnel of trees on Clark Street, the result of our jacaranda trees in full bloom. Their blooming season is short but brilliant. I'm mesmerized by the delicate blossoms falling like soft rain every time the breeze blows, showering the streets with a blanket of violet perfection.

WHEN I GET HOME SASHA looks like she's ready to roll out the door. My sister, despite being disabled from the car accident that changed our entire family's future, has a busier social life than I do.

"Where are you off to?" I ask with an encouraging smile. She's more dressed up than usual and she looks really pretty. I wonder if anyone will be able to look past her wheelchair to see how extraordinary she really is.

"Emily and I are seeing the new *Fifty Shades* movie with the girls!"

I can't help but feel a warmth flow through me at the big grin on her face. Nothing makes me happier than when Sasha is happy. And although I can't understand the allure of the romance books and movies that got her through her complicated recovery six years ago, I thank God for them. The friends she's made from the book groups she's connected with are meaningful to her. As it turns out, a group of them live in L.A. and she gets together with them frequently.

"Come with us!" she insists.

"Is this *welcome to girl power week*?" I tease. "You're not going to believe this, but the reason I can't join you is because I'm going with a group of women from work to a male strip club tonight."

Her eyebrows knit together as she bites back a grin. "Are you going to strip?"

I roll my eyes at her. "Of course not."

"You could you know. You're really handsome, and with all that soccer club stuff back in school, and now your time spent at the gym has paid off. You have a great body. Plus, you look like a cross between Chris Pine and Clark Kent!"

"Um thanks . . . but I really don't think this is a conversation I should be having with my sister." I'm also aware that she says this stuff to make me feel better about myself, so I know not to take her compliments seriously.

"Oh whatever!" she laughs. "Well, no matter what you're going to do, I'm happy you're getting out. You need to have a life that doesn't involve screen time. You know how much Mom and Dad wanted that for you." She reaches her hand out to me.

I walk over to her and take it, gently squeezing it in my hand. "I know." We share a meaningful gaze. I swear I don't know what I'd do without Sasha in my life.

The doorbell rings and I'm sure it's not Billy yet. Sasha rolls to the door and opens it, then rolls back so it will clear as her friend steps inside.

"Ready?" Emily asks Sasha with a grin, holding up an eye mask that appears to be shaped out of black lace. She finally glances over at me and waves. "Hey, Charlie."

"Hi," I say, hoping I sound friendly. Emily has been really good to Sasha and I'm grateful to see how their friendship has helped my sister build a new life for herself.

"You ready?" she asks, and when Sasha nods they both look eager to get to the theater.

"You want me to help load her up?" I ask Emily.

"No, I'm a pro at that thing. We're good," she replies.

Once I've made sure Sasha has the keys for the wheelchair-equipped van, and closed the door behind them, I head into my room to shower and change into clean clothes.

Billy arrives a few minutes early and scowls at me as I open the door to my apartment.

"What?" I ask, holding out my hands in frustration.

"You're wearing that, man?" he asks as he yanks on my oversized plaid shirt I've pulled over my favorite Star Wars T-shirt.

"What's wrong with what I'm wearing?"

I know he means well, but Billy's censure humiliates me—like I can never do anything right. Even something as simple as choosing something to wear for this type of event eludes me.

"You'll never score anyone but a virgin-geek in that get-up."

"I'm not looking to score tonight."

He shakes his head, then points to my bedroom. "You need to put on those jeans you have that you say are too tight, and the blue T-shirt that makes your shoulders look big."

"Oh, for fuck's sake," I grumble.

He taps his foot on the floor. "I'm waiting."

I return a couple of minutes later with my hands jammed in my pockets. These jeans reveal way more than I'm interested in sharing.

"See, now you're worthy of being my wingman!"

I study Billy. He's not the best looking guy in the world with his thin build and mop of curly brown hair, but his personality is really engaging. I have to give him credit, he carries himself with confidence, like he's all that. Besides, everyone at work seems to know and like him. He's also been really nice to me despite my awkwardness, which is really saying something.

MY NERVES FLARE AS WE approach the entrance to Wild Nights as I'm sure we'll be turned away, but then I calm down when the guard letting people into the club gives us a once-over, and immediately waves us inside. I guess guys coming to an essentially male strip club is encouraged and not that unusual. It's one of the benefits of living in L.A. where anything goes.

The entrance and lobby lead us to the main room; a vast space with a high ceiling painted black that's scattered with spotlights with different colored gels. There are also strands of silver balls and small mirror pieces that reflect the colored light throughout the room. Between the movement of the lights, the sparkles, and the rich colors, it's very dramatic.

The stage runs along the front of the room, framed with velvet curtains. The first three rows of tables next to the stage are for VIP seating, and near the middle and back there are rows of chairs.

Billy spots the group of tables up front where the girls from work have settled and he winds his way through the dark club to get to them. I follow close behind. He circles the group until he gets to Claire, and he gently tugs on a lock of her hair so she turns around. Her look of surprise shifts into a smile and the girl sitting next to Claire scoots down to the last empty seat so Billy can sit.

I stand uncomfortably behind them, wondering what to do, and Billy turns and points to an empty chair at the next table . . . so much for being his wingman. I wish I wasn't so damn awkward. In an intense moment of regret I contemplate leaving and Ubering home, but Davis calls out to me, pointing to an empty seat next to him. "Hey, Charlie, here's a seat."

I join him and sit down, then realize I'm at the table with the bride-to-be and her posse. They're already exuberant, and she's wearing this thing on her head that resembles a cheap Vegas wedding veil and a white satin banner draped across her chest.

I'm always amazed at the weird rituals that our society comes up with during significant life events. From what I can see, Brittany's tiny white dress, which I assume is to signify a racy wedding dress, is quite revealing. If I were getting married I'm pretty sure that I wouldn't want my bride-to-be wearing this get-up into a club where the air will soon be thick with testosterone and the feverish hope of female fantasies to be realized.

I remember Sasha watching that movie, *Magic Mike*, once and from the little bit I saw, this crowd looks tamer compared to the one in the movie. But then again the main show hasn't even started yet. I see tonight as a sociological study for me more than anything. This set-up is like an ancient Roman Coliseum fight featuring a brave gladiator trying to survive the claws and ravenous appetite of the wild creatures who circle him.

I'm relieved when the waiter stops at our table so the girls can order a second round. I order a shot and a Heineken in the hopes of loosening up. The waiter is shirtless with nothing but a bow tie from the waist up. He's tan, toned, and unquestionably good looking. As my gaze scans the room, I realize without surprise that this is the case of every man working here.

I'm quietly thankful that Billy wouldn't let me wear my *Star Wars* T-shirt. I feel much less conspicuous in what I'm wearing. I bet Sasha would say I could work here, but you'd have to hold a gun to my head to try to be professional at a job where you wear no shirt, have your body oiled up, and allow random girls to grab your ass.

The girl Alice, sitting next to me, is trying her best to flirt with our waiter and he flirts back, winking at her before he moves on to the next table. I notice her shudder with delight when he turns away. This guy clearly knows how to earn his tips.

About thirty minutes have passed, which I've spent mainly nursing my beer and watching various groups of girls tumble over to the dance floor, moving in groups in a pattern that reminds me of migrating birds. Suddenly the announcer comes over the loudspeaker, instructing people to take their seats because the show is about to begin.

My entire body stiffens when the boom of music blasts through the room and the line of men saunter across the stage in step with the heavy bass beat. An ego-deflating feeling hits me only moments later. Every single one of them is everything I'm not: confident, uniquely handsome, and aware of their allure in an intoxicating way. I swallow the word that comes to mind and lingers on the edge of my brain back. *Sexy.* They are blood-boiling sexy as they thrust their hips forward and flex their sculpted biceps. Each one's ass is tighter than the last, and an uncomfortable feeling starts at my toes and tingles up my legs until it's settled into my groin. I'm getting aroused, and the fact that I'm surrounded by women I work with—who could notice me getting worked up—is only making this worse.

The magnetic pull I've always felt toward men is so primal it's hard for me to define in this situation. I've never been attracted to men who strut down the street like sleek tigers choosing their mates. The tattooed men in gay porn, with their earrings and cocky confidence do nothing for me.

I guess I'm more comfortable with men in my league. I think of Leo, my shy science project partner in high school who taught me to computer hack, but more importantly taught me what it felt like to have another boy kiss and touch me. He woke something in me that made me feel heat and desire, and he made me feel whole. Leo never made me feel awkward or like a loser. That vague feeling of wrongness that ate away at me, could feel right when his lips pressed against mine.

I try not to think about Leo anymore, because those thoughts make me relive the worst night of my life. I hope he's okay . . . actually, more than okay, I hope he's happy wherever he is.

Grabbing my beer and slugging it down, I frantically scan the room to see if there's a waiter around to bring me another. I eye the bar but I can't possibly walk over there with this bulge in my pants. Holy hell . . . if only I'd stayed at home to avoid this potential soul searing, public humiliation.

In an attempt to calm my libido down, I try averting my gaze from the strutting men on stage, studying my chewed up cuticles and imagining our grocery list, but the pull to look back up at the tanned bodies, oiled so they shimmer under the theater lights, is a magnetic pull that I can't seem to resist.

My eyes widen as the front dancer yanks off his slacks, which are designed to pull apart, and is left with only a G-string on—a G-string that barely contains his package. It's like a bull's eye my intense stare is unable to shift away from. Embarrassed about what's happening in my pants, I'm lucky that everyone in the club has their gazes fixed to the gods on stage and they don't notice my hand slipping between my legs to adjust myself.

I can feel my blood racing through my veins and my heartbeat pounding so hard my chest feels tight. I'm feeling lustful things outside my comfort zone that I've never felt in public before. I wonder what it would be like to be pressed up against one of these men, to run my fingers over their oiled abs and then slide them down inside their G-string. The image makes me take a sharp breath, and I lean back in my chair and spread my legs farther apart under the table.

This isn't the first time I've wondered about what it would be like to be naked with a man sporting this kind of body and moves, but I'd never seen men who look like this, and are practically naked, only feet away from me. Sure I know lots of built guys from when I played soccer, but they were all about the game and didn't reek of this sexy swagger, nor have dark, handsome faces that made me sense danger and fueled a desire to abandon my restraint. The longer I sit mesmerized at the dancers' movements—the way their gazes burn through the audience, focusing on one woman at a time—the more I can't deny something I have tried to push down for a long, long time.

There's a primal thirst inside of me that no woman will ever quench, and until I've found my true partner, a man whose very touch leaves me breathless, I'll never be satisfied.

I've fought this feeling for years, and not only because I was teased about it in school. Being bookish and sensitive left me vulnerable to other kids' cruelty. At one point I thought getting involved with soccer would improve things. I developed a laser focus to get good at the game, and rise above my low place in the social pecking order. The result of my hard work was that I was talented enough to be part of an elite soccer club, but I still got teased as soon as they sniffed out that I wasn't fixated on girls. They were downright cruel about it, all but destroying any confidence or self-worth I still had.

As for family judgment, my parents are gone now . . . not like they would have been torn up about my desire to be with a man. They were as liberal and open-minded as a confused teenager could hope for. And my sister, the most progressive person I know, is active working social media to fight for gay rights, among other causes. But there's always been something nagging at me about the biology of humans and that natural order gives us urges to find our mates and reproduce, thus continuing the human chain. I'm someone driven to follow rules, do what's expected, not ruffle feathers. I also know that I probably adopted that mindset as an excuse because I was scared out of my mind that I'd be rejected. Denial of who I was became a way of life.

And besides, even if I wanted to pursue being with a man like I was with Leo, in this cutting-edge City of Angels I can't figure out a way to tip-toe into that world. When I drive through West Holly-wood on a weekend night the streets are sexually charged, and from my viewpoint the prowling men exude aggression and entitlement. Meanwhile, I'm like a toddler trying to figure out how to crawl before I walk. Surely I would be laughed at, or even worse, ignored. What if I can't find my place in the gay community either?

I manage to slowly calm down my urges by fixing my gaze on anything but the stage. I study the different tables of women, and take note of the random men scattered throughout the crowd. I wonder if they were coerced to come, like I was, or if they think the night holds some type of promise for them that allows them to sit patiently while surrounded by women distracted by the wall of testosterone seeping off the stage.

When I'm adequately composed, I wander over to the bar for another beer . . . anything to blur the vivid, lustful tableaus my mind keeps conjuring.

"What can I get you?" the bartender calls out.

"A Heineken," I answer, watching as he grabs a bottle and deftly flips the cap off.

I can't help but notice that his bright smile is dazzling against his warm-toned Hispanic coloring and smooth skin. *Is every single man in this place gorgeous?* His face is markedly appealing: large, friendly eyes, defined cheekbones, and full lips that when smiling create dimples in his cheeks. I can't help but stare at him wordlessly.

He's not tall, but incredibly built, and holds himself like he's a giant among men. He wears his confidence as impressively as his swagger and the perfect way he fills out his black, fitted T-shirt. I don't have to let my stare linger too long to realize he must lift weights or something equally rigorous to have a body in that kind of shape.

"Did you bring your girlfriend here tonight, or did she drag you here?" he surprises me by asking.

"Oh, I don't have a girlfriend," I reply, sounding too eager. I can feel my cheeks color.

"Are you looking for one?" he teases. "Because you wouldn't be the first guy to come here with that in mind. And believe me, there's every reason to think it's a good idea."

"No, that's not it. The girls at work dragged me here. It's one of those bachelorette things."

He rolls his eyes. "Yeah, we get a lot of those. It's like a license to get wild. I guess I can't blame them, though. We all know that whatever they do, their husbands-to-be are probably doing worse."

"I wouldn't know. I haven't been to one of those."

He shrugs. "They're definitely not my thing so I haven't either," he says, studying me while he does. "What's your name?"

"Charles, but my friends call me Charlie." I take a swig of beer, trying to come off as cool and detached. It's a long shot that I'll pull that off. "What's yours?"

He extends his hand over the bar to shake mine. "I'm Ramon. So, Charles, that sounds like a prince's name. Are you ever called Prince Charles?"

I laugh. "Hardly!"

"Well, Charlie, this place is about fun, so relax and keep an open mind. You may be surprised and have a better time than you imagine."

He winks at me and I'm so flustered that I take a sharp breath.

I'm about to ask him another question when a girl calls out to get his attention from farther down on the bar. I lean forward, trying to be subtle as he walks toward her. He fills out his jeans so perfectly that my mouth starts to water. I quickly turn from the bar so he doesn't notice me lusting after him. The last thing this bartender needs is someone interfering with his job. Besides, he's probably just being nice to me for the tip.

I return to the table to find Davis, but my mind is on Ramon and that dimpled captivating smile.

As the numbers continue, I keep glancing back at the bar while I finish my beer. My gaze searches for Ramon, but another handsome man has replaced him as the bartender. I'm taken aback by how disappointed I feel. I was hoping to talk to him more.

Suddenly everything shifts because despite the music still booming the room lights come up. Three of the performers from the stage are combing the audience and they approach our group of tables. The tallest of the dancers approaches Brittany and holds out his arm to escort her to the stage. Another dancer behind him has picked out Katie. And a surge of panic blasts through me when a beautiful girl in what could be described as a very minimal bikini approaches me.

Her hand glides along my shoulder before reaching out for me. "Come on, handsome," she coaxes.

I sit frozen in my seat, trying to figure out how to get out of this, when several of the girls from the party join in the effort to get me up. Rather than put up a fight, I take the woman's hand and follow her toward the stage.

My heart is racing and not in a good way. I start to wonder how sexy these shows get. Is she going to dance around me while I watch? I swallow hard, trying to convince myself that I can take one for the team . . . can't I?

Everything becomes a blur to me as my panic builds. I am passed off to a stagehand and then led down a short walkway and flight of stairs until we step into the blinding light of the stage. The handler directs me to sit in a sturdy chair that says "Best Man" on the left side of what looks like a throne and another chair that says "Maid of Honor" a little past it that looks identical to mine.

I slowly sink down until I'm sitting, and I'm blinking rapidly trying to manage my flight or fight instincts. People are going to laugh at me; I just know it. The guy leans down close to me.

"Okay, dude, just relax. The first part of the number is all about the bride-to-be. Then the dancers will do their number with you and the other girl. You don't have to do anything but sit there. You don't touch or talk to them as they dance, unless they encourage it as part of their act. Let them do their thing. Got it?"

I numbly nod.

"Good," he says. "I'll come get you and direct you back to your seat when it's over."

"But—" I start to say in protest.

"No worries, dude. Stacy is hot as hell. I'd be happy to trade places with you right now, but I've got a job to do and I've got to bring home the bread. You know what I mean?'

I nod again.

I try to look out at the audience to see if I can spot Billy, but everything is a gray haze under the glare of the light. So my gaze shifts to the stage and Brittany who looks thrilled about the whole thing.

Brittany turns toward me, and waves. "Ready, Charlie?" she calls out.

I wave back. "Sure!" I reply with the most manufactured enthusiasm I can muster under this freaky circumstance. *Why didn't I stay home?*

The stage lights dim and the music pumps up. I can feel the beats of my heart synchronize with the music and throb through every part of my body. A wave of dread washes over me knowing I'm going to regret this in profound ways.

A new set of roaming lights move across the stage and then I hear cheers erupt as a male and female dancer strut toward Brittany. Because they're in a position closer to the front of the stage I can't see exactly what's happening, but from the roar of the crowd it must be good. Squinting my eyes, I glance over their way to see the female dancer behind the throne arranging her veil, but the spotlight is on the male who is straddling Brittany's legs as he towers over her while thrusting his hips forward.

I hear squeals from the audience, but none as loud as Brittany's. *Good lord, what is he doing to her?*

Distracted by what's happening to Brittany, I stop worrying about what lies in store for me, but I shouldn't have relaxed because next thing I know the male dancer is on stage approaching Katie, and the woman dancer sashays over to me. Part two of this spectacle is apparently about to begin.

My fingers dig into my thighs as she starts to run her hands all over me and swing her hips from side to side. My gaze is fixed on my hands until she slips her fingers under my chin and lifts my head, so that I'm forced to look her in the eye. Leaning into me, she skims her breasts against my face, while the audience sitting closest to us starts to hoot and holler.

I close my eyes until I feel her back away, but when I glance up she's now practically on my lap grinding her hips. She smells like a combination of flowers and that goopy stuff girls put in their hair. I guess she's pretty enough, and she has a great body as girls go, but she also looks worn out under her fake smile. I'd be willing to bet that she came to Hollywood to be an actress, never thinking she'd have to end up here to pay the rent.

My mind shifts to a program I had worked on once for an on-line matchmaking site that was suffering from a sluggish algorithm. My efforts may have increased their online visibility and upped their click-throughs, but in the end there's either chemistry and a primal attraction between two people matched up or not, and in this case there is less than zero.

She slows down and maybe it's because I'm not responding to her, or maybe it's the way the number goes. But she doesn't seem into it . . . just going through the moves. I can relate to that feeling. It reminds me of the two times I tried to sleep with a woman, the result of which was the confirmation that the female species did nothing for me sexually.

When she touches my face again I give her a tight smile of

encouragement. After all, this public humiliation has to be ending soon. Sure enough, after a few more grinds and rubbing her tits in my face again, she backs off, accepts the tip I managed to remember to give her, and dances toward the other side of the stage.

Turning in my chair, I look behind me to see the stagehand watching everything going on with a protective eye. I was hoping we were done, but he isn't giving any indication that he's about to come get me. When our gazes meet, he grins and gives me a thumbs-up like I must be the happiest guy on earth right now. He has no idea.

There's another round of cat-calls from the pent-up audience when the dancers step to the front of the stage and dance provocatively to amp up the viewers. Suddenly, they split apart again and move toward us.

My mind is momentarily jumbled, and when the images sort themselves I realize that the second male dancer is approaching me. I can't help but stare at his incredible body as my gaze slowly works its way up from his muscular thighs, to his abs, built chest, and shoulders . . . and when I get to his face I realize I'm blinking repeatedly.

Apparently, the confusion that must be evident in my expression is amusing my dancer, because he nods and winks at me before leaning in closer, and I feel a flush from his hot breath against my ear. "Hey, Prince Charlie . . . ready to have some fun?"

I can feel my eyes bug out and a lump form in my throat. It *is* him. "Ramon?" I ask in a strangled voice.

"The one and only," he answers seductively. "I thought you could use a little loosening up." He widens his legs and steps closer, straddling me, then runs his fingers through my hair while he slowly rotates his hips.

"You're gay?" I ask, my mouth gaping open.

His bold laugh makes my cheeks color. "Oh, baby," he croons, "you're so damn cute. Ask me again when I'm done with you." He winks and then slowly rocks his hips forward, making me want to rip his briefs off. They fit like a second skin, the dark fabric clinging to every flexing muscle and bulge.

"Oh God, oh God, oh God," I whisper, feeling like my face is on fire.

He backs away again to dance around me, brushing his hand over my shoulders and down my thighs while he moves. Every sweep of his touch electrifies me until I'm sizzling like a lit fuse.

I've never seen anyone—other than on music shows or videos—who could dance with such a natural rhythm and sexual vibe. He turns toward the audience partway through the dance and then bends forward so his ass is presented to me, and I'm in agony not to touch it. He has the most perfect, gorgeous ass I've ever seen. I blush thinking about what it would be like in this moment if we were alone, and he wasn't wearing the tiny briefs. *Oh God,* I think with a sigh.

I'm trying as best I can to hide how turned on I am. Has there ever been more proof that I'm so completely gay?

I'm having trouble catching my breath when he straightens and swivels, then straddles my legs as he thrusts his pelvis tauntingly close to my face.

Shifting back until he's almost sitting on my knees, he then slowly drags his way up my thighs until his ass is against my crotch and he sinks down firmly enough to know I'm painfully hard for him.

The edges of his mouth turn up with delight. "Oh, Charlie," he moans. "You feel so fucking good."

I swallow thickly as he slowly grinds over my erection. I feel like I'm going to lose my mind I'm so turned on.

He runs his fingers along my jaw. "I had a feeling you'd like this," he says in a deep, sexy voice. "You do, don't you?"

I nod frantically, desperately hoping he won't stop. In my lustful haze, I don't care that there's an audience watching me come undone by this man. As much as I'm trying to restrain myself, in this moment his touch, his masculinity is everything I want and need. If only I could touch him the way he's touching me.

And as if he could hear my thoughts, he lifts himself off my lap and while still straddling me, he takes my hands and guides them up and down his sculpted thighs until my palms are burning, then slides them to his rear and presses against my fingers until I have one of his perfectly tight, round ass cheeks in each hand. *Holy hell.* As I grasp him, he slowly thrusts his hips while I gape open mouthed at his crotch.

There's no mistaking the thick, long bulge in his tiny shorts. Ramon is hard and I have an overwhelming urge to taste him, to slowly suck his cock in between my lips. I have never seen a man as sexy as he is. The way he moves has me hypnotized.

I want him, I want him, I want him.

I'm on fire, every part of me burning to consume him. As he gyrates slowly into me, I crave to run my tongue over his bronzed abs, to bite my way across his muscular shoulders until my teeth scrape up his neck and along his chiseled jaw. *I want . . . I want . . .*

But suddenly I realize the song is winding down and he's slowly pulling away from me, out of my grasp and in a moment, out of my life. I feel a surge of panic. I can't lose this feeling of hope for more, this physical ravaged hunger of a neglected and desperate man.

"Ramon," I whisper, as I watch him move to the front of the stage, down the stairs, and into the audience with the other dancers.

I'm so stunned that I almost don't notice the stagehand shake my shoulder.

"Come on, dude. Time to get you back to your seat."

I blink to determine if I'm awake or if all of this has been a dream. If so, I wish I'd never woken. In my dreams, I would've followed Ramon until we were in the dark hallway leading to the bar, and I would pull him into my arms and kiss him with every ounce of passion I have.

I clench my jaw as the guy takes my arm and leads me off the stage. In the dark hallway, I have an epiphany as he leads me toward the bright light of the theater. No matter how hopeless my prospects, I can't keep ignoring my desire to have intimacy and a connection with another man. I shut all that away after the accident, which in the end has caused me to lose much more than just my parents. I'm not really living, and I need to claim my life . . . whatever it's meant to be.

As soon as I return to my place at the table, the girls are going on about the female dancer who danced for Katie.

"She even touched my boobs!" Katie exclaimed.

"And you liked it!" Deb called out.

Katie shrugs with a grin. "Maybe I did."

There are more squeals until Deb brings up my racy experience and they erupt in excited moans over Ramon's seductive dance.

"I'm sure that was uncomfortable for you, Charlie, but it was friggin' hot," Katie croons. "That man is perfection!"

"He can thrust his hips against me any day!" Deb says with a heavy sigh. "It's not fair that all that hotness was wasted on another dude!"

I bite my tongue. There wasn't a single second of his performance that was wasted on me. I'm startling awake now and I may never sleep again.

That night I lie awake for hours. I stroke myself thinking of Ramon and come twice, not even caring that my growing obsession with him is completely irrational. I've never been an irrational person; I've followed the rules and taken care of my responsibilities. Now none of that seems to matter. All I want is to have Ramon straddle me again and whisper in my ear, "Hey, Prince Charlie . . . ready for more of me?"

"Yes, yes . . ." I moan as I come again with a ragged breath and a flood of need for more and more.

2. The Beautiful Man

THE NEXT FEW DAYS I'M a walking, talking mannequin, my head as empty as an abandoned house. Most of the weekend I stare at my computer screen in a lust-filled stupor. Monday I do just enough to make my team think I'm working, but my mind is back with the caramel-skinned, beautiful man who made me feel more.

By Tuesday I've decided that I can't continue on like this and I have to take action. After work I go home and shower, play a video game I couldn't give a fuck about, then shower again until it's late enough to go back to Wild Times. The door guy narrows his eyes when I approach him alone.

"My girlfriend and her friends are already inside," I lie.

He pauses for a moment, then lets me in.

Once I'm in the main room I realize how awkward this all is. Where will I sit? How can I blend in until I see Ramon?

I approach a table to the far right that is empty other than two middle-aged women who look embarrassed to be there. I pause, and then gather my courage and sit down. I gesture to the stage. "I'm writing a sociology paper on the exploration of sexuality with the modern woman."

They nod and seem to relax a little with my declaration. I now have a safe place to navigate my next move. I keep glancing back at the bar, hoping to see Ramon, but there's only another man there I don't recognize. For a moment, I panic with the idea that he isn't working tonight, but I'm soon rewarded with my first glimpse of him as he steps behind the bar and starts checking on anything that needs attending to. He's even more beautiful with his serious expression than the man I fantasized about touching me while my fist moved up and down my cock.

Have I elevated him into an unrealistic fantasy? *Yes. Yes, I have.*

Watching him unabashedly, I study him as each customer competes for his attention. So far everyone who's approached the bar has been a woman, and he serves them with a friendly demeanor but doesn't initiate more, even the one in a lime green tiny dress that keeps leaning over the bar, blatantly flirting. His lack of dynamics with the women makes me hopeful that he paid me more attention last week for a reason. I know it's irrational, but it bolsters my confidence so that when the first number starts and all eyes focus on the stage, I take a deep breath and rise out of my seat. I'm silently giving myself a pep talk, so I don't give up and sink back down into my chair. I can't fumble my words and intentions in front of him, this may be my only chance to make him think I could be worthy of his attention, even if I'm not.

Approaching the far end of the bar, I watch him wipe the counters down until he finally looks up and our gazes meet. The way his smile breaks across his face fires a flare of hope in my chest. He saunters over to me. "Hey, Charlie. You're back."

I nod. "Indeed, I am."

"Here to see the hot dancers?" He nods toward the stage, where the guys are lined up along the edge of the stage, thrusting their hips synchronized with the beat of the dance music. Leaning in closer to me, he winks.

I slowly blow out a breath, my nerves electrified. "No, I'm not here to see them. Actually, I came to see you."

"Is that so?" he says; his dimples deepen into his smooth skin, enhanced by the shadows cast with the overhead spotlight. "But there are lots of great dancers here."

"But they aren't you," I state simply, before my gaze drops. I must sound ridiculous. He danced for me last week, five, or ten minutes tops.

When I look up our gazes lock for a moment and his interested expression makes me feel like I matter. It gives me a surge of courage.

Settling down on one of the stools, I lean in toward him. "Hey,

I was so flustered last time that I forgot to tip you."

Ramon shrugs. "No worries, man. That one was on me."

"Heineken?" he asks, as he pulls it out of the fridge.

I nod. "So I was hoping to talk to you."

He arcs his eyebrow. "Okay, and what did you want to talk about?"

I take the chilled bottle that he offers me and turn it in my hands nervously. "Do you always bartend and dance in any given night?"

"No, not usually," he replies with a shrug.

"Then why last time I was here?"

"Because I felt like it. The owner and I are friends and he gives me a lot of latitude."

I push a twenty across the bar top, and gesture toward the beer before I take a swig and set it down. "So why did you feel like dancing *that night*?"

He takes the bill, turns to ring up the sale, and then slides the change toward me. "Because I was curious."

"Curious? Has anyone every told you that you're maddeningly vague?"

"Maybe."

I can't read the wide grin—if he's having fun teasing me or he's purposely getting me worked up.

"Because . . ." I prompt.

"I like intrigue. It keeps things interesting. Don't you think?" He rolls his shoulders back, which pulls his T-shirt snug across his chest. "And you intrigue me, Charlie." His dark eyes smolder as he waits for my reaction.

At his bold stare and frank declaration, my lips curl over my teeth to quell my hunger for him. I have an overwhelming urge to lick him along every smooth curve and bulge of his flesh. I feel a flush work up my neck. I've never engaged in conversation with anyone this blatantly sensual. He exudes sex and I'm feeling drunk with his pheromones, which are curling around me, teasing me into a man who can barely think straight. For a moment, it's like I don't even know who I am anymore.

I nod, pressing my lips tightly together. Taking a deep breath,

I try to refocus on the conversation. "Well, you're very intriguing, too, Ramon."

He lets his gaze slowly slide over me, making me feel naked . . . not only emotionally, but physically.

"Can you tell me what you're curious about in regards to me?" I ask.

"Lots of things."

"Like what?"

"Well, for one, you look like a professional. I'm curious what you do."

I shrug. "Yeah, I guess you could say that. I'm a high-level programmer."

"Mmmm. No wonder you're so intense."

My eyes grow wide. "Really?"

"And I take it you don't have a lover, since you came back here alone to talk to another man. Not just any man, but an erotic dancer." He studies me. "And you don't seem at all like the cheating kind."

"Definitely not a cheater," I agree.

"So what are you about? And who are your people, Charlie?"

"People?"

"What's your background? Is your family in L.A.? Do they know what you're about? Do your friends?"

Something frozen starts to spread through me. I want more from Ramon, but how much do I really want to reveal to a bartender who works in a male revue club?

As if he senses my reluctance, he takes a step back and glances down the bar, noticing two women approaching. He raises his hand at me, and nods toward the girls. "No worries, man. Sometimes I cross a line without meaning to." He taps his temple with his fingertips. "I like knowing what a man like you is about. You clearly are so much more than just your handsome face and hot body."

I have to stop myself from looking over my shoulder to see who he's really talking about. *Handsome? He thinks I'm handsome and hot?*

Suddenly I can feel my heart pounding in my chest. But before I can put a response together, he nods toward the girls and walks away to take their order. My mind frantically spins as to what I can say if he comes back here.

Sitting for several minutes while slowly nursing my beer, I try to watch him as he takes care of customers without being too obvious. He's naturally charming and so comfortable in his body. I could watch him for hours like this and never get bored.

When the intermission is over, everyone heads back to their seats and he approaches me again. "Can I get you anything else?"

"A shot of Jameson, and another Heineken," I respond.

He watches me down the shot, his gaze fixed on my lips as I lick them clean.

"I live with my sister," I blurt out. Clearly the alcohol is rendering its intended effect.

His eyes narrow as he studies me. "Okay. That was a little random."

"You asked about my people," I try to explain. "Sasha *is* my people."

He nods in rhythm to the music. "Anything else you want to share?"

My gaze falls to the countertop. "There was an accident." My fingers tighten over the beer bottle. "She's a paraplegic now."

His whole face shifts and the compassion in his expression gives me the courage to look him in the eye.

"An accident? So you take care of her? And your parents?" he asks.

"They died in the accident." I hold my breath, anticipating his response.

"Damn," he whispers. "I'm really sorry, Charlie."

"Thank you. My sister, Sasha, she's really something though. The truth is I feel like she takes care of me, more than I take care of her."

"Well, I think the fact that you are there for her says a lot about the man you are. Your parents must've raised you right."

Feeling my eyes glaze over, I have a moment of clarity where I can't believe I'm telling this stranger my story. Somehow, the rusted latch over my heart got loose and now these emotions are pouring out of me in a flood with no barrier to slow it down.

"My parents were really good people."

He straightens up, projecting complete self-assurance. "Family is everything. That's how I was raised, and all of this," he waves his hand across the club, "tries to make you believe that fun and gratification are worth losing your true self over, but believe me, they're not."

His expression looks bitter for a moment, until his face calms again.

"You sound like you know from experience," I say softly.

He nods silently. "So, your sister, Sasha . . . what does she think about you being back here tonight?"

"She doesn't know. She doesn't know I'm gay either."

"Are you sure about that?"

I have to consider what he's implying. Sasha is very observant and bright. Could she have known about Leo and me? Does she wonder why I never date girls?

"Maybe, I'm not sure."

He nods, seeming to understand. "Maybe it's time. How do you think she'd react? You could tell her about how you're feeling."

"Like that I needed to see you again?"

"Needed?"

"Yes. This is going to sound stupid, or dramatic. But there's something about you that makes me feel like I can be myself and not judged. That night I felt like I was awakened from a very long sleep."

At first something flashes across his face that looks like concern, but then that fades and he smiles. "Good. Now stay awake."

I laugh. "Like it's that easy."

He shrugs. "It doesn't have to be that hard."

I garner my inner strength to boldly ask him, "So what did you think about me that night?"

Shifting on his feet, he pulls the long sleeves of his T-shirt down tight over his chest, and then smoothes the wrinkles out with his powerful looking hands. "There was something about you that made me want to know you."

"Yeah?" I ask, feeling hopeful.

"Yeah." He gives me a devilish grin. "I also wanted to touch you."

My eyes widen in surprise by his offering this jewel box of words, so sparkly and seductive that I'm coming undone. *He wanted to touch me.*

"Why?"

He leans over the bar, close enough that I can feel the heat radiating off of him as he chews on his upper lip. "Well, besides the obvious, there's something about you. So much restraint pushed down for so long. It's like a challenge . . . what would it take to set you free?"

I swallow hard, unable to make eye contact with him. He makes it sound so easy, like I can suddenly be someone else. Not Charlie the placid programmer—responsible, cautious Charlie—but a man willing to take risks to feel something as the man I aspire to be. There's a powerful feeling, of desiring someone special that I've searched for yet never found. Ramon is highly desirable and clearly likes a challenge. *But if I surrender to that feeling, and if he doesn't reject me, will I be ready for the outcome? Will he?*

He glances at me with a curious expression. "The thing is, now that you're back, I wonder if I danced for you once more if you'd get that turned on again for me."

I squirm for a moment on the uncomfortable bar chair. It's overwhelming how intensely aroused I am. "Right now, Ramon . . . I'm already turned on," I whisper with a groan. "I need—"

He shakes his head with a frown, cutting me off. "Believe me, I wish I could, but it can't be tonight. We're short staffed, and I'll be tending bar all night."

My disappointment cuts me open. "What about tomorrow night?" I ask, trying to mask the desperation in my voice.

"It depends on what you want." He rubs his hand roughly over his chest, making my cock twitch. "The club offers private dances."

"How private?" I ask. "I'd only want you."

He nods. "Completely private. You'd have thirty minutes completely alone with me." He tips his head. "It's pricey."

"That's not a problem," I reply tersely. "What time?"

AFTER PARKING NEXT TO SASHA'S van at our complex, I pull the folded cocktail napkin out of my pocket and smooth it over my thigh. Seeing the words, *Ramon 8:30, Private Room 4*, makes my heart pound. I can't believe I'm really going to do this tomorrow. Every nerve ending in my body is sparking. I could barely breathe the whole time he was securing the room for us on the club's computer program.

Desperate to ask Ramon what 'private' really means in this context, but feeling too awkward to ask, my mind reels at the possibilities. Maybe it's exactly like how he danced around and over me on stage, but without the audience. Or maybe more is allowed. And what if *more* can happen? I wish I knew if that were even possible. The idea of *more* . . . me touching his bare skin wherever I want while his dark eyes watch me is going to keep me up tonight, and every night in the foreseeable future.

Tapping my foot nervously the whole ride up from the garage to our apartment, I open the door to our condo to find Sasha reading, but I can also tell she's been waiting up for me.

"There you are!" she exclaims. "Everything okay?"

I nod nervously. "Yeah, everything's fine. When did Lucia leave?"

"Around seven-thirty."

Lucia and Estella are Sasha's caregivers that come to the condo and help with her care. Estella has the morning shift, and Lucia the early evening one. We also have Carmen, who has a flexible schedule and can fill in when one of her primary caregivers needs a day off.

She cocks her head to the side. "Where've you been? I missed you this morning when I slept in, and then got your text that you were going out tonight."

Damn, what am I going to tell her? Why didn't I plan this out ahead of time?

"Umm . . ." I stutter.

"Charles Andrew Morgan! You cannot hold out on me. I want details!"

Sinking down on the couch, I take a deep breath while I rake my fingers through my messy hair. She follows me until her wheelchair is facing me, only inches away from my kneecaps.

"So that strip club I went to last week . . ."

"Yes . . ." she says breathlessly.

"I met someone there that I'm interested in."

"Did you have a date with them tonight?"

I shake my head. "No, nothing like that."

"So you went back tonight to see that someone again? Do they work there or something?"

"Yes. They're a dancer."

"You're interested in an erotic dancer?" She claps her hands together with a squeal. "That's so hot! I didn't think you had it in you, Charlie!"

"I didn't think so either," I admit.

"So what's she like? She must be really special if you like her."

"Yeah, well . . ." I rub my hands over my knees.

Her eyes light up. "It's a guy, isn't it?"

Swallowing hard, I nod my head in affirmation. "Yeah."

Thrusting her finger in the air, she leans toward me. "I knew it! I knew it! Emily kept telling me I was wrong about you being gay, but I think it's because she secretly has a thing for you!"

I'm overwhelmed by her enthusiasm and revelations. I knew she wouldn't have an issue about me finally admitting I'm gay, but I didn't think it would excite her so much.

"I want to meet him!" she declares.

"No way," I say, shaking my head.

Knowing any sign of disappointment in her gets to me, she immediately pouts. She's normally not manipulative, so I have to think she really does want to meet my potential conquest.

"Sasha," I say tenderly, "I really don't think he's interested in me, so no introductions yet."

"So you don't have a date or anything? How could he not be interested in you? You're everything awesome, Charlie!"

My heart swells at my sister's pure adoration of me. She has no idea how her absolute belief in me is what's kept me going through all the rough times we've forged through.

"Why don't you ask him on a date?" she asks. I can see the wheels in her head already turning. "There's that new restaurant on Robertson that's supposed to be really romantic."

"We have a date, but it's one I'm paying for." My cheeks heat with shame. It sounds so bad now that I'm explaining it. "He's going to dance for me again."

"Dance?" Her expression is a combination of puzzlement and intrigue. "Like sexy dance?"

"Very sexy dance," I confirm, picturing Ramon thrusting his hips toward me. "I got pulled on stage when I was with my group from work, and once I was under the spotlight I realized he was the one dancing for me. You can imagine how freaked out I was, but he's amazing and he made me feel incredible. So I'm going to do it again with him privately and hopefully determine if there's actually something more between us or if I've simply lost my mind."

"Don't be silly. You haven't lost your mind. It's normal to be attracted to someone who I assume is very attractive."

"He is," I agree.

She reaches out for me and I take her hands in mine. "Charlie, you know that I love you all the more for telling me about how you're feeling. There's no judgment here." She waves between us. "I don't care if he's a stripper, if he makes you happy then I already like him. You know that, right?" She squeezes my hands tighter.

I nod. "I know."

"So what are you going to wear tomorrow night?"

I roll my eyes. "I don't know. What difference does it make?"

"You have to show you're putting effort in! I say either that gray V-neck T-shirt or that dark red button-down I got you for Christmas."

I can't help but get a kick out of the fact that she's trying to style me for what she wishes was a date.

"And wear that really good cologne. You know which one. Fancy pants Aunt Beth got it for you."

"The Armani?"

She nods. "He won't be able to keep his hands off you!"

I grin back at her, and for a brilliant moment I feel hope for something new and exciting to look forward to.

3. Say My Name

THE NEXT DAY I PUT my gym bag in the car, figuring I'm going to need to burn off some of this anxiety before I head over to the club for my time with Ramon.

It's been one of those rare, rainy Southern California days, but in the late afternoon our glass box of a building suddenly lights up when the sun breaks through the dark clouds and makes all the rain-drops clinging to the glass shine like scattered crystals. People actually scamper out of their cubicles to see what's happening. Rain in L.A. overwhelms people. It's usually more than they can handle. I swear if you dropped them down in Chicago in January, they'd probably die. I like to think of myself as an exception, but if we get a brief bout of humidity from our usual dry, pleasant weather, I get edgy.

Billy approaches me and gives me a thumbs-up. As I try to figure out what that gesture means in this circumstance, a couple of guys from the new virtual advertising team follow right behind him. "Hey, Charlie, after work we're going to Barney's on Santa Monica Blvd. for burgers and to watch the game. Come with us."

I like that Billy shatters the stereotype that computer nerds hate macho stuff like watching football. I challenge the nerd thing in my own way by working out a lot.

I shake my head. "I'll have to catch you next time, guys. I'm heading to the gym after work."

"Screw that," Billy says. "I thought you worked out in the morn-ing before coming in here? Besides, you can blow it off one night."

"I can't, working with my trainer tonight. If I blow him off I'm punished later," I lie.

He scowls. "Trainer? Okay then, next time!"

By five-thirty I'm trembling inwardly with anticipation to leave work because that will mean I'm that much closer to seeing Ramon again. Then after thirty minutes of waiting for the proverbial shoe to drop with some last-minute work issue, I grab my bag and head out the door.

I can barely focus at the gym, so I take extra care with the weights because the last thing I need is to get injured before the most promising night I've had in years. I wonder if Ramon is nervous or excited to see me, but then I chastise myself for imagining such ideas of a guy who I assume does this kind of thing frequently, and on top of that can have whomever he wants in West Hollywood or any gay borough in L.A.

My thoughts of him get so X-rated, while in the gym's steam room, that I have to bunch my towel in my lap to cover-up my arousal. I feel like a pent-up teenager, all the hopefulness raging through me, edged with a healthy dose of self-doubt.

I try to imagine Ramon sitting across from me in this thick, hot mist, his caramel skin soft and dewy with the moist heat. With only a towel around his waist I could gawk at his every defined ab and bicep ripple while he watches me slowly pulling off his towel . . . his hooded gaze heavy with want and a fierce need for *me*.

I'm such a dreamer.

Ironically, near the lockers a good-looking guy starts to flirt with me while I'm getting dressed. In all my excitement, am I projecting a hormone that suddenly makes me desirable? I can only hope so with Ramon in mind.

"Is that Armani?" he asks, sniffing a little too close to my neck and far beyond my comfort zone.

I nod, trying to avoid looking shocked at the way his gaze travels over me, lingering on my crotch.

"I thought so. You smell good enough to eat," he delivers with a grin. "You want to grab a drink or something?"

"Thank you, but I've got someone important waiting. I'm not

going to let him down."

His eyes go wide with surprise. "Good for you. I wish more guys in this godforsaken town were loyal like that."

Twenty-three minutes later I pull my Audi up to the club valet, too impatient to circle the lot for a prized parking space. Besides, what good is having money if you don't spend it on things to make life easier? After an awkward time checking in, one of the guys at the front desk leads me down a hallway to the far left of the lobby and opens the door to room number four. "Have a seat," he says, gesturing to a chair in the back part of the modest-sized room. "I'll let Ramon know you're here."

"Okay, thanks," I reply, suddenly questioning how I put myself in this insane situation. I am essentially paying money to a man I barely know to make me feel something again. Hopefully he'll help me uncover a part of me that had been denied so long, I wasn't sure if it was still in me.

I sit silently, except for the vague rustle from the nervous tapping of my heel, causing my thigh to rhythmically rise and fall off the seat. My gaze moves around the bare room with low lighting and a simple table off to the side that holds what looks to be an iPod dock, a stash of water bottles, a box of Kleenex, and a trashcan tucked neatly beside the table's thick legs. The walls appear to be lined with a burgundy type of fabric and it occurs to me that this room must be sound-proofed. I wonder what type of sounds are shielded from the crowds that file into this club to see the dancers.

Some of the bolder women guests must reserve private times as well. Suddenly I feel really awkward to be here, and not in a gay club where this type of thing, I imagine, is a dime a dozen. Right as my nerves start to get the better of me, the door slowly swings open and Ramon steps inside.

He carefully closes and locks the door, and then turns toward me. "Hey, Charlie," he says with a sexy smile. "I'm glad you're here."

"Wouldn't have missed it," I reply, trying to come off relaxed and failing due to the quiver in my voice.

"Good." His gaze slowly moves over me, appreciation in his

expression. "You're especially handsome tonight," he murmurs.

I try not to roll my eyes, knowing this is the start of his performance, but part of me is intoxicated by the way he's already making me feel . . . even if it isn't sincere.

He takes several steps closer to me, and stops to take a stance, his feet spread hip width apart. "Would you like me to start?"

My mouth falls open at the question. I'm not sure what I expected . . . that he'd dance right into the room. But now he's asking about what *I* want and I hesitate.

"Can we talk for a minute?"

"Sure." Walking over to the far wall, he lifts up the free chair and carries it over to place it a few feet in front of me. His grace in every movement has me hypnotized. He lowers himself to the seat and leans back, his legs slowly spreading apart as if he's laying himself open for me.

I swallow back a surge of desire that rolls through me.

"Do you do this private thing a lot?" I ask, gesturing loosely across the room.

He shakes his head. "No."

"But when you do, is it mainly women? I mean . . . considering who most of the patrons of this club are."

He shrugs. "Women like me. I make them feel safe, and they make me feel appreciated."

I nod. "You're very charismatic."

"Thank you." His huge brown eyes shine as he watches me like I'm someone fascinating.

I fumble my hands together. "I was meaning to ask you. Does this . . ." I pause, at a loss for words.

"Yes?" he asks, patiently waiting for me to continue.

I let out my held breath. " . . . involve actual sex."

"No," he says, his seductive gaze piercing mine. "No touching each other's genitals."

I can't hide my disappointment—I feel it etch its way across my face.

"But you can touch yourself." He bites his lower lip. "I'd really like to watch that."

I'm so instantly aroused that for a moment I'm actually dizzy from the lack of blood flowing into my brain. I lean forward, considering dropping my swarming head between my knees before I faint.

"You okay?" he asks.

I nod numbly.

"Hey, do you always wear those glasses?"

I finger the edge of my black-rimmed glasses. I've worn this style for years, liking how serious they make me look. "Yeah, well except for in bed or the shower. Why?"

He shrugs. "I don't know. I think they're hot. I've always had a thing for brainy guys, so to me it's a very sexy look."

I feel a flush work across my face.

"Can I see what you look like with them off?"

"I guess," I say softly, as I carefully pull them off. I suddenly feel naked.

"Damn," he hisses. "You look even sexier without them."

I inhale his flattery like a starved man. "Do you want me to keep them off?"

He stands. "No, baby, I want you to see everything with perfect clarity. You ready for me?"

My hard cock, already clearly outlined along my denim-clad thighs, throbs at his words. He glances down to my thigh and then back up to my eyes, letting out a ragged sigh as he slowly shakes his head. "You're so damn sexy, Charlie. I've got to start before I lose it."

Damn he's good at this.

"Okay," I whisper.

After setting the chair back in the far corner, he slides his iPod out of his pocket and programs it before setting it in the doc. Once the music starts he adjusts the volume. I immediately recognize the music since Sasha used to watch the music video over and over. It's that Justin Timberlake guy singing "I'm Bringing Sexy Back". And damn, I'm pretty sure Ramon is on a mission to bring my sexy back, or at least find my sexy in the first place.

Walking to the far end of the room he stops and stands with his back to me, about ten feet away. After a few seconds where he's completely still, he starts rocking his hips and then rolling his shoulders back. My heart is already thundering.

Slowly turning around, he looks past me, as if his mind is taking him someplace else dark and mysterious. Mesmerized, I watch him move as he gets pulled into the music, the expression on his face like he's the one being seduced.

If I had any doubt that it mattered at all to him that I was sitting here, that insecurity is blown away when his eyes lock on mine, and the heat that ignites his gaze scorches me.

The way he dances toward me prolongs my agony to feel his touch, even something as simple as his fingertips brushing my arm. I need the connection, like I need to breathe. I'm so twisted up that I have to monitor myself to keep from panting.

Who am I? Only hours earlier I was analyzing codes, searching for the breach in the system that could wreak havoc with a leading corporation. Now I'm reduced to a desperate animal . . . all my decorum and reserve peeled off of me until I'm a raw bundle of nerves and desire.

Only two steps away now, Ramon stops moving forward and fingers the edge of his T-shirt tauntingly.

I swallow hard realizing I'm going to see his perfect chest again, smoothly sculpted into a Michelangelo god-like man of marble. I think of glorious sculptures of warriors and heroes poised for battle, their chests broad and muscled, their swords drawn. Instead Ramon is poised for a different kind of battle and surely he will win. In the presence of this man, I have nothing to fight against, and everything to surrender to.

His shirt is pulled high enough now for me to see bronzed, smooth skin over abs cinched within his narrow waist. My fingers tingle to glide over that patch of heaven. Rolling his hips languidly, he continues to pull the shirt off, and once it's off he steps closer to me and winds the shirt around my neck, sliding it back and forth a few times so his masculine scent fills my nostrils before he finally lets the edges go.

Lifting one of the edges of fabric so I can press my face into the softness, I breathe him in even deeper as my gaze meets his. I can tell this pleases him, and that pleasure captured in his narrowed eyes is my reward.

My gaze settles on his chest and how the low light beams down, rendering every muscle and ripple of his abs and powerful chest like a work of art. I've never wanted to run my hands over bare skin as much as I do in this charged moment. This man is incredibly beautiful, and he wears it well.

His hips are still rolling but more subtly as he takes my hands and places them on the waistband of his jeans. "I want you to unzip me, Prince Charlie," he murmurs in a smoky voice.

Such a declaration could feel cruel, like I'm being teased, but instead it feels sexy because he says it in a tone that makes me feel worshiped . . . like I really am a prince.

My fingers trembling, I unfasten the top of his jeans and then grasp the pull on the zipper to tug it down. It takes effort—both because I'm flustered, and it's clear he's hard, which tightens the denim and slows everything down.

"I like your hands there," he whispers as he watches me struggle. As I press in a bit too firmly against his erection to work the zipper, he bites his lip and takes a sharp breath.

When I'm finally done, my hands are poised in mid-air while he loops his thumbs inside his jeans and slowly drags them down as his hips start moving again.

"Oh God," I whisper, realizing his pants are down.

His dick is hard all right . . . so tantalizing trapped inside his narrow briefs. It's tantalizing but torturing, because every part of me wants to wrap my fingers around his hard cock to feel him pulse in my grip.

"You like?" he asks, his muscular thighs bare now as he rocks his hips forward.

"God yes," I sigh. I feel his fingertips skim along my jaw and then across my lips.

"Your lips are so pretty," he says with his gaze fixed on them. "I bet it would feel amazing to fuck your mouth."

My mouth waters at the idea of it. "Please," I moan, not even recognizing the sound that vibrates out of my throat. I'm already painfully hard, like I could come any second.

"Please," I whisper louder, not even trying to hide the desperation in my tone.

Reaching down, he cups a hand over each cheek. "No, handsome, it's not allowed, but you can't imagine how bad I want to."

My mind is racing—so frantically trying to figure out a way around the rules that I barely realize that his jeans are off and tossed aside, and a different song is playing. He's dancing again, swept up in the rhythm and heavy bass beat. He's the most natural dancer I've ever watched up close. It's like that saying, *the music lives in you.* I always thought it was so corny, but now I can see that music definitely lives brilliantly in Ramon. He is a conduit to the musical, sultry magic swirling around me.

From behind I can feel his fingers in my hair as he leans against my back, sliding to one side and then the other. I moan as his fingers work across my scalp.

"Yes?" Ramon whispers before he skims his lips across the back of my neck.

I gulp in air. "A thousand times yes."

"You are so easy to please, Charlie," he says tauntingly in my ear before grazing his teeth along my neck. "I love that about you."

"I love *this*," I say as he trails his hands down my chest from behind, and when he drags them back up he scrapes his fingertips along my nipples.

"Oh fuck," I groan.

"So sensitive," he replies, sounding very pleased as he continues to stroke my sensitive skin. "Open your shirt," he purrs, tugging on the fabric so it's released from where it's tucked into my jeans. I pull the buttons from each buttonhole until he can slide the sides of my shirt apart. A loud groan escapes my lips as his warm hands run up and down my chest, stopping at each stroke to circle and flick my nipples. "Oh, baby, you're so damn cut. You must work out a lot, yes?"

I nod frantically, afraid a verbal response will slow him down. The song that turns me on so much fades, and another pumps up with a louder beat. His body reacts and I feel him lift off me as I mourn the loss of his hot hands . . . only to find him seductively dancing along my side until he's in front of me again. Once front and center, he turns so his back is to me and then his hips come to life, rolling and grinding, his fingers edging his briefs down until I can see the crack of his ass.

Is it weird that I want to lick it, bite it, and own it? I want to own all of his ass, and actually the way he's presenting it to me, makes me feel like it's already mine. Tentatively, I reach out and place a hand on each cheek like I did two nights ago. But this time I can hear Ramon let out a low moan as he presses his ass deep into my grip. My fingers explore as he moves, pressing into the curve of muscle meeting flesh, running along the seam of his crack.

"Can you imagine how it would feel if my hands were on your bare ass?" he asks breathlessly as he does this move that makes his ass quiver like the only thing that will satisfy him is taking me.

Oh, I can imagine Ramon's hands on me but right now I have no words—just a parched mouth from panting and a thick tongue that can't form words. Instead, I let out a long, mournful groan.

"Yes," he hisses.

I sense he knows I'm losing my composure and he carefully turns, my touch never leaving his hot skin. I settle my hands on his hips as he faces me and lowers himself to my lap. I wonder about how much time has passed, and how much time is left. I can't let this end, I need it to go on and on until I've been completely transformed into the sexual being I was meant to be.

"I wish you could fuck me," I blurt out.

"Hmmm," he moans, sliding his ass forward until he's pressed over me, but this time he rocks his hips aggressively. I can picture it so vividly in my head, my legs spread open for him . . . gasping as he pushes inside of me, one slow inch at a time. I dig my fingers into his hips to pull him down tighter.

"You're close, aren't you?" he groans, rocking his hips back so his hard-on rubs over mine until he sinks his ass back down hard.

"Yes," I say, my voice tense.

His hands press down over my chest, his gaze full of appreciation.

"So fucking sexy," he whispers.

My cock throbs, and I soak up his appreciation and revel in his obvious lust as he pinches my nipples and then watches me come undone with a quiet, satisfied smile.

He rises off my lap, but continues to straddle me as his hips rock with sharp thrusts. A moment later his fingers are cradling my head to urge me closer so he can roll his hips right up to my face until I feel the fabric of his briefs sheathing his hard cock make contact with my face again and again. All I'd have to do is slide down his briefs and open my mouth wide to make my life complete.

"Please," I groan.

He bends, leaning over me until his hot lips skim my ear. "You have no fucking idea how much I want to, Charlie. You're making me crazy, baby."

I keep telling myself this is part of his act, but part of me doesn't believe that. The desperate look in his eyes and the way his warm hands grab me are not the moves of a man in control.

Hypnotically to the beat of the music, he lowers his ass to my lap once more, but this time he slides back and forth more aggressively. Each time he's up against me, his weight settles over my throbbing cock; he slowly grinds until I'm right on my edge.

He slides back toward my knees and nods to my crotch. "I wanna watch. Take it out for me."

"What?" I mumble, making sure I heard him right.

"I want you to show me how you get off, and when you come I want to hear my name."

A hot flush moves its way up my chest and neck. *How can I possibly do this without humiliating myself with my awkwardness? What if he laughs at me?*

His eyes get stormy like he's not going to give up on getting what he wants. "Will you do that for me?"

I bite my lip and nod nervously before shutting my eyes and letting my head roll back. "Oh God," I whisper as I reach for my fly. I can't even be embarrassed at this point because my desperation to get off is so intense that I have no options left. If he can't touch me,

I'll have to, and he can watch exactly what he's done to me. I make quick work of it, pushing my boxers and jeans away as best I can so my hand is free to fist my dick firmly and start the rough strokes that are the only thing I'm capable of when this man has wrecked me.

His gaze is fixed on my cock, slick with pre-cum. "Can you imagine me sucking you right now?"

I nod frantically, my fist now blurring over me.

He groans with a raw hunger. "I wish I was, handsome. I'd suck your big cock so deep."

And holy hell, that's it. That's fucking it . . . Ramon and his filthy words have pushed me right off the highest ledge.

"Say my name," he growls as I start to come.

"Ramon! Oh fuck . . . Ramon . . ."

"That's right," he croons, encouraging me on.

I have a vague sense of my eyes widening as I soar and my head falls back, the come spilling over my fingers while Ramon says dirty, sexy words about what he wants to do to me that sound like a Shakespeare sonnet in my stupor because I want him so damn much.

My final moan is primal and echoes through every part of me. I'm an animal in heat with this gorgeous creature who could be my mate, and I never want to be a mere man again.

4. Finding My Man

MY HEAD FALLS FORWARD AS I gasp to try to catch my breath. I feel Ramon's hands on my shoulders, massaging and kneading, then working up to my scalp. It feels so damn good. Is there nothing about this guy that doesn't feel fantastic? Is there any way on earth from this moment forward for me not to be obsessed with him? I think not.

I finally open my eyes and lift my head so my gaze meets his. "Is there anything you aren't amazing at?"

The corner of his mouth twists up and his eyes spark. "Plenty, but I've got to say, Charlie, you're really inspiring."

"No one has ever made me feel like you do," I boldly state as he hands me tissues so I can clean myself up.

His warm gaze does something to me. "How long has it been since your last lover?"

"Oh, you wouldn't believe it if I told you."

"Try me. I've stopped being surprised by people's secrets a long time ago."

I add up the years in my head since the night of the accident. "Six years."

His mouth gapes open and his expression can only be described as shock. "What? Are you kidding?"

I shake my head, my gaze falling to the ground. "I've messed around a few times in school, but it was meaningless . . . just getting off, and never seeing the guy again. I've only had one guy I really cared about and he was my first and I can't exactly say we were full-on lovers yet. But we intended to be."

Ramon already has pulled his jeans on, but now he's putting

on his T-shirt and shoes. He shakes his head while he ties his laces. "That's so wrong. I would've gone nuts by now. Do you watch a lot of porn or something?"

I shrug. "Sure, there's that, but maybe I've gone nuts. I had to pay you to get some time with you, and now all I want is to do it again."

He arches his brow at me. "Which means?"

I can feel my cheeks flush with embarrassment. "Can I book you for tomorrow and the day after . . . I mean if your schedule allows it."

He holds up his hands. "Whoa, wait a minute. More sessions with me isn't what you need, Charlie."

Rising, I pull up my jeans. "Believe me . . . it is. It's exactly what I need. I already feel like a different man from these two experiences with you."

There's a knock on the door and Ramon cracks it open. "Yeah, give us a sec." He turns back toward me. "Don't get me wrong, you are damn hot, maybe my most responsive audience yet, which is a total turn on, but what you need and deserve, Charlie, is something real, not paying me so you can feel something."

I can feel my contentment fade, and I turn away. "So you won't let me book you anymore?" My heart freefalls from feeling so high and exhilarated, to now flattened with rejection.

"Oh damn," he says, noticing my expression as he grabs his iPod off the doc. "Come on. Follow me."

I don't hesitate, but instead follow him wordlessly out the door and down the hall, until he pushes open a side exit door I hadn't noticed, and we're suddenly outside. The cool night air and openness startles me after being enveloped by all that lustful heat in an enclosed space.

"Come on. I'm going to grab something to eat. You like fish tacos?"

"Sure," I say enthusiastically, amped up to pretend that this is a date.

We silently walk side-by-side two blocks down Sunset, before he approaches a non-descript door with a sombrero painted on it and opens it for me. "After you."

The interior is dimly lit, yet with an explosion of color. Delicately stenciled paper flags and streamers in bright hues crisscross the ceiling, and stained-glass lanterns are mounted on the walls above each booth. The hostess, wearing a wildly decorative Mexican skirt and embroidered top, hands us our laminated menus as we slide into our booth. "Drinks, boys?" she inquires, as she pushes her thick, black, wavy hair off her shoulder.

"Water for me," says Ramon.

"Dos Equis," I reply.

After she's left, I ask him, "You don't drink?"

"Not like I used to, and never on work nights. Now I enjoy a good glass of wine once in a while." He pushes the menu away without looking inside. He must eat here a lot.

"So are you from L.A.?" he asks after taking a long sip of water that the waitress left when she took our orders.

"Paso Robles." I shake my head. "After the accident, my sister and I moved down to L.A to live with my Aunt Beth. The best facility to deal with my sister's injuries was down here, and in the beginning my aunt really wanted to help."

Ramon nods, and remains quiet. Undoubtedly processing the oversharing of information I've dumped on him. I have friends at work, like Billy, who don't even know as much about me as I've shared with this guy, who's essentially a stranger even if he watched me jerk off.

"Do you still live with your aunt?"

"No, after a couple of years it was too much for her. And neither of us were easy, so I can't blame her. That's when I got the place where Sasha and I live now. She checks in on us and does what she can for Sasha."

"How's your sister doing now?" he asks with an intense gaze, like he really wants to know the answer.

"Pretty good," I reply. "I mean considering everything she lost in the accident, her determination to make something of her life frankly blows me away."

He nods his head somberly. "Wow. I admire that."

"Me too," I agree. "So how about you? Did you grow up here?"

"Hell no. I was raised in San Antonio, Texas. My parents crossed the border from Mexico and I was born here. My mom and sisters are still there."

"What about your dad?"

"He was killed in a construction accident when I was ten. Being illegals, we couldn't get any assistance, and my mom was too scared of being deported to seek legal advice. That's when I became the man of the house, doing whatever odd job I could. Mom cleaned houses to keep food on the table. I still send money back to them regularly."

"Is she upset you don't still live there now?"

His expression gets somber. "Yes. But she knows I don't belong there. I haven't lived in San Antonio since I left for college on a football scholarship in Utah. She pushed me to go. Her dream has always been for her kids to have a better life than she had."

I shake my head. "I can't believe you played football. That's such a macho sport, especially in Texas, right?"

He nods, but his eyes take on a harsh look.

"What did they think of you being a gay football player?"

"Are you kidding? I couldn't be out when I was playing. That would've been the end of everything. I had to wait until I graduated and finally got my ass to Miami."

Our conversation halts when the waitress brings our plates over. He has a big combo platter with fish tacos, rice and beans, and sautéed vegetables.

"Do you always eat that much at night?"

He shrugs. "I don't eat before I dance. And you, my friend, gave me an appetite." He winks at me and my heart actually flutters. I thought that shit was made up for Victorian romance novels, but no, I'm pretty sure my heart is jumping in my chest and I'm feeling things for this guy that defy logic.

I take a chunk of my nachos, scooping up the melted cheese and plunging it into the sour cream and guacamole before shoving it in my mouth.

He grins as he watches me.

"You like those nachos, I take it?"

I grin back. "I love Mexican food. Give me a tamale and beef enchilada combo plate and all is right with the world. This is dessert tonight. I had a big protein shake earlier at the club to fuel my workout."

"Mama makes homemade tamales for Christmas."

"Oh, I bet they're amazing."

He nods. "Wait, you worked out before you came to the club?"

"I was working off my nerves."

"Awww, you were nervous? Why?"

"I've wanted this feeling so much and had gone a long time without it. How would I deal with it if the whole thing was incredibly awkward on my part, and going through the motions on yours?"

"Well, then you must be pleased that your fears were for naught?"

I stuff another nacho in my mouth and grin. "You don't think I was awkward?" My face heats up as I remember how frantically I jacked myself off while he watched.

"You were fucking hot, Charlie. Seriously. You saw how hard I was for you, didn't you?"

"I just assumed . . ."

He scoffs. "What? That I get that way with everyone? After all this time dancing, I can tell you that it hardly ever happens."

"Really?" I ask, my eyes widening at his confession.

He winks at me. "I'm getting hard right now thinking about it. That's why I was so shocked you haven't been shacked up all over West Hollywood. You're the total package. Can't you see that?"

My eyebrows knit together as the frustration boils up inside of me. "Are you teasing me?"

"Hell no, I'm not. Yes, you're handsome and smart. You've got a career and integrity, and a hot body that any respectable gay man would want to have in his bed. So what's stopping you from finding your dream man and living your happily ever after?"

I arch my brow and scrutinize him. "I could ask the same of you."

His expression falls and he shakes his head slowly, his gaze heavy with sorrow. "I had my happily ever after, and I lost it."

"Really?" I ask, feeling his pain as if it was my own. "How'd you lose it?"

"He died. It was cancer, and really fast and gruesome. We never had a chance."

"I'm sorry . . . really sorry."

His gaze seems focused on something far away. "Thanks, me too. It's been almost two years, but it feels like yesterday."

I nod, and push my beer bottle forward. "You sure you don't want this?"

He gives me a pained look, and shakes his head. "No, Luis was the one who saved me and got me to start making good choices, and being thoughtful about how I drink. I owe it to him to stay that way."

Snapping my bottle back, I feel ashamed that I tried to tempt him. Obviously this man he loved cared very much for Ramon. I don't know a lot about relationships, but what I do know is that to be loved like that must be an incredible thing.

We eat silently for a minute or two, but it doesn't feel uncomfortable. Now that I think of it, nothing about Ramon feels uncomfortable and that fact astounds me. Some days I feel like awkward is my middle name.

I finally break the silence. "So did you mean it? I really can't book you for tomorrow?"

He shakes his head, gesturing that his mouth is full. I marvel to see that he's almost cleaned his plate. I wait patiently, and when he finally swallows he shakes his head again. "No you can't book me."

"Why not? What if I do it anyway and then you have to dance for me?"

The corners of his mouth turn up. "You'd do that?"

"Yeah!" I reply, sounding more confident and forceful than I feel.

"You're fucking hot when you're assertive. You should put that out more."

I shrug. "Okay. I'm booking you tomorrow and you're not going to make any trouble about it. I want you on my lap, and I'm going to make you hard as hell again."

"Fuck," he whispers. His eyes are dark and stormy.

"I'd like that too," I respond with a smug look, belying the fact that my insides are flip-flopping.

"I bet you would," he says with a smoky voice. "But that's not going to happen."

"Ramon," I beg.

"I'm taking you to a gay club after work. Is eleven too late for you?"

My curiosity is sparked and I want to know more. "No, that's not too late at all. Why are we going to another club?"

"Because Wild Nights caters primarily to women, and I'm going to help you find your man."

5. The Rebirth of Charlie Morgan

OUR TEAM MEETING HAS WRAPPED up and I'm slow shutting down my files to head back to my workspace, while Billy is cleaning off the white board. I look up and notice Katie staring at me.

"What?" I ask, giving her a quizzical stare back.

Narrowing her eyes, her gaze moves down to my chest and up to my face. "You look different. I can't put my finger on it."

Billy turns around and studies me, too.

"Different?" I ask.

Billy scrunches his face and tips his head. "Hmmm," he sighs.

"Don't you think?" Katie says to him while pointing at me. "He looks more settled, like he's decided something."

Okay now she's freaking me out. I'm compelled to ask her, "So how long have you been thinking that?"

"I started to notice it the Monday after Brittany's party at Wild Nights. You seemed different after that night."

"Well who wouldn't after having that dude practically fuck you on stage. Maybe he's worried he's gay now," Billy says with a guffaw.

Katie nods.

I glance up at him, fighting not to show my anxiety. "Do *you* worry that I'm gay now?"

He shrugs. "Why would I worry about that? It wouldn't matter to me. As long as you're getting some and happy about it, I'm all good."

"Oh, it'd be so hot if you were gay," Katie states with a dreamy smile.

Are these two for real? I'm not going to out myself randomly at work, but I will figure out where and when it would be a good time to make that known. And now Katie's statement piques my curiosity. "Why would me being gay be hot?"

"When I was in high school I walked in on two guys making out in a classroom after school." Her cheeks turn bright pink. "I was so stunned I couldn't move, and for some reason they didn't say anything or tell me to leave. One smiled at me and they kept making out as I watched."

"Were you turned on?" Billy asks.

"Oh, you have no idea."

I stare at her, stunned into silence.

"Damn," Billy says. "You're pretty cool, Katie."

"Thanks, but those guys were the cool ones. Their names were Matt and Davis. Not long after that they'd take me dancing at this gay club in Silver Lake whenever I wanted. Those were good times," she murmurs with a faraway, blissful expression.

The whole way back to my desk I marvel, not just at the conversation we had, but how I suddenly feel lighter. It's like a heavy, weighted jacket has been pulled off of me. I like this feeling of freedom and it gives me another reason to keep moving toward figuring out who I'm really meant to be, and along the way I'll let the people in my life know. Then I'll finally be able to shed the shell of the man I've been until now.

THAT NIGHT AT HOME I find Sasha in her room working on her blog.

"Hey bro," she calls out.

"What's with this?" I point at a weird, oblong, tube-shaped thing fixed to the inside back of Sasha's wheelchair.

She sighs. "Estella is worried about a spot on the right side of my back. The thing is to make sure we've taken pressure off it so it doesn't get worse."

I feel that surge of alarm I always do when anything with Sasha is off. "Is it a sore?" I ask, knowing how quickly that can become a serious problem for a paraplegic.

"I don't think it is yet, she's being overly cautious."

"Well, better that than someone who isn't thorough since things can get out of control very fast."

Her eyes are wide and full of fear. "I know."

Stepping closer, I run my hand down her long, auburn, silky hair. She loves to be touched where she still has feeling. Besides her hair, her hands are her other favorite thing for me to play with. It took me a while not to feel awkward about it. She is my sister after all. But it's so soothing to her that how can I not do these small things that make her happy?

I glance over at her computer screen. "So what are you doing working? Shouldn't you be in bed?"

"I had an idea and I didn't want to forget it. Besides, you're one to talk. Are you really going out again tonight?"

It suddenly occurs to me that she's used to me always being around. "If that bothers you, I can stay home."

"No, I'm happy you're getting out. I'm just curious."

"My friend Ramon is taking me out dancing at a gay club."

Her face lights up. "Really? Look at you stepping outside your comfort zone."

Sighing, I rub the back of my neck. "You've got that right."

"Well, this is where it all begins. The rebirth of Charlie Morgan."

I arch my brows. "A bit dramatic perhaps."

She grins. "Maybe . . . or maybe not. So tomorrow I want to hear all about the club. If you like it will you take me there some time? After you take me to Wild Nights first though." She grins widely.

"Really? Why would you want to go a gay men's club?"

She narrows her eyes like she's imagining being there. "Well I hear they're the best clubs around. Emily told me about a place called the Abbey and said they seem very welcoming to everyone. I have a feeling they wouldn't treat me like a freak."

I sit up straight, full of fury. "Did something happen recently? Did someone treat you poorly?"

She reaches over and takes my hand. "No, people are polite for the most part, but I always get those stares of pity. But some of the gay guys I've befriended in the community aren't like that. They swear they're coming to L.A. one day to take me clubbing."

"Oh," I say, stroking her hair, then tugging gently on the ends like she likes. She lets out a happy sigh and then refocuses.

"Don't worry, I understand that I'll never be normal again, or have all the things I once assumed I'd be able to do in life, but that doesn't mean I can't do fun things . . . just now I have to do them in my own way."

I lean over and kiss the top of her head. "And you will," I say proudly.

Smiling up at me, she points to the door. "Now, don't you need to get out of here? As I understand it, you've got a date tonight."

"Yes, ma'am." I straighten up.

"And you tell Ramon I want to meet him. Maybe you can take me to the club some night, Charlie?"

"Maybe. We'll see about that."

IT'S FIVE PAST ELEVEN WHEN I pull over a few blocks from the club and text Ramon. A minute later he responds.

Almost done, I'll be outside in five.

I'll wait here. I'm only three blocks away. Text me once you're outside. I respond.

Will do.

When my phone pings with his text my heart speeds up. I wonder what this night will hold. I don't like this idea of Ramon finding a man for me, but I'm going along with this because it means that every time we're together is another opportunity to convince him to take a chance on me.

When I see him standing tall, scanning the street for my car, my mouth waters. Then my heart sinks as I realize that he obviously chose those fitted, lean jeans and ivory knit shirt that clings to every muscle to attract other men. He already knows I'd take him in a heartbeat.

A wide grin spreads across his face when he sees me, and he waves. I pull over and he jumps in the car. "Thanks for picking me up."

"Sure. So how was work?"

He shrugs. "Same old, same old. A few women were pissed they didn't get their lap dance . . . something about a reservation screw up. But otherwise it was a pretty regular night."

"Do you get tired of it?"

He sighs. "Sure, at times. Some women come in there thinking they can do or grab whatever they want."

"Well you've got to admit that the ads for this place sort of encourage that."

"Yeah, I guess. But I always wonder what their husbands or boyfriends would think if they saw what went down there."

"Does it make you feel objectified?"

"Yeah, but believe me, if you want a taste of objectification, any gay club will serve it up in spades. I've never been grabbed and man-handled roughly any place more than the gay clubs I used to work at in Miami."

"Wow. That must've really bothered you."

"Yeah. Over time it got old. That's why I went with this place when I moved here. Plus, the women tip better."

"But it's still objectification, right?"

"Hmmm, I got past over-intellectualizing that a long time ago. I'm doing this work of my own accord. I know the customers appreciate that I'm fit and attractive, and if that fact objectifies me, so be it. I know when I walk out those doors I'm a lot more than that."

"You are." The glimpses that I've seen of the real Ramon have impressed me—his dedication to his family most of all.

"Besides, there's some form of superficial stereotyping everywhere in life. Hell, I probably wouldn't be taking you out tonight if you weren't hot. Is that wrong? I guess, but it is what it is."

"You really think I'm hot? You're not just saying that?" I ask, trying not to sound needy. Sometimes I almost wish he didn't say stuff like this to me. It makes me desperately wish for the very man I cannot have.

"I thought we were past this, dude. I mean, come on . . . last night?"

"What about last night?"

"When you tore open your pants and went at it I barely kept my shit together. You weren't merely hot, you were scorching."

"I could do that again for you some time," I tease, but I'm not really teasing. I'd do it again, any time, if Ramon was watching me with that hungry expression.

He grins, and then turns his focus out his side window. "Yeah, well we'll see about that."

The Lodge, Ramon explains, is the hottest new place in West Hollywood. I pull up to the valet and surrender my car to the best-looking valet I've ever seen. This guy has to be a model or something. Ramon laughs when I turn back to look at him once more before we head in.

"You haven't seen anything yet," he says, grinning.

I shadow Ramon as we go in because I can tell from the appreciative stares he gets that he's more than welcome here. The bouncer waves us in without any hesitation. I have no idea why they called this place The Lodge when everything in this place is upscale and stylish from the dark brown walls, terrazzo floors, and sleek modern furniture of dark woods and leather seating. The lighting is strategic, warmly reflecting off mirrors and giving enough light so that once our eyes adjust we can see everything, but dim enough to keep a sophisticated, sexy vibe.

Ramon appears to be scoping out the crowd as we pass a wide entrance to a large open area in the back with a long bar and dance floor with dancers lost in the loud hypnotic music. I'm happy to be here, but equally nervous because there's no question I won't fit in with this hip, upscale crowd.

After scanning the dance floor, Ramon leads us back to an area more near the front and we approach the bar.

"What's your pleasure?" the tall blond bartender asks us, dropping cocktail napkins on the bar top. His eyes are icy blue which render me speechless for a second.

"Umm, a Jameson on the rocks. Actually, make that a double."

"Soda water with lime for me," Ramon says.

After paying, I lean into Ramon. "This place is fancy. I can't imagine meeting anyone here that would be interested in me."

Ramon rolls his eyes.

"I'm serious," I insist. "Why did you think this was the place to take me?"

He shakes his head. "Okay, I get it . . . I'm never going to convince you how good looking you are. But you're damn smart and you're a professional, and that's who these people are. There are lawyers and agents, business men and doctors who can go to anywhere on Santa Monica Boulevard to pick up a boy toy to fuck, but here they can find people they can both talk to *and* fuck."

"And you think that's what I want?"

He pulls back for a moment and studies me, like he's trying to figure me out.

I get that he's trying to deflect me away from him—since I'm clearly not who he wants—but it's not just that I want him. Even if Ramon wasn't in my life I don't think this would ever be my crowd.

Looking past me, he nods his head to my left. "Like what about that guy in the gray shirt. Couldn't he be your type?"

I turn and look, not too subtly either, because right in the same moment the guy glances up and sees us staring at him. The corners of his mouth turn up and he takes a sip of his drink. His gaze, which moves between Ramon and I, never wavers. When I turn back to Ramon, his brow is arched and he gives the guy a quiet smile. Panic bubbles up in me when gray shirt man with broad shoulders and a narrow waist starts coming our way.

He's good looking in a cool, serious-guy, New Yorker way. His hair is the color of strong coffee, wavy, and on the long side of short. He's pushed the unruly part off his face, and on one side it's tucked behind his ear. He's got those professor-style, tortoise shell glasses that makes him look brilliant and the knower of all kinds of obscure things.

"Hey," he says once he's in front of us.

Ramon nods his head and presses his open hand to his chest. "I'm Ramon, and this is my friend Charlie. He was telling me how you look like his type."

My eyes widen as I give Ramon an embarrassed stare, then nervously push my glasses up my nose.

"Oh, don't be shy," the gray shirt guy says with a sparkle in his eyes. "I like it when people are direct. I'm Michael, by the way." He's looking at me like he likes what he sees. "I haven't seen you around here before, have I?"

My fingers tighten over my tumbler of whiskey. "No, actually I'm new—"

Ramon cuts me off. "He's been working all the time. It's crazy. So I made him come out tonight. He's promised he's going to change his work-obsessed ways."

"Well, lucky for us," he replies. "What do you do, Charlie?"

"I'm a programmer."

"What kind of programmer?" he asks.

"Well, most of our clients are high-level manufacturers or major retailers. I've also created two apps that are in development."

Ramon shifts on his feet, and I sense this is the very kind of conversation he expected bringing me here. I also sense it's one he probably thinks he can't contribute to.

"How about you, Michael?" I ask, sounding more suave than I feel.

"I'm a sound engineer for Dolby. But I want to hear more about your apps."

"You haven't told me about your apps, Charlie," Ramon points out. "I'd be interested to hear about that, too."

"So you and Charlie don't work together?" Michael asks.

"No. We don't. Programing isn't my specialty." I can sense Ramon's nerves vibrate around me.

Michael takes a sip of his drink. "What is?"

It suddenly hits me . . . *What is Ramon going to say?* He has a Master's in Business and Club Management, but he's now an erotic dancer at a male revue club catering to women? *Damn.* I suddenly feel so protective of him. Surely he knew this could happen. Yet he put himself in this uncomfortable situation to help me.

But Ramon surprises me by his quick recovery. "I had a business venture in Miami, and now I'm trying to duplicate it here in L.A. But I'm at an early stage still, so I'm not sharing details yet."

"Nice," Michael replies right before his phone buzzes. "Excuse me," he murmurs while he reads a message. He looks up at me. "Hey, are you guys going to be here for a while? Some friends of mine are heading over and I'd like you to meet them after they arrive."

"Sure," Ramon pipes in. "We're going to check out the dancing in the back. You'll find us there."

"Great." Michaels turns and walks toward the front of the club.

Ramon gives me an enthusiastic pat on the back. "See! What did I tell you? We were only here ten minutes before you found someone."

"I didn't find anyone! You're the one that lured him over here."

Laughing, he takes my hand and doesn't let go while he pulls me to the room in the back, and toward the dance floor. I put up no resistance. After all, the idea of dancing with Ramon, where I can move freely with him close to me, sounds incredibly appealing.

Downing the rest of my drink so I can abandon my glass, I feel a rush from the booze, and a thrill from our hands being clasped together. His hand is so warm and strong, and in his powerful grasp, we're connected. He navigates us to the center of the dance floor.

Ramon immediately starts to move and he tugs on my hand as if to encourage me. I smile inwardly because this is the second bit of arsenal with me combatting the stereotyping of tech geeks. I'm actually a pretty good dancer. I mean I haven't danced in a while, only a couple of times during college when Sasha would force me to get out and quit worrying about her. But in our earlier teens she decided that we were going to be on one of those dance shows, even though we were too young and lived way out in Paso Robles. She was unrelenting, making me practice with her almost every day.

She always talked about dancing as her future career, and she was naturally great at it. Somehow, she coaxed the rhythm out of me that must have been there all along. It occurs to me that this is perhaps a theme in my life that I need to change. People like Ramon shouldn't have to take on the challenge of drawing my desires or talents out of me. . . . the very desires that I was clueless about.

So I take a sharp breath and start to move. I picture in my mind the YouTube videos Sasha still watches, which are shot in a studio in L.A. that a book friend of hers works for. Those videos feature some great dancers and so I now mimic their moves and find that I like the feeling. What I like even more is the huge grin spreading across Ramon's face.

Reaching out and grabbing a fistful of my shirt, he pulls me toward him. "Dude! You were holding out on me! Look at you!"

I hold back a satisfied smile. "Look at what?" I say, feigning innocence.

"You've got the moves, man!"

I shrug. "I've got all kinds of talents you aren't aware of."

His gaze gets heated, like a fire is lit behind his eyes.

It feels good for that brief moment, feeling like I'm holding my own, and not tragically dropped into a situation completely out of my league. Meanwhile, my moves have inspired Ramon and he's electric, the circle of men around us now all turned our way.

For the most part Ramon dances independently, his eyes closed as he grooves and sways, like he's swept up in the music. Other times he comes toward me with a magnetic pull until his arms are stretched up with his hands woven together behind my neck. Those times our hips rock in unison like a well-oiled sex machine. I can feel the heated gazes of the men around us focused where we thrust and I can almost imagine the erotic pictures they've conjured up in their imaginations.

We're two songs in when I feel a hand clasp my shoulder. Turning to see Michael and two other guys, I step back so our circle widens to accept them. Despite the loud music, we all take a moment to share our names and handshakes. And then just like that, it's the five of us dancing, moving around each other, happy to be dancing. I roll my shoulders back and in that moment I feel like I've never felt more free.

Michael is one of those dancers who doesn't move much, barely enough to call it dancing, but that's okay because his shorter friend with the shaved head appears to have taken Ramon on for a dance-off.

There's a potent energy created by the five of us that makes me feel like we're the brilliant center of this dance floor universe.

When the song changes to a slightly slower groove I pause, and Michael takes my elbow. "Drink?" he mouths over the loud bass beat. Nodding, I turn to Ramon and point to the bar, then follow Michael out. I feel a little weird leaving him with that aggressive guy, Paulo, but Ramon seems pleased to see me go off with Michael.

After getting our drinks, we stand in the archway to the patio so we can both get fresh air, and hear each other talk.

"So how do you know your friends?" I ask.

"I used to work with Fredrick at a recording studio and he knows Paulo from college. They're good guys. And Paulo loves to dance."

I turn back and watch him doing some kind of move around Ramon. "I can see that."

"So you and Ramon?" he casually asks.

"Umm, yes?"

"How'd you meet?"

"Oh, at a thing for one of my co-workers."

He nods, clueless how different the picture in his head probably is from what actually happened that night. Thank God, he doesn't ask for any details.

"So tell me about your apps," he says, pushing a wavy lock of hair off his forehead.

"The first one I developed is an investment app for teenagers. It's an educational tool to teach them about the stock market and investing, but in a format and with graphics that are more their language. I'm working with a video game company now to create a game around it."

"That's fucking brilliant!" he says enthusiastically.

It feels great that he's impressed. "Well, my dad was really into the stock market and investing, and he started teaching me early about how it works. But I'm great at math and statistics and a lot of kids are super smart but that may not be their strength. I started thinking what if there was a way to make it all more accessible?"

"Was this work done at the company you're working for?"

"No, it's mine. I actually started developing it when I was at Cal

Tech. So I wouldn't take the job until they signed paperwork that I own 100% of the projects I began developing before I started there."

"Smart." His gaze moves over my chest, and then back up to my face. "Then it must be true that you work all the time. No wonder I've never seen you in the scene."

I suddenly feel awkward, and try to imagine how to explain myself without sounding like a total loser. "Yeah, well . . ."

"It's okay. I'm a workhorse myself. But I'm glad you're out now. Don't get me wrong, I love my work, but what's life if we don't let our hair down once in a while?" He winks at me before taking a long sip of his drink.

Ramon and the guys are suddenly next to us, loud and laughing about some move Paulo tried that went awry.

"Dude, you are wild," Ramon exclaims, laughing. His bright gaze meets mine and he glances over at Michael and back at me before subtly nodding in encouragement. I wish he didn't look so happy that I was spending time with someone besides him. I like Michael all right, and maybe another place and time I'd feel that kind of attraction that sinks over you until it's all you know. But with Ramon, he's already under my skin and running through my veins, leaving no room for anyone else. If I wasn't sure about that, I am now with him on one side of me, and Michael on the other.

Michael seems to be a strategic thinker like me, and perhaps sensing that with the group here now nothing can happen, pulls out his phone and opens it up. A moment later he hands it to me and I look at the screen with my name already spelled out. "Type your number in there for me. I want to talk to you another time about the apps idea."

I nod and input my number in, but I'm doubtful that's really why he wants my number. I can tell by Ramon's expression that he doesn't think this is about business either.

I've finished off my drink when a tall, striking man walks up behind Ramon and leans down and says something in his ear. This guy has a chiseled face and tailored look like he stepped off a runway while sporting all black, but not in a Goth looking way. Wearing what appears to be expensive shoes, slacks, and a button-down shirt that has a subtle sheen from the fine threads of the fabric, he has that perfect stubble on his face that's just so, and dark eyes with lashes so thick they look fake. I already hate him.

Ramon's eyes widen at his words, and then close tightly as if he were wishing to be somewhere else. When he doesn't turn toward the guy, the guy takes his shoulder and turns him, then pulls him a step away from us.

The guy says something else into Ramon's ear. Ramon shrugs in response, and nods with a look of regret before turning back to us.

Ramon looks solemn when his gaze meets mine. "Go on, Charlie. It's okay. I'll be back." And before I can decide to be worried or not, they are swallowed up into the crowd.

I try to focus on anything else but Ramon being gone. Paulo starts demonstrating to Fredrick one of his dance moves that apparently Fredrick was intrigued with since it made Paulo's spine look like rubber. Michael shakes his head and laughs. It's clear they've all been friends for a while and I wonder if I could be friends with them, too. They seem like good guys.

A Lady Gaga song comes on and Paulo howls and suddenly we're back on the dance floor in a circle. I don't feel the same pressure to up my game without Ramon here, so I dance lazily, which seems to fit Michael's mood more. Meanwhile, Fredrick is doing his best to get Paulo riled up. I've got a good buzz from the two drinks and suddenly this fancy place isn't as intimidating. Michael has stepped closer to say something to me over the loud music when I sense a blur of movement and sharp tug on my arm.

Swinging around, I see Ramon with a frantic look. His eyes are wild and unfocused as his free hand tugs his hair hard.

"I have to go," he mumbles.

His expression has me completely freaked out. *What the hell happened to him?* "Are you okay? What's going on?"

He shakes his head, pressing his eyes tightly shut. "I fucked up. I have to get out of here." And with that he darts away, leaving me standing still with my mouth gaping open.

6. The Dreamer

"WHAT'S UP?" MICHAEL ASKS WITH a concerned look. He apparently saw enough to be worried, too.

"Sorry, man. I've got to go make sure Ramon's okay."

He seems disappointed, but I also see compassion in his expression, and he nods. "I'll call you."

I give a brief wave to the other two guys and turn to find Ramon. I'm immediately regretting that I didn't grab him right away because as I fight my way out the front entrance I realize he could be anywhere by now. "Damn!" I mutter under my breath.

I rush up to the bouncer. "Did you—"

He cuts me off. "He went that way." He points west. I guess he sees a lot of this kind of drama.

I rush to the corner and turn, noticing Ramon about twenty feet away leaning against the building. I approach him slowly as to not startle him.

When I get close I'm stunned by his expression. I could never imagine Ramon looking this defeated. He turns away from me as if he's humiliated to be seen like this. "Leave me alone," he says in a low voice.

When I don't leave he glances up with a harsh expression. "Didn't you hear me? Can you give me some space?"

Reaching out and grasping his shoulders, I say in the steadiest voice I can muster, "I'm not leaving you alone, Ramon."

A stream of cursing explodes out of him in a fury, as he slams his fists against the stucco side of the building next to us.

I'm starting to panic for him. Whatever went on in that club must have really been bad.

I step up next to him. "Please tell me what happened."

He shakes his head.

"Did that guy in black hurt you?"

He lets out a heavy sigh. "Hurt me? It's not like that. Screw with me? Play me? Piss me off? You have your choice. Any of those can describe what he did to me. And I'm a goddamn idiot for letting it happen."

Grinding my teeth, I'm trying to push down the rage surging through me. Other than Sasha, I've never had such an overwhelming instinct to protect someone. My fingers curl into fists.

Peeling Ramon off the wall, I turn him toward me. "Let's go back there and I'm going to kick his ass." Taking off my glasses, I hand them to him. He looks down at them with complete bewilderment. "Watch those for me, okay?"

The effect of my pronouncement creates a reaction I never would've predicted. A laugh bordering on hysterics bursts out of him, but as I surge forward he grabs my shoulder and yanks me back.

"Thanks, Charlie, but that would be a really bad idea."

I straighten up. "I know that guy is huge, but I was an eighth degree black belt in high school and feel this . . ." Flexing my bicep, I take his hand and press it over the hard muscle. "I may not be able to fully kick his ass, but I'll leave him in pain and make a point."

I can't believe I'm not only blathering this shit, but I'm feeling it from all the testosterone surging through me . . . and maybe a bit of whiskey buzz. I may not know Ramon that well, but I can't imagine anyone hurting him enough to put that look of total defeat on his face. I want to kill that guy, or at least maim him. But when I glance at Ramon again, I can see that me charging off to the club may not be what he needs right now.

Ramon carefully opens up my glasses and slides them back on my face. His tender expression deflates my killer instincts. Instead I want to hug him.

"Charlie, you wouldn't be fighting him alone, and his guys fight dirty. I'd never forgive myself if they messed you up."

Straightening my glasses, I take a deep breath and place my hand on his shoulder. "Okay, I'm not going to be an idiot if that's the case. Hey, I know. Let's go to Canters. I think we could both use a bagel and bowl of matzo ball soup. They're open twenty-four seven."

He looks at me like I've lost my mind. "I'm not going to a deli right now," he insists, shaking his head.

"You have to. I'm not good to drive yet, and we have to get my car."

He mutters something under his breath but turns and starts walking toward the club. "Let me have the valet ticket," he demands, outstretching his hand, but not meeting my eyes.

We're silent all the way back, and I pull out a twenty at the valet stand to pay the fee and get change for a tip. As we approach the car, I notice Ramon hesitate and focus on three men in the distance that appear to be watching him. The tallest one has his arms folded over his chest and a scowl. Suddenly it hits me that this is the good-looking guy that approached Ramon in the club—and he's definitely not happy that we're leaving together.

"Charlie, get in the car," Ramon commands in a stern voice.

Part of me wants to ask him what's going on, but I see a glimpse of fear in his eyes as his gaze darts from the men, to me, and back again, so I do what I'm told.

As I get inside, Ramon quickly slides in, and puts the car in gear. Looking up, I see the guys on either side of the tall man react to something he's said, and they rush over to a car parked alongside the building. Before I can see what happens next, Ramon curses under his breath, hits the gas, and tears out of the club's parking lot.

"What's going on?" I ask, my voice tense because I'm freaking the hell out.

"Don't worry. I've got this," Ramon's responds tersely as he takes a sharp right turn onto a side street off Robertson Boulevard. He's driving way too fast down a neighborhood street. Thank goodness it's late at night and the residential streets are nearly empty.

"Slow down," I say, and regret it when he scowls. I glance over and see his eyes are narrow and focused in the rear view mirror.

"Mother fuckers," he growls.

If I thought he was going fast before, now everything is a blur as he zig-zags down streets and alleys across West Hollywood. I cling onto the door handle and focus on breathing, while I imagine the horrific crash that could happen any moment.

I glance over at Ramon and he seems in complete control. He must have nerves of steel. We're in Carthay Circle off La Cienega when his grip on the steering wheel finally relaxes.

"We lost them," he says sounding relieved while I'm considering whether I need to step out of the car and throw up or not.

"Canter's is on Fairfax near Beverly, yes?" he asks, his voice surprisingly steady.

I nod. And let my death grip on the door handle go, as he makes a U-turn and starts heading east.

He's turned onto Fairfax and he looks over at me. "You okay?"

"Yeah, sure. I'm great. That felt like I was in a bat-shit crazy video game and my time was running out."

Ramon gives me a pained smile. "Sorry about that."

"How do you know they won't find us at Canters?"

"It's not like that. Marcus just wanted to scare me . . . like a warning."

"A warning? Are you going to tell me what he's warning you about?"

He deftly parks in Canter's lot and we get out of the car.

"Why don't we go inside?" he replies before patting the hood of my Audi. "Nice car."

THE HOSTESS WITH BRIGHT BLUE hair and an old-school waitress uniform on, seats us in a booth in the big room, which is a hodge-podge of retro design depending on what decade each upgrade was done. The booths may be vinyl and the tabletop Formica, but I explain to Ramon that the food is as real and hearty as it gets. I'm glad I decided not to press him for answers right away because after a few minutes of being there I'm noticeably calmer, and he seems more relaxed. It's almost chill enough that I can pretend we're on a date. I think the change of environment was just what we needed. We both order plenty of food when the waitress checks on us.

After the meal arrives I slather my bagel with cream cheese, tear off a chunk, and dip it in my soup.

Ramon wears a dubious expression. "What the hell are you doing? I may not be Jewish, but I sure know that's not kosher what you're doing there."

I shrug. "Who cares? I'm not either, but even if I were I'd do this. You should try it. It's so good."

He shakes his head and continues to eat properly. "So did that guy Michael at the club get your number?"

Dipping another chunk of bagel long enough for the cream cheese to start melting off, I nod.

"Are you going to go out with him?"

"Do you want me to?"

"Well that was kind of the point, don't you think?"

"Honestly, I went there with you tonight because I wanted to be with you."

He lets a long sigh out and rests his chin in his hand, his elbow perched on the table.

Not being able to hold off any longer, I push my soup away. "Ramon, can you tell me what exactly happened with that guy? And why did they follow us?"

His head falls forward, his free hand joining the other to cover his face. When I cough, he parts his hands far enough so I can hear his words even though he's staring down at the table. "He wants something from me, and I'm sure he didn't like seeing me with you. He's very territorial."

"What does he want exactly," I ask, feeling discouraged that there's a new potential roadblock between Ramon and I.

"It's complicated," he says.

"How so?"

"It's a long, messed up story. You see I met Marcus right after I moved to L.A."

I twist my napkin that's resting on my lap into a tight coil. "Did you date him?"

Ramon nods. "He was sexy, mysterious and demanding, and I was intrigued by him."

I don't like where this is going. Sexy and mysterious is everything I'm not. "Did you date a long time?"

"Longer than I should have. I quickly learned that he wasn't a good guy, but I was in such a bad place that I actually felt like I deserved the asshole way he treated me."

It's hard for me to picture Ramon's behavior so self-defeating. "Things were that bad when you arrived here?" The feeling that swells up in my heart reminds me of Sasha and my shocking relocation to L.A . . . At the time, I tried to act like I could handle it, but I was a total wreck inside. I wish I could express to Ramon the depth of my sympathy for sharing a similar experience of loss and then being forced to leave home.

"Really bad. About a year after Luis died, I got involved in a business deal that went south and the assholes took my investment money, which was most of what Luis left me. I should've known not to be so stupid, but I was still grieving and Luis had encouraged me to open my own club. It was part of his dream, too. I would've done anything to make it happen."

The wheels in my head are spinning. *Ramon was trying to open a club in Miami?* "So how does this Marcus guy play into it?"

"He's tied into some kind of network with his business deal-ings . . . some of them in Vegas and Miami. When we were involved he said he was going to help me recover the money."

"Did he have new information for you tonight?"

"He said he did, but then when he had me alone I realized he had duped me again. And then . . ." His hands close over his face again.

Everything in my stomach is souring. Ramon is a tough guy, if he's this upset it must be really shitty. Reaching out, I take hold of his forearm. "Hey, it's okay."

He starts wildly shaking his head. "No, Charlie, it's not fucking okay! He wants to control me and I'm done with all that. I promised Luis I would stand tall in his memory and not sink back into the fucked-up life I was living before we met and he showed me my worth. Instead, back in that room after feeding me tiny scraps of information, Marcus had me on my knees begging for his help again, and instead, he tried to force himself on me and then laughed in my face."

"Damn." I groan.

He presses his eyes shut and shakes his head. "Luis would've been so ashamed of me. He probably knows. He always told me he'd be looking out for me from up there." He tips his head up to what he intends to be the heavens, and not this strange pattern of faux stained-glass panels over the fluorescent lights of the deli.

I scratch my chin in thought. "So you're fighting for what is rightfully yours, and I get that. But I watched a news report recently about the massive problems with the Cuban gangs and Russian mafia in Miami. Do you think somehow your deal was connected to people like that?"

He nods mournfully. "I didn't connect that at the time obviously, but now I do. I think most of the independent clubs are run through their networks."

"So you can see that fighting them to get your money back may not only be impossible, but you could put yourself in serious danger?"

Releasing out a long sigh, his shoulders hunch forward. "That's how I ended up in L.A. I had arranged a meeting in South Beach to talk to the three men I'd done the deal with. A friend told me I was crazy if I thought anything good would come out of it—that it was more likely they'd rearrange my face. A few days before the meeting I had a very vivid dream where I woke up on a couch in an unfamiliar room and noticed a patio door open to a balcony. In the dream, I stood up to see where I was, and there were Luis and his childhood friend, Hector, sitting in the sun looking out over the view. Hector lives in the Hollywood Hills, so I was amazed, wondering if that's where Luis's idea of heaven was. In the dream, I glanced down at my clothes, realizing that I was disheveled and unshaven, and I felt terribly embarrassed for Luis to see me in such bad shape. He turned to me, his gaze intense and penetrating. It was as if he knew I was in danger. 'Ramon, mi amor, this is where you *have* to be *now.*'"

Completely taken by the image, I suck in a sharp breath and lean toward him. "Whoa. So you felt that the dream was prophetic?"

He sits up straight, focusing on me with wide eyes. "I knew it was. I got up right then and started packing my stuff. I called Hector in the morning and was out on a flight that afternoon."

"And here you are," I say, feeling gratitude that this message came to Ramon and he took it seriously. Otherwise, he could be dead.

"For better or worse, here I am."

I change the subject for the rest of our meal in an attempt to get Ramon's mind off things. At one point he asks me what Michael and I had talked about, and I mention our conversation about my investment app.

"That's so cool you follow the stock market and know so much about investing. I wish you'd been around when I was trying to figure out what to do in Miami. I'd learned a lot in school about running a business: starting capital, overhead, city licenses, advertising and promotion, sales projections and door draws. But my finance professor was so incompetent that the class was a wash."

"It's never too late to learn," I say. "I can help you. Do you plan to ever try to open a business again? If so, I could help you with that, too."

"You'd do that?"

"Sure."

He sits up, his whole mood lightening. "My goal is to try to open an all-inclusive dance club, but this time here in L.A. It's going to take a long time, though, because I don't have nearly enough capital saved yet to justify drawing in investors."

"Was that always your dream?"

"When I was younger I wanted to own restaurants or cafés. It wasn't until I became part of the gay scene in Miami that I realized I'd be better suited for a club. Like I said, I was a business major in undergrad, but Luis encouraged me to go back to school and get my masters in hospitality management with a focus on club management. I finished the program a few months before he got sick."

"Smart to get that education about the business side. Too many people jump into business ideas without the foundation they need."

"But I still screwed things up by putting my trust in the wrong people. If only I'd followed my gut."

I shrug. "Live and learn. Look, I'm not going to minimize the horrible stuff that happened to you, but I'd wager that you've learned a lot from it."

He nods. "And Gene, the owner of Wild Nights, has taken me under his wing and taught me a lot. He was another friend of Luis's and that's how I got the job. There's a lot I admire about how he runs his business."

"Well, you know I'm a fan of his club, thanks to a particular guy who works there."

Walking out of Canters, I'm both proud and amazed that not only was I not awkward tonight, but I was able to really help Ramon after what happened with Marcus, and that makes me feel great. He tosses the car keys to me and I do my regular thirty-minute check on my phone to make sure I didn't miss a call from Sasha. All appears to be good.

"So where do you live?" I ask, as I pull out of the lot.

"Near Franklin and Beachwood. You don't mind dropping me off?"

I look at him like he's nuts. "After that thrill ride where you saved me from the forces of evil it's the least I can do."

Laughing, he settles down in the seat.

I've turned onto Vine Street when I remember something. "Hey, Sasha keeps asking me to take her and her best friend Emily to Wild Nights. Would you be okay with that?"

"Sure, but will you be okay with that?"

I laugh. "I think so."

"How do you think she'd handle it if one of the floor dancers gave her some attention?"

"Hmmm, knowing Sasha I'm pretty sure she's hoping for that."

"I can't wait to meet your sister. How about the night after to-morrow? I'm not sure about comp tickets, but I can look into it."

"I think that night will work. I'll check with her and let you know. And don't worry about the tickets, I'll take care of that."

We're quiet for a few blocks and an idea occurs to me. "Hey, do you mind if we go up near the Griffith Park Observatory for a minute? There's a great spot to look at the view, and with these winds clearing the atmosphere, it should be the perfect night for it."

"We won't get arrested? It's pretty late," Ramon responds, his eyebrows knitted together.

"No, I've done it before a few times when I couldn't sleep. The spot I found is far enough from the guards that I've never had a problem."

He blinks a few times and sighs. "I guess. Not like this night could get any weirder."

Turning off Franklin onto Los Feliz, I feel a surge of excitement thinking about how Ramon and I are hanging out tonight. It's almost like a date. Yes, he may have had an agenda the first part of the eve-ning, and we had the scene with the bad guys, but the second half belongs to me. I not only got him to go to Canters with me, but soon I'm going to share with him one of my favorite places in L.A.

I take Vermont northbound, passing the Greek theater. Finally, near the top of the hill, I pull off a side road and park. Gesturing for him to follow me, I lead the way as we hike up the rest of the paved asphalt to Observatory Road.

"Don't you have to get up early in the morning?" he groans. "It's late, you know."

"Yes. But it's fine since I'm not a good sleeper anyway. I'd probably be lying in bed awake if I weren't out here with you."

When we climb high enough, we see the art deco form of the famous Observatory rise up into our view.

"Oh wow . . . look at that," Ramon exclaims.

Grinning, I nod. "Pretty great, yes?"

"Yes."

When I finally lead him to the landing—where only a waist-high, minimal fence is between us and the dramatic city view—he takes a sharp breath.

"Wow," he whispers, his expression positively stunned.

"You've really never been up here?"

"No, and now that I'm here I can't believe it." He sweeps his hand across the jewel box of lights sprinkled from one side of the city to the other. "It's cool, it look like it shimmers."

"It does." I agree, smiling to see him so happy. I point out Downtown L.A. in the far distance to the east, and he joins in as we move west: Hollywood, Beverly Hills and Century City, with Santa Monica and the now black stripe of ocean on the edge of our view.

He takes a half step closer to me so our hips are touching. "Is it crazy to think there's something magical about this city, like anything can happen here?"

I shake my head, my gaze still fixed on the view. "No, not at all. They say L.A.'s a place for dreamers."

He lets out a regretful sigh. "And I guess that would be me. I've always been a dreamer . . . wanting more than I deserve."

"Why would you think you don't deserve to dream big? That's the motivation that can propel the human spirit to accomplish amazing things. There's nothing wrong with dreaming, Ramon. How else do dreams have a chance to come true?"

The corners of his mouth turn up as he faces me. "I guess you're right."

I swallow hard, trying to get my courage up before I reach out for his hand. "What if I told you that I really think you can make your dream of having your own club happen?"

His fingers close over mine and his hand is so warm and solid—just like Ramon.

"I would tell you that I don't think you have any objectivity about me at this point."

"You mean like you've dazzled me until I've lost my senses?"

He laughs. "Something like that. I think tonight you've revealed that under that business-like, linear exterior, you're secretly a romantic guy."

"Really?" That's the last way I'd ever think of myself.

"Yes, really," he says, laughing.

I pause for a moment, thinking that if I'm ever going to take a chance, this very moment, while we're brushed by this gentle breeze and illuminated by the silver light of the moon, would be the perfect time. The City of Angels sparkles just for us. Maybe all the dreams between us could be spun into something real and true.

I clear my throat so my voice is clear. "Well, dazzling and romantic guy aside, I wish you'd let me kiss you. I mean I get it if you aren't looking for a relationship, but just one kiss wouldn't hurt anything, right?"

"Oh yeah, sure . . . one kiss? I'm not buying that."

"You're so confident. How do you know that I won't find your kissing style to my liking and the result will be that I'll never kiss you again?"

"Umm, I'm sure that's not going to happen."

"So confident," I tease.

He tips his head and throws his hands up. "Just stating the facts. I'm an epically good kisser."

"Can I be the judge of that?" Nervous as all hell that he'll reject me, I turn to face him, and I watch as his gaze travels over my face, in particular my mouth. I slowly slide my hand across his shoulder like I've seen in movies, curving around his neck where it rests possessively. I remember the first time Leo and I kissed it was awkward and sloppy with teeth clashing, and I nipped my lower lip on his braces. I'm determined that this kiss is going to be nothing like that. And when our lips meet the feeling is smooth like sweet cream and just as delicious. Much to my surprise and delight, he doesn't push me away or resist. My lips fit his perfectly, our breaths short and sharp . . . every bit of my pent-up longing for this man wrapping us together tightly.

My fingers explore up his neck, into his short, thick hair. His sculpted chest presses firmly against mine, expanding with his ragged breaths. I close my eyes, as if this moment will never end as long as I can't see him pull away. He kisses me back passionately, making me feel like there's no one he wants more. He's hungry and wanting . . . his touch an invitation, not a command. I could kiss him forever.

When we finally need a breath, we part, a sliver of moonlight shining between us. I feel his lips skim along edge of my ear.

"My romantic prince," he teases in a dark whisper. "And all that talk earlier about you saving me . . ."

"Did that turn you on?"

"You know it did."

"Mmm," I moan as his lips continue down my neck. "Yes, I would have saved you, as long as you keep saving me, too." I'm hoping he can't see my skin flush because I feel like I'm on fire.

The weird part is that I actually mean the truth of these words, probably more than I've been willing to admit until now.

We both turn toward the view. I can't tell what he's focusing on in the distance, but that the intensity of his stare lets me know his mind has gone somewhere important.

"What?" I finally ask.

His fingers tighten over the guardrail. "You know the last thing Luis said to me?"

I shake my head gently and wait as he takes a deep breath.

It's disconcerting, if not heartbreaking, that he would be thinking of his ex after kissing me. I thought he was as swept up in the moment as I was. But instead of crumbling, I soldier on, waiting to hear what he has to say.

"He said I was golden, and that he wanted me with someone who deserved me."

"He said that? I mean, not the golden part . . . I get that. But he was already thinking about you with someone else?"

"He had accepted his fate at that point, but he was really worried about me, and he knew I'm the kind of man that is better with a mate."

"Interesting," I whisper.

"And he made me promise I'd wait for that man."

"Wow. No pressure for you or anything," I can't help but point out. "And you're still waiting?"

Not giving me an answer, he leans over the railing, gazing at the brilliant world at our feet. A million lights shine for us from towering office buildings to mom-and-pop businesses, tiny Compton apartments to Holmby Hills estates, random dive bars to Beverly Hills hotels, and everything in between.

I let my gaze travel upwards to the starry sky. In L.A. you don't see a lot of stars in the night sky because the city glows so brightly, diminishing the necessary darkness. But on a clear night like tonight the sky shimmers, too. I think about Luis's spirit soaring up there watching over Ramon, and I silently speak to him, sending word of my deepest desire. I imagine a floating fire lantern etched with my secret message and released from my hands with a hope and prayer as it ascends.

Please let me be the man he's been waiting for, Luis. I'll be good for him, you'll see.

7. Like Romeo and Ramon

I CALL RAMON AT LUNCH on Thursday to make sure he's working that night. Also, it sounds goofy to admit, but I really want to hear his voice. His voice is perfect, warm and smooth like a thick sweater wrapped around you on a cold day. But more than that, there's something in his tone when he says my name that sparks bolts of excitement right up my spine.

Besides, I don't want to go through all the steps to get Emily and Sasha to Wild Nights, let alone how thrilled Sasha is at the prospect, only to find out that it's not a good night after all.

"Hey Charlie," he answers. "You guys are still coming tomorrow night, right?"

"Yeah, I was calling to make sure it was still good for you, too."

"Sure, it's good. Are you *sure* Sasha would like some extra attention? Because I've arranged something."

I'm suddenly overcome with a troubling thought and my stomach cramps up. "You're not going to dance for her, are you?"

"Are you seriously asking me that? What kind of guy do you think I am? After the things we've done together it would be wrong to dance with her."

I let out the breath I was holding. "Right . . . I knew that. I wanted to make sure."

"So what time will you get there?"

"My plan is by seven, or seven-fifteen, depending on how smoothly things go. I want to have them there with plenty of time before the show."

"After you get them settled at the table come get me at the bar."

"Will do. Hey, Ramon?"

"Yes?"

"I'm looking forward to seeing you tomorrow, whether you dance or not."

I can hear the smile in his voice. "Me too."

After hanging up I lean back in my chair with a satisfied stretch. It feels like my whole life is opening up and getting bigger, and instead of fearing the unknown, I'm exhilarated. Suddenly I realize there's someone leaning against my cubicle's half-wall and I startle.

"Damn, Billy! How long have you been standing there?"

He gives me a crooked grin. "Long enough. So you and the dancer are a thing, huh?"

This really isn't something I'm ready to talk about, so I give a safe answer. "No, we're just friends."

"Sure you are." He winks at me. "But tell me, what do you talk to a stripper about? The best place to buy G-strings?"

My fingers tense around the arms of my chair. He likes to give people a hard time, and I try not to let it get to me because it's stupid stuff, but I'm compelled to defend Ramon. "You don't know what he's about, Billy, so stop being an ass. Has it occurred to you that he has bigger dreams than you do?"

Taking on a defensive look, he slaps his chest dramatically and grins. "Hey, I've got big dreams!"

Crossing my arms, I lean back in my swivel chair. "Like what? Didn't you work at Dodger Stadium in concessions for several years to save money for school? Would you like it if I thought the only conversation you could have back then was talking about hot dogs?"

"All right, point made," he laughs, good-naturedly.

"For your information, Ramon has a Masters in Hospitality Management with plans to open a dance club. So that job is great exposure and training for him."

"And I bet all the tail he gets is an added bonus."

"You know what they say about people who assume, Billy," I say with an exasperated groan. "You're making an *ass* of *u* and *me*."

"You know how much I like to rile you up. I seriously am getting off on how you're defending him. You really have a thing for him, don't you?"

"There's no *thing*," I reply, waving my hand toward him, all the while thinking that there actually is a *thing, a* very real thing.

Earlier I was daydreaming and thinking about all that I've learned about Ramon since I first walked up to him at the bar. Each bit of knowledge has piece-by-piece built an impression in my head of a man I respect. He's worked hard, both to get through school and chase his dreams, he's dedicated to his family, has been in a committed relationship, and lives a clean life despite the scene he works in. He has goals and dreams, making him a man worth taking seriously. Frankly, he seems like someone who has a lot more to offer than I do.

Billy's expression softens as he studies me. "Seriously though, dude, I'm happy you're doing stuff . . . getting out and living. It's about time. And I never was able to influence you to go have fun often enough, which worried me a lot, so I give major props to Ramon for how much he's accomplished in so little time."

I narrow my gaze at him until I realize he seems sincere, and a wave of warmth flows over me. Apparently, I was so disconnected that I didn't know my friends were worried. "Are you serious about that, Billy?"

He nods and shrugs. "I am."

"Well, thanks. That means a lot to me."

THE NEXT EVENING AT OUR condo, Sasha holds up two articles of clothing on hangers for me to see. "Should I wear the lower-cut black shirt, or the red?"

"I don't know—the red one?" I say. "As your big brother, it's out of what's acceptable for me to encourage you to wear anything low-cut. I may be gay, but that doesn't mean I don't understand how straight guys work."

She arches her brow. "And how do they work exactly?"

"Like maybe they'll be trying to look down your top when you're not paying attention, or even while you are." I give her an exaggerated look of horror.

"Okay, thanks. It's the black one then. Tonight's about rolling out of my comfort zone!"

Well she certainly put me in my place. I grin inwardly. I like this rebellious side of her.

She pivots her chair and heads back to her bedroom. Lucia has stayed overtime to help her get ready. I think the false eyelashes were a bit much, but I have to admit that Sasha looks really pretty, especially with that exceptionally happy expression on her face.

In all the different places I've taken Sasha, or places I still want to show her, I never thought a male revue of dancers/strippers would be the highlight of the year. *Wow, I wonder what Mom and Dad would think of all of this?*

A minute later the doorbell rings repeatedly until I finally yank the door open.

Emily is bouncing on her toes, and when she steps inside she gives me a hug, which I awkwardly accept. "I can't believe you're taking us to Wild Nights." she says. "Thank you, Charlie . . . this is such a treat."

"Really?" I ask. My mind tries to recall how old Emily is since she seems so young right now. Maybe she needs to read less and get out more. But then again, until a week ago you could say the exact same thing about me.

What's happening with my life? I think, and then grin like a fool.

"Sasha said you have a friend who works there. Is he going to dance for us?"

"Um, no. He's bartending tonight, but he does want to meet you two."

She lets out a long, happy sigh. "Oh yes. We want to meet him."

I observe that Emily has tamed her wild, curly red hair into something intentionally sleek. I'm impressed with how great she looks tonight, especially her hairstyle, which is stylish as opposed to her usual look, like she strolled through a tornado and her hair took the brunt of the beating.

Sasha calls out for her from the other room where Lucia is helping her with finishing touches, and Emily gives me a little wave and slips away.

I listen silently, the entire drive to the club as they go on about exactly how disrobed the men will be, the potential size of their manhoods, and whether they stuff socks in their briefs or not. I had no idea that women were actually worse than men with this stuff. From what I can tell, they are far more descriptive and critical about their expectations.

Emily, who is sitting in the front passenger seat, but is turned sideways for her conversation with Sasha, glances over at me. "Will any of these guys be dancing close to us? Do you think we can touch them and stuff?" she asks, her cheeks turning bright pink as she giggles.

I guess now that they know I'm gay, it's a free-for-all in the conversation topics.

"I'm not sure about *'and stuff.'* You're better to avoid that."

"I've heard stories," Sasha says quietly to Emily, apparently not caring that I'm right here listening.

"You mean that cover model who got wild in New Orleans?"

Sasha nods her head with an arched brow.

What exactly happens at these book events anyway? I wonder.

When we arrive at the club, the valet lets us pull into the driveway so I can get out to release the latch securing Sasha's wheelchair in place. It's situated behind the two front passenger seats. From there she can direct her electric wheelchair down the mechanical ramp extending from our customized mini-van. A couple of onlookers marvel at the technology, but Sasha is pretty used to gawking by now. Emily takes a moment to smooth out Sasha's skirt and then turns to nod at me.

"Ready, ladies?" I ask, and they grin and nod enthusiastically.

"You look sharp," Sasha says as her gaze travels over me. "I haven't seen you wear that jacket in forever."

I shrug. "I figured it was a special night."

Warning them to pull out their ID's, Emily hands hers to the bouncer before he can ask for it. When she passes through and the big, burly guy sees Sasha, his expression brightens. "Hey there, pretty lady, are you ready to have fun?"

"I'm so ready," she replies with a huge smile.

I swear I want to hug the guy for putting that joyful expression on my sister's face.

"Okay then, I want to hear about it later," he teases.

She nods with wide eyes. "I'll come looking for you."

When she rolls past him, I give him a thumbs-up. "Hey, thanks, man." I'm almost choked up that this bruiser took a moment to make her feel like she belongs, which is everything.

"Anytime," he responds with an understanding nod.

One of the shirtless guys with the bowties scans our admission print-out and then guides us to a reserved table near the front where they've adjusted the table's proximity to the one behind it. Now Sasha's wheelchair easily fits in.

"These are amazing seats!" Emily exclaims. "Are they really going to dance right there?"

"Yes. And see that staircase?" I point about six feet to our right. "At some point they'll come down the stairs right there to go into the audience."

"Wow! Can you believe this, Sasha?"

"What would you ladies like to drink? I'll go to the bar since we're a little early for the waiters to work the tables."

"Maybe a Sprite for me for now," Emily answers.

"Same for me," my sister adds.

Although I'm not sure if Ramon is supposed to be here yet, I'm hoping he is. I'm really anxious for him to meet Sasha. But when I approach the bar a shot of excitement zings through me. He's opening a bottle of wine, and I watch his forearms flex, every muscle defined where he's folded up his sleeves. I'd love to be that wine bottle with his nimble fingers wrapped around me while he twists and turns until he eases me open.

Feeling awkward, I push my glasses higher up the bridge of my nose, and run my fingers through my mess of hair. It's that moment that he looks up and sees me, and the resulting smile not only turns the corners of his mouth up, but it lightens his gaze as his eyes connect with mine. A second later I see his eyes trail across my shoulders and down, taking in my sports jacket, and the button-down blue shirt underneath.

He glances on either side of me with a curious expression. "Are the girls at your table? You brought them, didn't you?"

Is he thinking I made that up to have another excuse to see him here again tonight? "I sure did. They're back at the table and I've gotta say . . . me bringing them here is the biggest win."

"I bet," he says, grinning. "And I've set some stuff up, and I think they'll really love it. You promised they won't be too shy. Right?"

"No worries in that regard. I swear, if there was a handicap ramp to the stage, Sasha would be happy to be up there in the middle of everything. She is way cooler than me, Ramon."

He tosses his dishtowel on the counter below the bar top. "I really want to meet her. Let's head over there now."

My fingers curl, wanting to take Ramon's hand, and he follows right behind me, weaving between tables now filling up with women amped up for the evening ahead. When we finally reach our table, I surmise that he should be the one called 'prince' for the way he charms them.

He starts by leaning over Sasha and taking her hand, then gently placing a kiss on her fingers right where a ring should be. "Sasha," he says. "I've heard so many wonderful things about you."

She studies Ramon for a moment, and then glances up at me, and then back at him with a wide smile. "Well, you're certainly everything my brother said you'd be."

"I hope that's a good thing," he replies with a wink.

"Oh you have no idea. It's awesome. Ramon, let me introduce my best friend, Emily."

He takes her hand and repeats the gesture, and I observe Emily's eyes grow wide as she watches him.

Grabbing a free chair from the table behind us, he pulls it up between the two girls so he can talk to them eye to eye. I sink down in my chair, mesmerized to watch Ramon cast his spell over them, as he did with me the night we met. His magic skills are substantial, and watching Sasha's eyes light up as he asks about her having to fight guys off since she's so pretty, feels like too much to me, but then I look at her adoring gaze and realize that it's just right.

He manages to also equally charm Emily, asking her about boyfriends he assumes she has, which delights her to no end. At one point Emily and Sasha are giving each other wide-eyed looks, and Ramon glances over at me, giving me a conspiratorial wink.

Warmth unfurls in my chest for this man. He has no idea that him charming my sister, making her feel like a regular girl who stands out for nothing other than being so pretty, even if only for one night, means more to me than any attention he could give me.

Sasha reaches over and rests her delicate hand on his forearm. "Ramon, you have to come to our place for dinner. Did you know what a great cook Charlie is?"

His look of surprise is almost insulting.

"What?" I ask. "I already warned you I have all kinds of skills you have no idea of." I cross my arms over my chest, hopefully to project a cocky confidence that I'm actually lacking.

"So what are you going to cook for me, Prince Charlie?" he asks.

"Prince Charlie!" they both squeal, and I flash him a dirty look.

"Food," I reply dryly.

Sasha leans into him. "He's a natural in the kitchen. I keep saying he should have his own show like Gordon Ramsey."

"You mean like the shows where Ramsey tells people what fuck-ups they are?" He turns toward me. "Is that what you have in mind, Charlie? Because I'm not sure you could pull that off."

I scowl at him. Is he giving me a hard time so his tender ways with the girls seems that much sweeter?

"Do you cook, Ramon?" I ask.

"Not really," he admits.

"Well then I'd suggest that you lay off me."

His surprised expression aggravates me, and I realize that I don't like Ramon teasing me, no matter the reason. It brings back shitty memories from middle and high school where I got picked on a lot. Not because my growth spurt came late, but it was like those assholes figured out I was gay even before I was sure of it. The memories of their cruelty from that time still burn.

All I want in life at this moment is for this guy to think I'm amazing and to say as much. Not to pick apart things that don't even matter.

Pushing my chair back, I stand up. "I'll be back in a minute. Where are the restrooms?"

He gestures toward the far back left corner.

"Thanks," I say somberly before waving my hand. "Continue on."

When I exit the bathroom after washing my hands, I stop in my tracks realizing that Ramon is leaning against the wall, waiting for me.

"Anything wrong?" I ask, automatically worrying about Sasha.

"You tell me. When you left we were all worried that something was wrong with you. Are you okay?"

I shrug. "Why wouldn't I be?"

He looks down with a sheepish expression. "Well, Sasha told me that you hate to be teased."

"I guess," I murmur.

"And that you take pride in your cooking."

"Hmmm. She's probably right about that, too."

He steps up to me and wraps his arms around me. "Charlie, I'm sorry if I hurt you."

I'm having trouble letting go of my tension from feeling defensive; my body remains stiff as he holds me.

"Teasing is a sore spot for me. I had it pretty rough when I was younger."

Pulling back, he fixes his gaze on me like he's looking for the hurt reflected in my eyes. He must see it because he winces. "When I look at you I see an amazing man. You're smart and accomplished, you have a good heart . . . shall I go on?"

I edge the corners of my mouth up enough that he notices. "By all means, do continue."

"Shall I point out that you are very desirable, handsome and built, and you kiss like a passionate Romeo, only not with Juliet?"

"Romeo and Ramon. That sounds like a bad porn movie."

"A hot porn . . . and to top it off, you're a prince. I mean, how many guys can compete with that?"

"True. I've pretty much got the edge on the prince thing." I suddenly realize my body is relaxing the more we talk.

He gestures to the hallway. "Shall we get back to the girls?"

I nod, and step in line behind him as he leads the way.

The music is pumping and the dance floor is filling up as rounds of drinks are served and everyone loosens up. I get some whiskey and the girls agree to glasses of champagne, and it makes the two of them even more giggly. It's damn cute. I don't bring up the dance floor because it looks like it would be precarious for Sasha considering how crowded it is. Instead we keep drinking, and before we know it the announcer gives the warning that the show is about to begin.

To say I had no idea where to focus is an understatement. Although my appreciation for the beautiful, shirtless men marching across the stage is profound, my eyes are continually drawn to Sasha and Emily whose mouths are gaping open.

"Oh my gawd," Emily whispers.

I'm pretty sure I hear Sasha moan.

Glancing over my shoulder, I see Ramon leaning over the bar with his eyes fixed on the girls. When his gaze moves to me I nod, and he smiles.

Feeling warm and relaxed from my drink, I lean back in my chair and ponder how much my life has changed in a week. Although I have no idea where I really stand with Ramon, I know he likes me at least a little. I'm pretty sure he wouldn't kiss me if he didn't.

And now tonight, and the way he is being with Sasha . . . I swear if he continues treating us like we're more significant than mere friends, but like we're special, how can I help but fall head-first, hopelessly in love?

But then a chill runs through me as my insecure mind starts up with the questions. *What if he's being kind to you? What if you're not his type? Does he have a boyfriend you haven't heard about yet? What's the real deal with that Marcus guy? What if this attention is because he feels sorry for you?*

The last idea is the harshest, because I don't want his pity. I just want him.

We're about halfway through the performance when the house-lights come up partially and my heartbeat surges. I glance back toward the bar and see Ramon moving toward us, but stopping about twenty feet away. He folds his arms over his chest, and his laser focus is on the guys starting to dance their way into the audience. I notice him nod abruptly and then look forward to see one of the best looking of the men approaching our table. I recall from the beginning of the show that he was introduced as Jess.

Jess approaches our table, and while smiling at Sasha, carefully pulls her wheelchair back, and turns it a bit so she's facing him and Emily at the same time. There's enough space for him to step between them and put on a show.

The guy is a friggin' god, so buff, tall, and handsome as hell. He entertains them both at the same time, although always lingering longer on Sasha. He does this movement where he rolls his body toward her until his face is inches from hers. She remains outwardly composed, but I know my sister. This is an experience she will relive in her mind a thousand times.

Emily, meanwhile, looks like she'd elope with him in a hot second. From the looks of the way his hips move, the man would be noteworthy in bed.

Once again, I glance back at Ramon who seems pleased with the performance. Jess takes the arms of Sasha's wheelchair, gently pushes it back, and then rolls it toward him so that it settles between his straddled legs. When he starts rolling his hips, I realize that Sasha's cheeks have never been so pink and she actually reaches up and slides her hands down his thighs. Jess rolls his hips a few more times, then grazes her cheeks with his fingertips and straightens back up. Before he joins the group back on stage, he leans over and says something in Sasha's ear. He grasps her and Emily's hands one last time and squeezes before returning to his place under the lights.

Emily doesn't disappoint with her dramatic reaction. She starts clutching her chest. "I'm dead! It's lust whiplash causing a complete internal collapse!" She starts fanning her face with her hand in a frantic motion.

Sasha, in contrast, is still as a statue, her face frozen in some state of supreme bliss.

Reaching over, I clasp her hand. "You okay?"

Her gaze connects with mine, her eyes glazed with tears. "Charlie, that gorgeous man told me that I'm beautiful."

"Well you are," I say very matter of fact. "That's never been disputed."

She shakes her head like I've completely missed the point. "You're my brother. Of course you're going to say that."

"Give yourself some credit. You know how good looking you are."

She guffaws. "Hardly."

"So what makes you think that he lied to you about thinking you're pretty?"

She gives me a rather pointed look and waves at her legs and her wheelchair. "Hello, Captain Obvious. Are you denying the undisputable truth that people feel sorry for me? Sometimes I feel like my wheelchair and useless legs are all they see."

"Please don't say that," I say, trying to be convincing, but my shaky voice gives me away. How can people not feel sorry for her? She's lost so much and will never have the life she was meant to have.

Her anxious expression fades. "You know what? None of that matters tonight. That guy Jess really looked at me. For that magical moment, I felt for the first time since the accident that maybe I could have more. You know what I mean?"

"I do, and you will."

When I look across the room, Ramon is still watching us. "I'll be right back," I say to the girls.

As I approach him, he glances over to the far wall on his left, and his expression is troubled. My gaze follows his to reveal the asshole Marcus leaning against the wall and giving Ramon a look I can't read. By the time I'm in front of Ramon I can see he's very unsettled.

"What's he doing here?" I ask, not hiding my irritation. Suddenly I'm worried about Ramon. Plus this is Sasha's special night, and I can't have anyone spoiling it. I glance around, but thankfully I don't see his goons.

"He came to apologize," Ramon says as he looks down at a mark on the floor when he should be looking me in the eye. *What's up with that?*

"Apologize for what exactly? I'm under the impression that there's a lot he should apologize for."

Ramon shrugs. "Well to start with . . . for being an asshole and territorial with me at the Lodge."

"Territorial?" I scoff. "How about sending his thugs after us?" I glance back over at him and he all but snarls at me. "If you ask me he still has a lot of issues."

"I have to finish our conversation, but I told him he'd have to wait until I knew Sasha got what I'd promised." He nods toward our table obviously trying to change the subject. "From back here it looks like things went well. I knew Jess was the right choice."

I can't help but give him a huge smile. "Thank you so much for arranging that."

He shrugs. "No biggie. I was happy to do it. She's a really great girl, Charlie."

"She's awesome. We were always close, and she was always the one looking out for me. Now, since the accident, of course our roles have switched some, but she's still my biggest support."

"Family is the best." He gestures to the bar. "Hey, I better deal with Marcus and then get back to work, but I'll come by during my next break."

The girls finish most of the champagne, and by the time the stage show ends both girls are dancing in their seats. Well, with Sasha it's more arm and head movements but it's still dancing. When the house lights come on there's photo opportunities and Jess comes over so I can get shots of each girl with him. It's been a long time since I've seen Sasha this happy. That picture will definitely be getting framed, and I'm betting it will be shared on social media with her book friends.

Despite all the epic-ness of the night, or perhaps because of it, I notice her starting to fade. This was a lot for her. After telling Emily that we'll be leaving soon, I go to let Ramon know. He looks even more distracted, I assume by whatever is going on with Marcus. I want to ask more about it, but now is not the time.

Gathered in a circle at the edge of the room, the girls thank Ramon profusely and he accepts their thanks graciously.

"So when are you coming over for dinner?" Sasha asks him. She sure doesn't beat around the bush. "I won't be there you know. I'll be spending the night at Emily's."

Emily glances over at Sasha with a surprised expression. "Awesome!" she says.

He looks flustered. "Uh, I'm not sure about my schedule."

I get a sinking feeling that he's got an issue about dinner. Does his reluctance have anything to do with Marcus? Or maybe it's just too much, too fast with me, and we shouldn't push him. But Sasha is unrelenting when she makes her mind up about something.

"When's your next day off?" she asks.

"Wednesday," he replies, but he looks even more distracted.

She claps her hands. "Okay, Wednesday it is! Are you a vegetarian or allergic to anything?"

"No," he states with a frown.

Now I'm really getting uncomfortable. I can feel my neck tightening and my palms sweat. "Sasha, don't push him. If he doesn't want to come over for dinner, he doesn't have to."

Her expression is crestfallen as she gazes at him. "You don't want to come?"

There's a pause, and then Ramon gives what seems to be a forced smile. "It's not that. Hey, I'll come, okay?"

Letting out a puff of relief she nods. "Great!"

8. The Vineyard of Broken Hearts

I'M OBSESSED. NOW THAT WE'RE home and away from the Marcus situation, I can't stop thinking about Ramon. My desire to be close to him is like a gravitational pull drawing my body toward his. Late that night I'm restless, still possessed by the sheer thought of him. Finally around two, I doze off.

Drifting out of a fog I realize that I'm wandering through a short hall and into a vast room that seems to be a club. Other than a spotlight shining on a single table in the audience area, and the row of small lights edging the stage, the room is pitch dark to the point that I can't see where the ceiling and walls meet. I feel like I've been sucked into a black hole.

I approach the table under the spotlight and note the single rose in a vase, a glass of Scotch, and a propped up envelope. It has my name written on the front in an elaborate scroll. Glancing around the room to fruitlessly see who left it there, I sink down into the chair and carefully tear open the flap and pull out the thick card with a hand-written note. It contains three words, and my mind searches for the phrase's deeper meaning.

Why not now?

Taking a gulp of the drink, I feel the warmth spread through me. Lifting the card up again, I whisper the words. "Why not now?" What in the hell does that mean? And how does it pertain to me?

The spotlight over my table dims at the same time a spotlight on the stage is illuminated. Suddenly music fills the space, and it's a hypnotic rhythm that immediately pulls me in. My gaze fixes on the stage light just as a figure steps into it. I'd recognize that smooth skin perfect body, and handsome face anywhere. It's Ramon, and my fingers ache with want to touch him.

"Ramon!" I say loudly, but he remains still, as if he didn't hear me call out his name. He's wearing a fedora, leather straps around his wrists and neck, and black pants that fit him like a second skin. I desperately want to pull the pants off him so I can trail my hands down his muscular thighs.

When he starts moving his hips to the music I'm overcome with this feeling of desire that thunders through me. I've never wanted anything or anyone more than this man. I want to feel his bare skin against mine, I need him inside me, all over me—taking me until I can't see straight and my body and soul have completely surrendered to him.

He begins to rock his hips and roll his shoulders in a provocative way. I never imagined being overwhelmed by such erotic feelings, to be willing to let this sexy man have his way with me. I'm breathless just at the thought of him fucking me.

The music amps up and Ramon turns so that his back is to me, and he runs his hands down over his ass as he slowly begins to thrust forward. I can vividly imagine my ass pressed up against him. I swallow hard, trying to get a grip on my lust that is spiraling out of control. My thoughts are darkly erotic as I imagine all the things he could do to claim me. Then I shock myself by wondering . . . what if I was the one taking him and claiming him as mine? I picture it, and feel my cock throbs just he pivots again so that he's facing me. He sensuously runs his hands up his thighs, then across the bare skin of his abs and broad chest.

"Welcome to the show, Prince Charlie," he calls out from the stage. "What can I do to entertain you?" I get a glimpse of his devilish smile.

"You can come over here," I boldly call out.

He arches his brow at me, and narrows his eyes. "Please Sir, can you tell me . . ."

Sir? Why is he calling me sir?

"Tell you what?"

"What you want from me."

Standing defiantly, I push my chair back abruptly. I'm aware of my chest rising and falling as my breathing gets heavier, while our intense gaze heats up. Realizing that the spotlight over my table is glowing again, I run my fingers down the length of where my hard dick is trapped in my jeans and straining against the denim. I watch his dark stare follow my touch. Even from a distance he can't miss how aroused I am.

"Why don't you come see for yourself?" I call out, in a deep, raw voice I barely recognize.

"I want to . . . so much," he murmurs, as he watches my hand move. "I'm going to approach your table."

I'm confused by his formality, but I nod my head. "Please do." I lift the glass of whiskey for more liquid courage and take a long sip as he slowly descends off the stage and approaches my table. The energy between us is electrified.

When he's in front of me he removes his hat and sets it on the table. Turning toward me, he gently runs his fingers down my chest, and as I press forward into his touch he slowly starts to undo the buttons on my shirt, and parts the fabric to reveal my chest.

"Mmmm," he moans when my shirt is fully open. His warm hands caress my pecs, and abs until his right hand trails down to where I'm hard for him.

"Charlie," he whispers as he presses his eyes shut, and I can hear his hunger in his ragged voice.

He starts to undo my jeans and I let him. By the time he's got them pushed down past my knees and his hand is stroking my cock, I'm on fire with raw desire. He takes his free hand and gently pushes me down until I'm sitting in my chair, my legs spread, fully exposed to him.

I watch him as he makes a show of slowly working his pants off. He moves in rhythm to the music, as each part of him is revealed: his hipbone, his taut pelvis, his erect cock, and the defined muscles of his thighs. I study every part of his glorious body. He is perfection.

When he's finally nude he stands before me brazen and unashamed. "Are you ready?" he whispers.

Words escape me so I merely nod sharply, as I watch him with dark eyes. He lowers himself onto my lap and just when I get used to his weight, he takes my thick erection in his hands, lifts up and with the music's bass beat syncing to my heartbeat, he slowly starts to effortlessly sink down over me. The incredible sensation of how he feels as he lowers himself—taking all he can, is mind-blowing. I'm filling him so full that he can barely breathe.

"How can this be happening?" I murmur.

Stilling, he rests his hands on my shoulders. He's flushed, as if drunk with pleasure as his bright eyes meet my gaze. "Don't overthink everything, Charlie. Tomorrow will be, or won't. The past is what it was. Just live in this moment."

"So why not now?" I ask, as I try to sort out in my logical mind what he's trying to make me understand. I run my hands down his back until I can grab his ass and pull him closer. What if this is our only moment? I know without a doubt that I'll never get enough of him, and I don't want to let him go.

"Yes, because life is a dream, and this very moment is everything."

I nod, as if a light has shone on the mysteries of the entire universe.

"We are everything now," he whispers with a sharp breath as he pulls me into an embrace and rides me in rhythm to the music until I'm wild. It's as if we're made for each other as our bodies become one.

He lifts up and sinks down, slowing fucking me like this is how we were meant to be. My body responds by rocking up to meet his stokes.

"That's right, Charlie . . . take me." He's thrusting his hips and taking me deeper to the music, murmuring the words to the song as if a reverent prayer.

I moan as we take each other higher, fucking harder, my hand on his hard dick stroking him, until I'm so out of my body with pleasure that I no longer know where I am. His words *why, not, now,* echo in my mind.

My final impression before everything fades to black is that our passion will never end, and part of me will always be held in Ramon's embrace.

The next morning when I wake all I want is to go back to sleep and relive it all again. It feels like I've seen what Ramon and I could be. I have to embrace this idea of living in the *now.* I've never wanted this beautiful man more, and Wednesday night can't come fast enough.

THE FOLLOWING MONDAY IS BUSY at work. We've been stressed out with a group project writing code for a major design and content revamp for one of the largest comic book distributors and retailers.

I haven't heard from Ramon, which makes me feel awkward and

insecure again. But by the afternoon I force myself to at least text him.

Hey Ramon, still coming for dinner Wed?

Yeah, sure. What time?

Is 7 ok?

Great. See you then.

I stare at my phone. What the hell? Surely he realizes that he doesn't know my address. I wait a minute and decide to text him again.

Would you like my address?

Oh sure. Sorry, I'm distracted here. What is it?

Distracted? I feel the hot lick of jealousy work its way up my spine. *Who is distracting him?* I start picturing things in my head to the point that I begin feeling nauseous, so I finally have to give myself a talking to. I mean sure, he could have met someone since I last saw him that he's taken a shine to, and Marcus has suddenly been back in his life, but that doesn't mean I'm out of the picture yet. Does it?

THAT NIGHT SASHA HELPS ME put a menu together. We agree not to make it too fussy. I'm going to grill a couple of steaks, then make potatoes au gratin, a kale salad with grapefruit and goat cheese, and warm rolls with garlic butter. For dessert, hot fudge sundaes. Since she and Estella were already going to Whole Foods today, Sasha adds my ingredients to their list.

Sasha also informs me that with help from Lucia and Estella, she's going to do a sleepover at Emily's. I'm tempted to talk her out of it because Ramon really isn't sounding that into dinner so I'm doubtful he'll be staying with me Wednesday night, but she seems so excited about all the plans that I keep my mouth shut.

Getting up extra early Wednesday morning, I do most of the prep work for dinner. Then at lunchtime I go to the wine store on La Cienega and buy a really good bottle of cabernet sauvignon that the shop owner, Pete, recommends.

I start daydreaming and hoping for how the night will go. I want him to like our place, and enjoy the dinner, but most of all I want to learn more about him as we talk, hopefully seeing that my instincts about him have been right. I imagine his warm smile and big brown eyes, and I picture kissing him—an idea that immediately warms me up. It could be the perfect start to something more for us, which right now I want more than anything.

Slipping out of the office early, I'm nervous as all hell by the time I get home. I put the potatoes in the oven, open the wine to breathe, and take a quick shower and shave. I take out the large white envelope containing a special surprise I have for Ramon, and put it on the edge of the counter to give him after dessert.

Debating whether to light the candles or not, at two minutes to seven I break down and light them, a minute later, blow them out, then light them again.

At ten minutes after seven, I straight the alignment of the silverware while taking deep, calming breaths. Twenty minutes after I take the potatoes out and set them on the cooling pad. Checking and rechecking my phone obsessively, at seven-thirty I pour myself a glass of wine. Five minutes later I sink down into a chair and text him.

Hey, Ramon, you were coming over at 7 for dinner. Are you on your way?

Ten to eight and I'm getting angry. I decide to fire up the grill and cook these damn steaks anyway. I'm on my second glass of wine by the time they're done, so I decide that the fate of these expensive steaks lies in his hands. I lift up my phone, my index finger vibrating with tension.

I'm worried something's happened to you, hopefully not an accident. Will you please call me and at least let me know you're all right.

I don't finish the sentence with a question mark because it isn't a question; it's a polite command. Shouldn't it occur to him that considering my history with tragic accidents that I can easily slip into irrational fear? But then I remember how hesitant he'd been about the invite. So when I don't hear back from him my anger goes into a red zone and becomes rage. Apparently three glasses of this cab is the deal closer. My dial has moved from pissed off to atomic fury. Maybe not eating wasn't the right choice, but my stomach is so sour now eating isn't an option, so I take the steaks and dump them in the trash, then throw the potatoes au gratin in the trash, casserole pot and all. Smelling something burning, I wander around the kitchen all muddled until I realize that the apparently defective candles melted down to nothing, dripping a sad puddle of wax everywhere, while a tragic thread of smoke signals their final demise.

Despite the wine-enhanced rage, a bit of common sense settles over me and I fish the expensive casserole pot that Sasha got me two Christmases ago out of the trash, dump the potatoes back in the trash, wipe the pot off with paper towels, then deposit it in the sink. *Fucking Ramon,* I curse.

The last glass of the forty-six-dollar bottle of wine poured, I whip out my phone one last time.

I really didn't think you could be this big of an asshole.

I stabbed at my screen three times before I actually hit the send button.

A wave of rejection slams over me like a Tsunami. *What the fuck? I thought he at least liked me. Why'd he kiss me back? Was that a pity thing, too?* I rub my face and then yank my hands away realizing that they're wet from my tears. I think it's this wine that's making me crazy. It must be harvested from the vineyard of broken hearts.

Since my mom died, there've been a handful of times where I would have given my right arm to have her sitting next to me again to give me advice. She was amazingly tuned into me, and knew I was upset sometimes even before I knew it.

The first time that I was desperate for another mom moment was three weeks after I'd lost her and Dad. The lead doctor overseeing Sasha called my aunt and I in to talk about whether to keep Sasha on life support or not. The three weeks after the accident she had been declining and not showing any signs of coming back to conscious life. The pragmatic scientist in me knew the odds and what little quality of life she appeared heading toward even if she did wake up, but the brother in me could no more let them pull the plug on Sasha than stab her with a knife. Sitting at her bed endlessly those first few weeks, I'd read and talk to her hoping she could somehow sense I was with her. At the time it may have been selfish, but I clung onto the idea of her coming back to me so we'd have each other and I wouldn't be left desperately alone.

It was the only time in my life where my supreme selfishness led to my most heartfelt prayer being answered, and I thank God for saving her every day.

Now the most current example of needing my mom again is tonight's version of freaking pathetic, drunk me. Yes, I'm the loser who finally decided to come back to life from my self-imposed isolation and then blew it completely. But naturally only someone this lame could fall for a stripper, who didn't even care enough to blow me off with a text. I wonder if he'd enjoy knowing that I've got melted wax all over my family's antique table, a trashcan full of a lovingly prepared food, and my very own shattered heart . . . all thanks to him.

My intuitive and compassionate mom would know exactly what to say to me to lessen my pain and somehow still give me hope. "Mom!" I cry out into the silence, sinking down into my crooked elbow that's resting on a wide patch of melted wax. I moan, wishing one of those movie moments would happen like I'd feel her presence or a sign or something. But instead it's only me in my cold, empty condo, the most alone person on Earth.

I REALIZE THAT I'M AWAKE from the moaning sounds coming out of my mouth. Next, I wonder why I have a vice tightened over my head. *Damn.* I wiggle my toes and fingers to make sure they aren't screwed up, too. Slowly blinking, I curse the brightness of the morning light.

Practically falling out of bed, I stumble to the bathroom and try to vomit into the toilet, but only end up retching instead. *Oh happy day.* Don't we have our big team meeting this afternoon?

After a very long hot shower where I start to recall my pathetic evening, I pad slowly into the kitchen to brew some coffee and a chew on a piece of toast barely scraped with butter.

I look at my phone, and other than several calls from Sasha, there's still no word from Ramon. I can't believe how bad it hurts. I feel ridiculous and desperate and broken, all adding up into an epic desire to go back to bed. But then my phone rings. It would be so cool and karma-like if the call is from Ramon, right when I was hurting over him, but it's not him, it's Sasha.

Suddenly my ingrained responsibility to her is all that matters, and no matter how queasy I feel at this moment, I still take the call.

"Hey Sasha. How did the sleepover go?"

"Fine. It was fun. How was yours?"

My stomach sinks when I realize that she doesn't know how the whole thing was a disaster when she had such high hopes for us. I can't bear to tell her about it when I haven't come to terms with it myself. It would break her heart, and then that would be two of us. I take the loser way out and totally lie.

"Well he didn't spend the night but the evening was great." I don't even recognize my voice due to this fake chipper sound.

"Was he impressed with your cooking?"

Damn, I'd give anything for a subject change. I'm a shit liar on top of being sick as a dog from all that wine and no food. "Yeah, he loved the food. He cleaned his plate."

"Mmmm. Was it romantic, with the candles and everything?"

I guess if almost setting a family heirloom on fire is romantic, I think with a heavy heart.

Kill me now. Having to relive the whole night as I'd hoped it would be, and not the disaster it was, is fucking torture. "Super romantic." I shake my head with disbelief. I can't believe I'm saying this shit. I suddenly realize that I'm already late for work.

"So what's your plan for today? I've got to get to work, but meanwhile do you need me to do anything?"

"No, I'm good. Estella's here with the van, we've done my morning care and she's got things covered. Emily already had to leave for work, so we're coming home soon."

Damn. I've got to get out of here. It's one thing to lie to Sasha on the phone, but there's no way I can if I'm facing her. "Okay, I'll have left for work by the time you get here, but I'll see you tonight."

I rush to the bedroom and throw on my clothes, then speed into the bathroom to brush my teeth. Fuck shaving and brushing my hair. Fuck tucking my shirt in or wearing clean jeans. Fuck it all, and most of all fuck Ramon.

I take a sharp breath and curl over because fucking Ramon was part of the dream. In this horrible haze of humiliation and disappointment, it's time to be a realist.

9. Sasha's Tears

EACH HOUR PASSING IS MORE tortured than the last. I thought things would get easier as the day went on, instead they've gotten harder. When Billy questions a particular code on the McKinsey project, there's a moment of inner rage where I want to storm out of the conference room. *This has to stop.* Self control and focus on my work is my mantra, so if this is what the let-down of a stupid crush can do to me, I'd better remain loveless my entire life.

I never took a lunch, so in the late afternoon I decide to take a break and walk down to Jamba Juice to see if I can stomach one of their smoothies. I pass Katie on the way out the building's front entrance but I keep my head down since I've got my earbuds in pumping a playlist of angry rap music and I'm in no mood to make conversation. Who knew that I'd ever actually *need* to listen to Crime Mob, Gunplay, and The Notorious B.I.G. to get through my day? I have a vague memory of Billy loading this playlist of angry rap on my iPod, and now finally listening to it, it's certainly eye opening.

Lingering at the office to avoid going home, I finally give up and get in my car. The sky is still bright and I realize that today is June twenty-first, ironically the longest day of the year. I know they mean longest day of sunlight, but that description also coincides with my emotions. *The longest damn day of the year, indeed.*

I drive home after work especially slow, the dread of having to keep lying to Sasha crawling up the back of my neck. I'd have to be an Academy Award winning actor to pull this off with a stranger, but Sasha can read me like a book.

When I slip in the front door I realize that she's quietly waiting by the couch. "Hey," I call out.

When she doesn't respond I freeze, and our gazes lock. "Are you okay, Sasha? Did something happen?" All I want is to go hide in my room, but she's freaking me out. I take a few steps closer to her. "Sash, are you okay?"

The sun sinks a degree lower in the sky, and as a result the light pours through our picture window and skims over her face. I squint and step closer realizing that she's got tears starting to trail down her cheeks.

Rushing over to her, I bend forward and wipe her cheeks with my thumbs. "What happened, honey? Please talk to me." I don't even recognize my own voice I'm so upset. If something bad has happened to Sasha, I'm not sure I can take it.

She gestures for me to sit down and then turns her chair my direction. Reaching her hands forward, she holds onto me tightly.

"What happened, Charlie? Did he do something to hurt you?"

I swallow hard, while my mind spins. *What does she know about last night?*

She waits patiently for me to speak.

Meanwhile it finally all starts computing in my numb brain. I know I was hungover and late for work this morning, but how could I have forgotten to take the trash out and clean up the candle wax? My heartbeat is speeding as I glance back at the dining table, and sure enough any sign of the melted wax is gone. I'm so humiliated. It's bad enough that I wasn't interesting or appealing enough to Ramon, so dull that he couldn't bother to come over, but Sasha knows I lied to her now and I never lie to her.

My gaze drops down to where our hands are joined. "I'm really sorry I lied about last night. I didn't want you to worry about me."

"Well, it's a little late for that," she says quietly, brushing her new tears away.

"I'm so sorry."

"Never mind that. I want to know what happened. Estella found where you'd trashed the whole dinner."

The words get stuck in my throat. It's so humiliating. I finally find my voice again. "He didn't show up."

"Oh Charlie." Her voice catches and her tears are breaking me.

"Please don't cry, Sasha."

Her expression looks like heartbreak, but I can feel the tension of anger in the grip of her hands. "Did he have a good reason?"

"I don't know, he didn't respond to any of my texts. He still hasn't." I let out a long sigh of defeat and lean forward until my elbows are digging into my knees as I hold my stupid head up.

She looks ready to spit fire. "Nothing? No calls, texts, emails . . . nothing?"

I shake my head slowly. "Nada, nothing. I guess I wasn't that interesting . . . not even worthy of a phone call."

She pulls her hand away and points at me with a stern expression. "Don't you dare say that about yourself! This is about him being screwed up. How dare he be so rude! How could he not even be man enough to text you an apology? And here I thought he was so charming and lovely. I couldn't have been more wrong."

"Well, he really fooled me. I thought he kind of liked me."

Damn, I sound pathetic.

"Oh, Charlie, he did like you. He docs! I know he does. There has to be a reason he did this. I'm not saying that makes it okay, but at least I'm sure it wasn't because he didn't like you."

"You're always such an optimist, Sasha." I give her a weak smile, but then it fades. "I can't believe how intense I felt about him so fast. It makes all of this hurt even more, and I don't want to put myself out there again. Can you believe I was even working on the beginnings of a business plan for him? He didn't know that, but I wanted to do anything for him that would make him happy. I'm such a sap."

She presses her hand on my knee. "You're not a sap! You're thoughtful and generous. So is that what the white envelope that Estella found in the kitchen is? She left it there."

"Maybe I'll burn it," I grumble. "There's no point in keeping it now."

She sits silently for a minute gazing out the picture window. When she turns back toward me I can tell she's made her mind up about something. "This is what I think, Charlie. You need to get closure with Ramon and show him the kind of man you are . . . the kind of man he's missing out on."

"Closure how?" I already feel my stomach churning.

"Go meet him face-to-face. Show up at the club before the show starts and show him the envelope. Tell him that you were disappointed, and even if he only considers you a friend, you deserved better. Then if he isn't responsive in the way you'd hope, say good-bye and walk away." She reconsiders what she said and then nods firmly. "Yes, that's what I believe you should do."

"Oh, I don't think so," I say, horrified at the idea. Talk about awkward and humiliating.

"Charlie, I'm going to say something to you I know you don't want to hear, but it has to be said."

"Can we do that another day? I think I've dealt with pretty much all I can handle today. It was one of the worst days I've had in a long time."

She sighs. "I know but this is important."

I lean back into the cushions and cross my arms over my chest.

"Remember that friend of yours in high school, Leo? He was the one you were with the night of the accident, right?"

I numbly nod my head. I can't believe Sasha remembers that detail. "You two were such good friends and he was such a nice guy. I remember he was always very kind to me."

I let out a long sigh. "He probably was the nicest guy I've ever known."

"Did you stay in touch with him?"

"No." What I don't tell her is that Leo became an emotional casualty . . . collateral damage because of the accident.

With Sasha's mention of Leo, the memories all come barreling back to me and I close my eyes as I start reliving that hell.

It was my junior year in high school and I was supposed to be on that long drive with the family down to Aunt Beth's in Los Angeles for her and her husband's twenty-fifth anniversary party. But two days before the trip I convinced Mom and Dad that I needed to stay in Paso Robles to work on the big chemistry project with Leo. The whole thing was Leo's idea, and he convinced me it would work. They reluctantly agreed.

What my parents didn't know is that we had schemed for me to get out of the trip so that Leo could stay with me those two days and nights. We had been sneaking around and making out whenever we could for several months. It had been thrilling and an awakening for each of us, a confirmation of confusing feelings that led to us falling in love. We never said as much to each other, but there was no question in my mind that I was in love with him and wanted to be with him whenever I could be.

The anticipation was so intense it took over my every thought. We had agreed this would be the time we would finally have full-on sex. Up until then there had been awkward kissing, and groping that lead to jerky, quick hand-jobs, and eventually sloppy, desperate blowjobs. But this was going to be something completely new and thrilling for us. We were going to not only have full-on sex with each other, taking all the time we wanted, we'd be able to sleep in the same bed and wake up wrapped around each other. We talked about it non-stop as the weekend drew near.

So that Friday night, Leo came over with his duffle bag, his parents thinking he was on another science camp weekend. We had pizza and Dad's beer for dinner like we were college boys or something. It was so cool and adult-like. After, we were making out on the couch, working up our nerve for our big moment, when suddenly the doorbell rang.

From that point on my memories are faded and flickering, like an old home movie with broken sprockets so the projector makes the images shaky and blurred. I vaguely remember the policeman who asked me my full name, and the grief counselor standing stoically next to him. Leo stood behind me, and apparently, he was the one who caught me when I fainted.

As they came inside and started asking questions, plans were made to reach my aunt so we could be at the hospital for my sister. It was explained that the eighteen-wheeler had lost control on the overpass, exploded through the cement wall, and soared down to the freeway below. My parents in their SUV didn't have a chance.

Later I took comfort when I found out that Mom and Dad's deaths were instantaneous. They never knew what hit them. Sasha, who was in the backseat, was broken but not obliterated like my parents were. She has no memory of it, thank God. After being cut out of the wreckage with the 'jaws of life' equipment, she died in the ambulance on the way to the hospital but they revived her.

It wasn't just that my life blew apart that night, my mind blew apart with it. I immediately determined that had I not been ruled by my lust and selfish needs, I would've been with my family under that eighteen-wheeler, living or dying with them but at least still with my home team. I never have and never will forgive myself for what happened.

If I had gone with them we probably would have left a minute or two later since I always had to run back in the house to get something I'd forgotten inside. That minute would've saved my family. I knew it with all my heart, as I knew I could never touch Leo again. Because of my shame and need to blame, he became as dead to me as my parents were.

I had a nightmare on the one-year anniversary of the accident in which a giant mass fell out of the sky on top of me. It was a Transformer-like creature with sharp edges, and layers of metal that were changing shape as it plummeted toward me. It destroyed me as it slammed into the earth, rendering me an abstract shape of human fragments and dust.

Sasha clears her throat, bringing me back into the moment. She lays her hand over mine. "You went somewhere far away. Didn't you?"

I shake my head sorrowfully. "The memories of those days are never too far from my thoughts. Leo is part of that."

"Why didn't you stay in touch with him?"

"It was a bad time," I say, assuming she'll put the pieces together.

"I saw you two kissing once in your bedroom. You didn't think anyone was home, but I was." Her expression is sweet and her gaze soft, while her tone is compassionate at the declaration.

I can feel my eyes grow wide until it feels like they're going to pop out. "You did? So all this time you've known I was gay?"

She twists her mouth side to side as she considers her answer. "No, I knew that you were trying out kissing with your best friend. I did the same with my bestie, Wendy, and I'm not gay. I guess I could be bi, I really liked kissing her, but the point is I didn't assume anything."

"Wow. Any other big thing you want to share with me? This has been quite a night."

"No, but I do think you should consider figuring out where Leo is and contacting him. Even if Ramon doesn't amount to anything, you've opened a door to a fuller, richer life for yourself, and it's time you step through that door and start really living. Maybe reviving that friendship could be a positive step toward that."

10. Closure is Bullshit

AT LUNCH THE NEXT DAY I pick up a burrito and Coke from one of the food trucks, and sit on a bench in the plaza area between the building and parking garage. Sasha's words have been on my mind, and my curiosity about what Leo is up to these days is getting the better of me.

As I eat I do a search on my phone and find Leo on Linkedin. It says he works at Google in Silicon Valley where he's a Senior Software Engineer. I'm impressed, but not surprised because Leo wasn't just brilliant, he had a lot of drive. A surge of warmth settles over me remembering how he made me feel like I was the greatest person he'd ever known, and he could never get enough of me. His love and attention made me feel special. Knowing how much he wanted me somehow redefined my self-worth at a time when my peers for the most part didn't have any interest in what I was about.

Impulsively, I decide to reach out to Leo through the Linkedin message system.

> Hi Leo,
> I hope this message finds you well.
> My sister brought you up in conversation last night and it made me wonder how you are. Our friendship back in high school meant so much to me, and I will always regret that I wasn't able to sustain it after the accident. I'd really like to hear from you if you're up for it. But regardless, please know that I wish you all the best and hope you are very happy.
> Best,
> Charlie Morgan

I add my phone number and email to the message before I send it.

Struggling a bit to finish my lunch, I realize that reaching out to Leo brings up a lot of complicated feelings, which are upsetting my stomach. The least of which is how my life was so bleak and hopeless after the accident, and as a result I pushed Leo away. I wonder if we would have stayed together if fate had played that day out differently.

I've emptied my trash in the bin and am walking back toward the building's entrance when my phone rings. My heart surges as I recognize his old number. It's him.

"Leo?" I ask, still not believing he replied so fast.

"Charlie! I couldn't believe it when I got your message! I'm so glad to hear from you. And you mentioned your sister. So is she doing all right?"

I'm flooded with happiness. He sounds as warm and kind as always. "She's doing well, thanks. I'm proud of her. With all of her challenges, she definitely focuses on living the fullest life she can despite her handicap."

"I'm not surprised to hear that. She always was a very strong, spirited girl."

"Actually, she was the one who encouraged me to call you, even though I figured that you wouldn't want to talk to me."

"Why would you think that? Of course I'd want to talk to you and know you are doing well. I'm assuming from your area code that you stayed in L.A. after your aunt moved you down there?"

"Yes, Sasha got the best medical care here, and I was able to go to Cal Tech. I work for World Tech Solutions. Is Linkedin right, that you work at Google?"

"That's right. The headquarters where I work is located in Mountain View."

"And how about the rest of your life? Is everything good?"

"Yeah, it's great. I'm happily married and we recently got a really cool modern house not far from here."

I can almost feel my heart freefall inside my chest.

Married. Of course I should have assumed that he'd be in a committed relationship. He was that kind of guy. But I'm still stunned he's with a woman. I'm so disappointed I can hardly breathe.

"Great!" I finally squeak out. "Any kids yet?"

"No, that's not going to happen. Thomas hates kids. You know what's crazy, too? He works for Yahoo."

I laugh, my heart strangely bruised . . . for although I'm happy he's stayed true to himself and is openly gay and in a relationship, it makes me wonder what we could've had.

"How about you, Charlie? Have you found your one and only yet?"

"Not yet," I admit, stinging at the thought of Ramon and how I may have answered that question differently only a few days ago.

"Oh, you will though, you're quite the catch," he says encouragingly.

"That's kind of you to say. Well, I better get back to work and I'm sure you're busy, too. Thank you for responding to my message."

"Of course."

"And if you and Thomas are ever in L.A., it'd be great to get together with you."

"And likewise to you, Charlie, if you're ever up our way. Really good talking to you."

"Thanks, Leo."

My hands are shaking as I slip my phone back in my pocket. Part of me is happy for Leo that he got what he deserved. The other part of me feels like a spotlight has been put on my threadbare life. I'm a shadow of who I could've been. What will it take for me to fill in all the empty spaces?

This feeling simmers in me all afternoon. I start to wonder, *What if I were brave?* If I could thicken my skin, I could start putting myself out there. Even though I have no faith in the science of the algorithms of dating sites versus the emotion and desire behind the algorithms of our hearts, I still have to try something. Maybe I should put up a profile and practice dating to build up my skills.

It's in that spirit and surge of faux confidence that I decide Sasha is right, I need to confront Ramon for closure or his silent rejection will carry into everything I want to do moving forward.

Remembering that he said he usually gets to the club by seven to either set up the bar, or go over the routine if he's going to dance, I decide to try to see him there. I arrive a few minutes after seven so it's before any of the patrons line up. I stop at home first to check on Sasha and grab the envelope with the print-outs of club prospectives that I'd put together for Ramon.

Circling the block twice before I get the nerve to park, I finally find an open metered space and pull in, then lean over my steering wheel taking slow, deep breaths to calm myself. Why did my infatuation with Ramon have to happen? Maybe I should blame Brittany for getting married, which created a reason for the women at work to throw her a bachelorette party, thus riling Billy so he'd insist on me coming with him, to the slow wait staff at Wild Nights that forced me to go to the bar to get my own damn beer . . . served by none other than Ramon, who then decided to dance for me and screw with my head. Yeah, Brittany is going to get a deluge of invisible daggers from me when she's back from her honeymoon.

There's no line in front of the club yet so I walk freely to the entrance, but then hesitate to open the closed door. Realizing it's not too late to back out of this exercise in humiliation framed as 'closure,' I seriously debate turning around but finally buck up, and pull the door open.

Two large men are inside the entryway, one I don't recognize who calls out in a gruff voice, "We're not open yet," to the other the bouncer who was kind to Sasha the other night.

"Hey man," he says, nodding to me with recognition.

"Hey," I respond, then hold up the white envelope. "I need to give this to Ramon. Do you know if he's here yet?"

"Yeah, he should be in the back bar. I'm pretty sure he isn't dancing tonight."

"Would you mind . . ." I say as I gesture with the envelope.

"It's cool. Go ahead."

My heart is pounding as I slowly walk through the half-lit club. The tables and chairs are in place and at attention for the procession of women who will soon excitedly rush in to get the best seats. Being in here before the club is fully open reminds me of the dream I had of Ramon and I alone here. It hurts to remember how erotic and fulfilling it was, so I try to push it out of my mind.

When I finally focus again and let my gaze shift to the bar, I see Ramon from the back, and it appears that he's checking the stock and adding some bottles to the shelves. It's at that moment that I realize that my desire to achieve closure is bullshit. It's a cover-up for the sheer fact that I still want him desperately and maybe if we talk there's still a chance for us. But what if there isn't? My humiliation and disappointment could be my undoing.

A surge of anxiety almost overtakes me, but I remind myself that at least he's alone and there's no reason I can't try to make this work. I continue to walk toward him. But a moment later another man steps behind the bar and right up to Ramon and smacks him on the ass in a proprietary way.

"Hey!" Ramon protests, but then the man who appears to be older, steps up behind Ramon and pulls him against his chest while wrapping his arms around Ramon's waist.

Ramon curses under his breath and then says, "Do you want me to get my work done or not, Gene?"

"Awww, you're no fun anymore!" the older man says with a pouty expression, still squeezing himself against Ramon.

What the hell is this about? Is this man someone Ramon is involved with? Why in the world did I imagine that he'd actually be interested in someone like me?

My head is spinning but the one thing I know for sure is that I don't need closure anymore. I need to get as far away from this club and my memories of what happened here as soon as possible before I fall apart. It occurs to me that now if I can figure out a way to hate Ramon his rejection may not completely break me.

I start to pivot around to leave and a voice booms toward me.

"Can we help you?" the older man calls out to me.

I shake my head sharply, and tighten my lips as I say, "No." But I have no sense if I whispered the word, or shouted it at him. In this moment, I acknowledge to myself that I don't know anything—just that it's time to leave.

There's a weird sound coming out of Ramon, which unfortu-
nately compels me to glance at him, and notice that even from this
distance his pupils look blown and his nerves frayed. That's more than
I needed to observe, so I quickly turn to walk as fast as possible to the
exit without drawing the wrong kind of attention to myself. Before I
reach the door I can hear movement behind me, so I grab the handle
and pull hard, the dark entry room suddenly flooding with light. As I
pass through I notice a trashcan to the right of the door and I dump
the white envelope inside before I rush out.

"Charlie!" I hear Ramon call out before the door falls closed
behind me.

It's like I'm screaming inside my head, and all I can think is that
I desperately wish I hadn't come, and I can't let him near me.

The bouncer is outside now, as a few women have started to line
up. Once I'm in the open air, I hit the ground running and I'm two
storefronts down before I realize I'm running the opposite direction
of where my car is parked. That slight pause and stutter in my step,
gives Ramon enough time to catch up. Grabbing me, he shoves me
against the store's wall.

Stunned, I push him hard so he stumbles backwards, but then
he lunges at me again, slamming his hands on my shoulders to pin
me down.

"Stop, Charlie!" He looks really frustrated which pisses me off
more.

What the hell does he have to be annoyed about? His groping dad-
dy-dude is probably waiting for him back at the bar, and I'm done
bothering him, so he should be fucking pleased as punch right about
now. My anger is a frail shield over the deep hurt I feel seeing his
beautiful face and all the hopes I had for us.

I'm wordless, so I glare at him with every bit of fury I can muster.
It suddenly occurs to me that the way he's standing with his feet spread
apart would make it easy for me to knee him hard between the legs,
buying enough time to break free. Imagining his reaction of agonizing
pain is satisfying. But before I consider really doing it, I glance over
his shoulder to see a police car has pulled up only feet away from us.

The passenger window rolls down and one of the cops leans out.

"Is there a problem, gentlemen?"

Ramon turns toward him. "No, sir. We've just had a disagreement between friends."

The cop narrows his eyes and studies me while Ramon eases his hands off my shoulders. "Is that true?" he calls out, looking only at me for the answer.

For a moment, I imagine what would happen if I told them Ramon was attacking me. But won't that make all of this worse? I'd probably have to stay to give a report. There's no way I'm going through all that.

"Yes, sir," I answer. "And I'm leaving, so if you'll excuse me . . ." and I take the opportunity to safely walk away from Ramon and toward my car. I'm almost to the front of the club when I hear the cop car pull away.

I consider running again, but I'm sick of this dramatic bullshit. I keep walking forward, not turning around, not looking to see what he's doing. The creepy thing is that I don't even hear him behind me, but feel his fingers wrap around my bicep and pull me to a stop. He leans into me, and hearing that voice and his hot breath on my neck really messes with my head.

"Look, Charlie, I know you're pissed off. But now that you're here let's talk."

"I don't want to hear anything you have to say," I grumble.

"I don't believe that, because if that were true, why did you come? Besides, there are things I need to say."

I shrug and shake my head. "You don't have to explain anything. You've made your feelings clear."

I try to meet his gaze with one of disinterest. I'm pretty sure it's not working though because he must see that my heart's breaking by the dejected reflection in my eyes.

He growls and slams his fist against the wall. "I knew this would happen."

I can't tell if he's directing this at me, or cursing the world.

"You must have come here tonight for a reason. Surely you can give me five minutes?" he insists. "I've been trying to figure out what to say to you."

"Sure you were. You know what, Ramon? You made your point the other night. Just let me go."

He takes half a step back and his gaze starts darting around like he's searching for someone. He seems nervous and edgy. He's not the only one.

He wraps his fingers around my wrist and tightens them as he takes hold. "We need to go inside," he commands.

"I'm not going back in there with you. This has been awkward enough."

He ignores me, and starts pulling me along. I don't have the slightest bit of emotional energy to resist. Apparently, I've had some type of breakdown or unraveling, because I don't have any fight left. He leads me back into the club, and of course we run smack into the older guy who was grabbing him. He's probably the new sugar daddy.

He gives me the once-over before turning to Ramon. "This is Charlie, isn't it?"

Ramon nods. "I need one of the private rooms so we can talk. Five minutes, and then I'll get back on the clock."

Gene throws his head back, laughing. "Five minutes my ass! Look, you can take room three, it isn't booked, but only if I can watch." A lascivious grin spreads across his face.

"Will you lay the fuck off, Gene?" Ramon mutters.

Gene throws his hands up. "Well, look at him. What did you expect?"

Ramon shakes his head and then pulls me down the hall.

Once we're in the room, he steps away from me, and locks the door.

I swallow hard, the fear rising out of the pit of my stomach imagining how this is going to go. Judging from our discourse until now, there's no reason to be optimistic, as desperately as I want to be.

Ramon digs his hands into the pockets of his jeans and lets out a long, ragged sigh. He sounds world-weary and like he'd rather be anywhere but here right now. Rubbing his hand roughly over his forehead, he narrows his eyes and studies me.

"Why'd you come here?" he asks, in a tone that makes me think he doesn't want to hear the answer.

I'm mute for a moment, wondering the best answer to give. I tip my head sideways and notice how tense his shoulders appear to be. I wish I could reach out and rub them for him. But I'm pretty sure he wouldn't appreciate that.

Clearing my throat, I finally answer. "Originally I was sent to come here for closure, but then after I arrived I realized that I don't want closure."

Ramon's gaze softens for a second, but then it morphs back to a cold stare. "Yeah? What do you want then?"

"Maybe to know if there's any way we can work things out. Can you tell me what I did to put you off?"

"What *you* did?" he asks, his expression edging on disbelief. "Charlie," he moans. I hear the slightest hint of sympathy in his voice, almost like he wished he could change the horrible direction this conversation was going.

"Well I figure I must have done something for you to just blow me off like that. Or should I conclude that there's someone else you'd rather spend time with?"

"What are you talking about?" he asks, now clearly irritated.

"Is it that man who was holding you at the bar."

"Gene?" he asks, before he seems to remember what I saw. Recognition spreads across his features.

"Is he who you really want?" I ask. "Is that why you didn't come to our dinner?"

He shakes his head. "Gene is my boss. I'm not interested in him like that."

"Well then, what did I do wrong? I can fix it if I know what it was."

He rubs his face roughly with his hands. "Charlie, you're just not getting it."

"Well, explain it then. I'm pretty smart, so I can't be that dense when it comes to relationships. I really like you."

"You shouldn't." His expression is miserable and it makes me feel pathetic.

"Why not?"

"I'm not the right guy for you."

"Yes you are." I see where this is going and I start to panic. Swallowing hard, my fear of being rejected is spreading through my veins as my heart starts beating wildly.

"Listen to me. You can't come to the club anymore."

"But why . . ." I start, before he interrupts me.

His gaze drops to the tabletop. "Because I don't want you to."

My heart stutters. For a moment I wonder if it's stopped completely. I didn't think Ramon had it in him to be so cruel. Despite that, I'm determined not to give up on him.

"Okay. I'll meet you other places. There are lots of places." I know I sound like a total loser, but my mind is racing as I can sense him slowly slipping out of my grasp.

Clearing his throat, I watch every muscle tighten along his shoulders and neck, and then his face, until he looks like a warrior. I try to steel myself for the battle he's armed up for and I have nothing left to shield myself from being blown apart.

"Charlie, I don't want to see you period. Not just at the club."

For a second the room goes black. I wasn't expecting this—that my heart would shatter in a padded room where people come for a little excitement. Instead I'm about to lose the one person I've wanted more than anyone.

My head drops because I can't bear to look at him. "Even as friends?" I whisper, sounding more pitiful than I thought I was even capable of.

"Even as friends. It just wouldn't be right. It's clear you like me too much, and you're not the kind of guy I'm into."

I have to fight curling over like I was just punched in the gut. My gaze shifts up to meet his. "Because I'm a geek and inexperienced? But I'm a quick learner."

He just stares at me, his eyes cold and empty, like every bit of light I ever saw in his eyes has extinguished.

"What kind of guy are you into?"

He turns away. "Not your kind." His voice sounds different now. But maybe that's to be expected because he's different than the Ramon I thought I knew. "You should leave now. You need to stay away from this club."

"I'm not ready to leave." I fold my weakened arms over my chest trying to give the impression of defiance. "I've been a paying customer so I can still come here any time I want you know." I have no idea why I'm saying this shit . . . maybe I'm stalling for time.

He walks over to the wall across from us and kicks it hard. "Okay then. Do whatever the hell you want if you don't care what happens to you, but I've got to get back to work. Just know it would be in your best interest not to come here. Forget about me, Charlie, I'm an asshole who's into the kind of guy you'll never be. You need to forget me, and I'll do the same with you. Believe me, you'll be much better off."

As he starts to walk heavy-footed toward the door I call out his name. I can hear the anguish in my voice and I feel a sting from the tear that I'm frantically blinking back. Ignoring me he unlocks the door, and pulls it open. He hesitates and half-turns back, then pauses, and in my heart I'm hoping he's changed his mind. But instead he takes a shallow breath and leans into the hallway light.

"I'll never forget you, Ramon," I call out just before he steps into the hallway and out of my life.

11. The Confusion of Cupid

CAN YOU DIE A BRUTAL death and still be alive? Each ragged breath is a betrayal when all you wish for is a silent emptiness, a quiet heart with no beats left.

I've known unfathomable heartbreak and loss. It has defined the last six years of my life. Losing Leo comes to mind, and I wonder if Ramon's cold rejection is karma for the way I treated Leo after my family's accident. Now I toss and turn in my bed wondering that very thing until the streets outside my bedroom window are quiet, and the soft light of dawn casts gray shadows across my room.

I don't remember how I got home last night after Ramon shut me out, or how I got to work today. My team seems to sense that something is terribly wrong, and so they walk on eggshells around me, and are overly kind.

Sasha is upset, perhaps because she was the one that convinced me to go see him in the first place. But last night I made it clear that I wasn't going to talk about what happened, and this time she listened and didn't ask more questions—well, at least for now. I think I've scared her with how dead the expression in my eyes has been since I saw him.

Now a week later there is heaviness in my gait as I pace through the condo before slipping out the front door for long walks after nightfall. Sometimes I don't come back for hours.

Week three Sasha has shifted her strategy from last week. Some days she swings back and forth, between tough love . . . going off about what a fool Ramon is so I need to forget him and get past this, to compassionate . . . trying to get me to talk about my feelings. I know she means well, but either option irritates me excessively.

I overheard her and Emily talking in the kitchen about going to Wild Nights, cornering Ramon and finding out what the hell is wrong with him. As much as I appreciate their support, just the idea of such a scene freaks me the hell out.

By the fourth week I'm climbing the walls as I torture myself imagining every horrible scenario like Ramon in Marcus' bed, or with some other beautiful man we saw that night at the Lodge. Any of them would surely be happy to have sexy Ramon between their sheets.

Thursday of that week during one of my particularly low points, I text Ramon.

Hey Ramon-I miss our friendship. Want to meet for lunch or something?

My fingers tremble when I hit send. As the minutes pass without a response, my stomach flip-flops, and I'm flooded with regret for sending such a pathetic text.

"Fuck! You idiot!" I curse out loud, even though no one is around for my self-loathing.

The next night my spirit sinks lower when after a substantial amount of whiskey I text him again.

Do you really think you gave us enough of a chance? I don't.

I suggest you reconsider your choices.

By midnight when he still hasn't responded to either text I send one final jab.

You're a dick.

And the dick didn't respond to that one either. After a few more days I stopped checking my phone, but I think it took several more weeks before I accepted that this thing between Ramon and I was really over. There's a part of me I'm sure will never accept it. I still go out of my way to drive by Wild Nights around the time the show would be gearing up. At least now I'm only doing it every other day, rather than twice a day, which was during my darkest stage.

During sleepless nights, I lie on my back and remember the way Ramon kissed me that evening at the observatory and my heart aches for him to hold me again.

But that longing isn't for the mean Ramon, who with a flippant wave of his hand, said things that made me feel undesirable and not worth his time. I was learning to hate *that* guy and sadly it's my resulting anger that finally forces me back on my feet.

ABOUT SEVEN WEEKS AFTER THAT last meeting with Ramon, I come home to find Sasha waiting for me after I'd taken an extra long walk. Even though it's late I'm not surprised to see her still awake since I know she's been very worried about me.

She studies me intently when I come into her room to see why her light is still on.

"That was a long one." She knows when I'm gone extra time it's been a particularly tough day.

I shrug.

"How are you holding up?"

"I'm alive," I say as I sit down on her desk chair, then swivel to face her.

"Have you heard from him at all," she asks, snapping her Kindle case closed. The question surprises me because she stopped asking that question weeks ago.

I shake my head. "No. I'm not going to."

"Can I be frank, Charlie?"

I want to dissuade her but I figure she's been good at giving me time in the last few days, so I decide to be open hearing what she has to say. "Okay," I murmur.

"You know how after Ramon didn't show up for dinner you were talking about moving on and putting yourself out there more. And maybe if you hadn't gone to talk to him that night you'd have been doing it already."

I suppose she's right if that is truly how I was feeling and not just trying to act like Ramon didn't matter, when he clearly was already under my skin. "But I did go talk to him that night." I point out.

"And you've suffered for that since. So I need you to hear me out before you say anything."

"Okay." Sasha has one of her ideas and there's no stopping her now.

She smoothes down her bedspread as she considers how to say what's on her mind. "So Emily and I did some research and found out that OKCupid is a very good dating website for gay men. I think it's time for you to try to get back in the game."

"Is that so?"

"Indeed it is." She gives me an encouraging smile. "So we've uploaded your profile and all you have to do is hit the button that activates your post and see what happens."

"You make it sound so simple."

"Isn't it? We used that great shot of you that Aunt Beth took at Thanksgiving. You're so handsome in that photo."

"Okay," I reply simply. Why put up an argument? Besides, I feel absolutely nothing about it: not nervous, not excited, not curious. But I know that if I try it, and go out on some dates it will be a step forward, and right now I'm just sinking.

"Really?" she cries out with a clap of her hands. "That's great, Charlie!"

I almost smile to hear her so happy. "So what do you need me to do?"

She points at my desk. "My computer's asleep, so once it's open you'll be on your page. All you need to do is review what we wrote and press the button that will make your profile go live."

Without a moment's hesitation I swivel in my chair, open her desktop and without reviewing anything, I activate the page. I lean in to read the message that's popped up. "It will take some time to upload."

She nods her head and claps her hands. "And what do you bet that in the morning you'll have a bunch of responses. Oh this is so exciting!"

I give her a warm smile. This is bringing her a lot more pleasure than me. But she's right—it's time to try to put myself out there again. *Get back on the horse*, our Dad would've said.

She lets out a big yawn, so I stand up. "It's late. You should be asleep."

"I know, but I wanted to make sure you were okay. You're pretty important to me. You know that, right?"

I step up to her bedside and lean over to kiss her forehead. "You're pretty important to me, too, kiddo. Thanks for looking out for me."

"Ditto."

SASHA HAS GOOD INSTINCTS—BY THE next morning I have several responses to my profile. I have to admit, I was pretty curious about the kind of men I would attract, and as the day goes on and I check my phone during breaks, I'm surprised to see a variety of guys responding. Some I even find appealing. As I scan through my prospects I realize that it feels good to have people show interest in me. Maybe I don't have to be doomed to a life without love after all.

Several days later, the first man I'm brave enough to respond to is named Jeffrey, and we agree to meet for coffee the following Saturday in the Toluca Lake, Burbank area. I learn over blueberry muffins and lattes that he works in merchandise licensing for a film studio, and works long hours and travels a lot. He's a Southern boy, and has all the charm one would expect. I find him easy to talk to, even though most of what we discuss is our jobs.

He's tall, lean and good-looking, but despite all that, I don't feel any sparks at all. I'm trying not to compare him to Ramon, but I keep doing it anyway. His movements are choppy where Ramon's are smooth and elegant, his smile toothy, while Ramon's is sexy.

When we part, I have a heavy heart. Will I always be looking for Ramon in the new men that I meet? If so, this is going to be a rough journey.

A couple of weeks pass before I'm inspired to try again. This time I take a completely different tactic. Rather than responding to people that have contacted me, I start scanning profiles to find a man as different as possible from not just myself, but from Ramon as well.

When I reach out to Christopher, who describes himself as outrageous and fun, I figure I've got the right guy.

Our first meeting is at a small bar in Silverlake where apparently he knows everyone. As awkward and embarrassing as that could've been, it ends up being fun as everyone wants to tell me a story about some crazy thing that Christopher, aka Cray-Cray-Chris, has done. I can't remember when I've laughed that much. He seems to get a kick out of shocking people, and is determined to loosen me up.

It's a fun night—the first one I've had in a long time, and that feels good.

On our next date I agree to take a big personal step and meet him at The Abbey, a very colorful gay bar in West Hollywood that opened over twenty-five years ago. It's exactly the kind of place I've been afraid to go to since we'd moved to L.A. But Christopher gives me courage and when he texts that he's arrived I look up from the bar and he storms toward me, like he owns the place.

He gives me a quick tour, and my mouth drops open as I take in both his big personality and this vast club that has a rich history. Beautiful men in tiny boxer briefs are dancing on risers, as couples dance together or in groups on the dance floor. The crowd is mixed with gay men and women, and straight women looking to dance without being harassed by single men. It's a large space with several bar set-ups, an outdoor patio and an adjunct space that seems to mainly have gay men inside called the Chapel. I recall that the Abbey is the place Sasha mentioned once for being all-inclusive, and she's right. I feel completely accepted without judgment, and it's a great feeling.

I'm glad I Ubered here, because with Christopher's encouragement I drink too much too fast and before you know it he has me out on the dance floor. I feel truly alive for the first time since Ramon abandoned me. It's funny because half the time Christopher is winding through the crowd, getting reactions from everyone he grabs or brushes up against. He even jumps up on one of the risers and starts to coordinate his moves with one of the dancer's. The booze must have gotten to me, because I laugh and keep dancing like I don't have a care in the world.

At one point I wander up to the bar because suddenly my desire to let go of my conventional restraints is all I care about. I down my drink and turn back toward the dancers when my eye catches a familiar face, and I have to blink to make sure I'm seeing clearly. *Fuck.* I stumble back into the crowd and try to get lost—both lost in the music, and lost from the one man I can't face.

I'm grateful that at that very moment Christopher finds me again and pulls me to the middle of the floor. He's pulled his shirt and shoes off but that doesn't slow him down. He dances like it's our last night on earth and I'm his co-pilot for our great journey. I close my eyes and sway to the rhythm, sensing everything: the taste of good whiskey in my mouth, the *boom . . . boom . . . boom* of the song syncing with my heart as it blasts from the speakers, the air thick with hunger and want, my need for something *more . . . more . . . more*. It's at this very moment that I feel a man step up from behind, and press up against me like a second skin.

A whiff of his scent fills my nostrils, and I want to step into a shadow and let the light fade to black so I'm undiscoverable in the dark. *Ramon.*

I wish Christopher was right here in front of me, but he's distracted by something else already. I swear the man must have ADD.

Gritting my teeth, I don't turn around. I just keep dancing hoping Ramon will figure out that I'm not going to acknowledge him, and he should back off. But instead he moves in sync with my moves, and I can't breathe.

"Go away," I say in a voice just loud enough to be heard.

"I can't," he says, leaning in, his hot breath on my neck, heavy with the smell of booze.

"What do you want?" I snarl, hoping to show I'm fierce now, that he didn't break me even though he tried.

"What I can't have," he says with a sigh.

"Well that makes two of us."

"I can't have you. And I've missed you," he says woefully as he rests his hands on my hips and then slides them down my thighs, and back up almost between my legs. We're in a club for damn sake, and he's acting like he hasn't noticed that we're surrounded by people who can see how he's touching me.

I roughly push his hands away. "Don't touch me," I hiss right before he slides his hands back over me. But this time he's pressing his hand down where I'm already getting hard. *Damn.* I'm aroused just from having him so close. My dick has defied me. It's then that I realize that Ramon, the man that barely drinks, is drunk. Very drunk.

"You still want me, Charlie," he groans, grinding up against me, while biting me along my shoulder blade.

"I hate you," I sputter as I spot Christopher, and then watch him get lost in the crowd again. I need to get away from Ramon, but it's as if my shoes are glued to the floor and I can't go anywhere. My body is reacting to him even though my heart says no.

His fingers tighten over my hard dick. "Yes, but love and hate can wind together into a knot in your gut. And feel this . . ." His hand is now stroking me. "You still want me, baby. Don't you?"

I glance over my shoulder for another glance at him and he looks like hell. All of his prettiness is gone. Instead he appears to be a man who's been broken and is barely hanging on. I should feel sorry for him but my anger is too hot to cool off. "Quit fucking with me," I growl.

His eyes get darker than I've ever seen them. "Do you want me to fuck you? Or we can switch it up and you can fuck me. I'll take whatever I can get. Hey, I bet you'd like that."

I wedge my eyes shut and repeat his words in my head. Who is this nasty, spiteful ass? Is this what being drunk does to him? And what the fuck did I ever do to deserve being treated like this? The Ramon I knew had a kindness that ran through to his core. This isn't the Ramon I knew. And it's freeing realizing that I'm better off not caring anymore.

"I'm here with Christopher," I murmur as I push his hand away again. I look up to see Christopher back up on one of the risers and his jeans are open.

"That crazy guy is busy, and he's not worth your time. You're better off with me anyhow."

"You made me feel that I wasn't worth your time, so fuck you,"

I curse as he takes my arm firmly, and leads me off the dance floor.

At this point the excess whiskey is numbing my brain, so as he pulls me down a back hallway and into a storage room, I'm still trying to figure out what the hell is going on.

"Nice," I murmur, my gaze taking in the piles of leftover furniture and restaurant supplies. "How did you know this room was here? Is this where you've taken your club hook-ups?" I mumble as he pushes me against a wall and leans into me.

He rolls his eyes. "There were no hook-ups," he says. "I told you . . ."

I try to push him off me, but damn he's determined. "Don't roll your eyes at me, asshole," I warn him.

He does it again and I shove him away. But this time he falls back into me hard so my head snaps against the wall.

"You dumped me. Why are you fucking with me now?"

"Because I want to fuck you," he slurs.

He leans his head on my shoulder and presses his forehead against my neck. "I never stopped wanting to fuck you," he confesses.

"Really?" I ask. "So I'm not your type and I don't interest you, but you still want to fuck me? Am I understanding that right?"

"Yeah. Well no. You want the truth? You're actually very interesting. Honestly I liked you too much. That's the problem isn't it? He knew how much I liked you."

"Who knew? What the hell are you talking about?"

He shakes his head dramatically. "Can't say."

He reaches down with his free hand and slides it under my shirt. Next thing I know he's pinching my nipples and it's making me harder. I realize that I'm panting loudly. *Damn it!*

"You're drunk," I state simply.

"Uh huh. Luis must be so angry. Sometimes I think he's talking to me."

"What does he say?"

"That I'm fucked up. I've pretty much fallen apart since you left me."

"What? I didn't leave you. You left me. Are we dealing with

selective memory here?"

"I had to leave you. It was the only way."

I must have a sharp response for that insane commentary, but it all goes fuzzy when he starts undoing my jeans. Within seconds he's got his fingers wrapped around my cock and he's skillfully squeezing up and down my shaft sending shivers along my spine.

"Would you come back to me?" he asks, perhaps feeling hopeful that I'll answer through the haze of my arousal, and not my anger.

I narrow my eyes at him. "No, of course not. I was a fool for you once . . . never again."

He skims his lips along my jaw and over my lips. Damn, I loved his lips, and actually I still do. "Never, ever?" he whispers into my parted lips.

My heart immediately hardens. "It's a peculiar thing about me, Ramon. I like being treated like I matter, like you actually care about me enough to be nice. You made it very clear that you couldn't give a shit about me. That's not something I'll ever forget."

His gaze is full of torment and confusion, and I wonder why I'm trying to speak rationally with a man who is blitzed out of his mind.

Surprising me, he sinks down to his knees, and drags my pants down along with him. Before I can form words his hands are on me, and he takes a long lick from the base of my cock to the tip.

"Your cock is perfect," he whispers. "See, I can be nice."

I lean back against the concrete wall and take a shuddering breath as he slowly sucks me in deep. "You call that *nice*?" I ask, disoriented to look down and see his mouth full of my hard dick. His gaze is dreamy—as if he's satiated. *Damn.* There's no question how much Ramon likes cock, and apparently he really loves mine.

I'm high from the lust blasting through me and I only have a vague feeling that I'm still standing with my feet hip width apart while he rubs the head of my cock over his lips and along his cheek just before he sucks me so far in he's almost deep throating me. I shudder with the bolt of pleasure that blows through me. As intensely hot as this is, my mind is clear enough to know that this is fucking with my head, and that's not a good thing. If he keeps this up I'll come for sure, but

I could end up a basket case.

I put my hands on his shoulders and push him back so we're separated, then pull him back up to standing. "I can't do this, Ramon. You're screwing with my head."

His head drops into the crook of my neck. "Please," he moans. "Please." He starts to fumble with his fly and while I'm deciding my next move he rocks his hips forward until our dicks are aligned. Before I can pull away, he wraps his fingers around our erections, now pressed tightly together.

"What are you doing now?" I groan, gazing up at the ceiling like I'll find spiritual guidance or some shit up there. I must be more intoxicated than I thought.

Against my better judgment I glance down to watch his strong hand firmly stroking our cocks that are slick with pre-cum. I'm mesmerized even though this isn't what I want—not how I wanted to be with him. We're in a fucking storeroom. This is sleazy and twisted and I know tomorrow I'm going to have nothing but regrets.

But with each minute passing his strokes speed up and my breaths turn into gasps. A fire is burning across my chest and down to where he's touching me. His hot hand is a blur, and his groan low and gravelly as he watches my hips buck. I can't stop now, my insides twisting tighter and tighter until I can't hold back and he moans with satisfaction as I start to come.

My eyes are shut tight so all I can know is the sharp high of release as my body seizes so intensely that I want to cry out but I swallow the sound instead.

"Damn, Charlie," he groans. "You're fucking hot." His fingers have gradually slowed to a light stroke, rubbing my release over where we're still joined, and at that moment I realize that he isn't going to finish.

"You aren't going to get off?" I ask, pulling back and yanking my pants up. It's not like I care if he does. I'm angry with myself, and him for using me. He only wanted me because he's drunk, and I was an easy target.

He watches me pull myself together, while he just leans against the wall next to me with a defeated expression, his clothes still in disarray. "I haven't since that night," he murmurs.

"What night?" I ask.

"When you came to the club. I haven't gotten off since then."

I narrow my eyes as I stare at him. Is he lying to me? What the fuck? Does he expect me to feel sorry for him if that's true? And besides, I'm sure it isn't.

I push myself off the wall and start toward the door.

"Charlie?" he asks.

"I'm done."

"Please," he says reaching his hand out to me.

Who's pathetic now?

"Done." And I do my best to hold my head up as I walk out the door.

12. The Visitor

THE FOLLOWING WEEK I FOCUS on pushing thoughts of drunk Ramon touching me out of my head. The weak side of me gets aroused at the thought of it, but the rational side of me is getting stronger every day. I also decide to take an OKCupid break and figure out the following week if I want to continue. I never found Christopher to say goodbye that night at the Abbey. I was over everything when I walked out of that storeroom, as a result nothing about Christopher seems charming or fun anymore. Maybe I'll get past my bitterness in a week or two.

But that Thursday afternoon, I'm pulling my reports together for our team meeting the next morning when Jenn from the reception desk, leans into my cube. "Hey Charlie, you've got a visitor."

I look up startled. I never get unscheduled visitors, and I've never had one escorted to my cube. If anything they'd call from the front desk and have us come up and meet them. I stand up abruptly. "I wasn't expecting any . . ." My mouth gapes open and I snap it shut.

"Hi Charlie." Ramon gives me a timid smile.

It's like Jekyll and Hyde, and I have whiplash seeing what appears to be the old Ramon again.

He turns to our receptionist, and gives her the big smile. "Thanks so much for helping me find him, Jenn."

"Oh no worries at all, Mr. Diaz."

"It's Ramon. And remember what I told you."

She gives him a flirty grin. "I will!"

After she wanders back to the elevators I fold my arms over my chest. "What did you tell her?"

"That her boyfriend Sam is an idiot if he can't see how terrific she is."

I roll my eyes.

"What? I meant it, and that dude is an ass."

"How long did you chat her up anyway?"

"Long enough to charm her into helping me find you."

I instinctively tighten my arms over my chest. "What are you doing here?"

"I really need to talk to you," he says. He's rocking back and forth on his heels, like someone about to sprint.

I wave my arm over my desk. "I'm working."

He sighs. "I can see that. But this is really important. As soon as I got the news I had to come over."

I can hear that Sheila in the cube behind me has stopped typing and is likely listening. She's one of the nosiest people I've ever met.

I shut down my computer and grab the jacket off the back of my chair. "This better be worth my time."

He glances at me, blinks, and then his gaze drops to the floor. "I hope you think it is."

I don't say anything to him—I just start walking to the elevators and he follows behind me. Our ride all the way down in the elevator is full of awkward silence as I chastise myself for not just insisting that he leave. If he'd protested I could've called security. But it's too late for any of that.

When we exit the building I head to the plaza that connects our building to its identical twin building that faces us. In the center of the plaza there's a huge fountain and I drop down onto the bench just past it. Ramon joins me a second later.

I figure I'll start out this conversation being clear about something that's been bothering me. "I didn't like what happened at the Abbey last weekend."

He scrapes his fingers through his hair. "I know, I'm sorry. I just . . ."

"Don't," I reply, stopping him mid-sentence. But he continues on anyway.

"I was at the end of my rope, and so shocked when I saw you there with that ridiculous guy. But I really wish you hadn't seen me like that, and I'm sorry for my behavior. I figure you really despise me now, and I deserve that."

I remain silent, watching the fountain for a minute before I respond. "You've shown me who you really are through all of this, and frankly I don't like that person, and I wish I'd never met the other nicer Ramon."

Glancing over at him, his cheek is bright red like he's been slapped and there's a deep sorrow reflected in his eyes. "I don't like that Ramon either, Charlie. But there's more to all of this than you know."

I abruptly stand up. "You know what? I've got to get back to work. You've apologized and I don't need to hear any explanations, so let's just leave it here."

Jumping up, he takes hold of my arm. "Please hear me out, Charlie. You may still hate me, but at least you'll know the truth about how I really felt about you all along."

I turn so that our intense gazes meet, my expression angry and his determined.

"Please," he whispers, his fingers warm as they tighten and pull me back.

I drop back down on the bench and glance at my watch. "I've only got a minute." My stomach is starting to churn.

He fumbles for his phone and begins tapping the screen while he talks. "Remember the night you brought Sasha and Emily to the club?"

"Of course."

"And you remember that guy Marcus was there?"

My face hardens. "You said he came to apologize."

He winces, but nods. "Yes, that's what I said."

"Did he apologize?" I narrow my eyes waiting for his response.

He lets out a pathetic laugh. "Ah, no. Marcus doesn't ever apologize for anything."

"Whatever. I'm not sure what that matters now. It has nothing to do with me."

And suddenly it hits me that the charming Ramon who was brought to my cubical a while back, is nowhere in sight. This Ramon isn't charming, or a drunk asshole, he's a man that's broken. He looks like he's about to cry.

"It has everything to do with you." He taps his phone screen and hands it to me.

I study the screen and then glance back at him. "Why do you have this picture of the World Tech building? Are you planning on stalking me?"

He taps the top of the screen. "Marcus sent it to me two days after you guys came to the club. Now read the attached message."

"Do you know what the body looks like after *accidently* falling off a thirty-three story building?" My voice breaks on the last word, and I clear my throat and read it silently to myself two more times while my blood pressure soars.

When I look up at Ramon his eyes are wide with terror, and he's clenching and unclenching his jaw.

"What the fuck?" I say, the panic clear in my throat.

He takes the phone, and moves it to the next message, then hands it back to me.

"Meet me at Il Fornaio on Beverly Drive tomorrow at one. I demand your complete focus."

I glance up at Ramon as my fingers tighten over his phone. "Is this psycho for real?"

He swallows hard and nods. "Scroll further," he whispers.

All the air whooshes out of my lungs when his screen reveals a picture of our condo. I spread my shaking fingers across the screen to blow up the two figures in the foreground. It's Estella pushing Sasha in her wheelchair down the walkway. A low cry comes from somewhere deep inside as I read, "You know what I need. So let me be clear. Crossing city streets can be dangerous for innocent pedestrians when large trucks lose their brakes."

My body collapses forward and I want to crush the phone, but I need the evidence preserved. My mind races, imagining rushing home, and how long it will take to throw things together so I can load Sasha in our van and tear out of this god-forsaken city as soon as possible. I'll figure out where we'll end up once we're on the road.

I'm about to sprint to the parking structure when I realize Ramon is shaking me. "Charlie, Charlie. You have to hear the rest."

I'm so full of fury that it's like my head is on fire. "You've known about this for how long and you didn't tell me? This fucker is threatening my sister and you do nothing?"

"I did everything!" he cries out. "I broke up with you even though it almost killed me to hurt you like that! I did all the things he demanded, and I almost had the information he needed on Ernesto. You have to believe me, Charlie, that I know how these guys work. If you'd gone to the police you'd both be dead now. I did what I had to do to protect you and Sasha."

"If all that's true, then why are you telling me now?"

Ramon lets out a sigh that sounds like relief, and suddenly his entire countenance is different. "I'm telling you because yesterday Marcus and his guys were arrested in a raid that has nothing to do with all of this. They're being extradited to Nevada, and bail was denied."

"Nevada?" I ask.

"It's bad. You don't mess with the Vegas underground. I imagine that's why he'd been back in L.A. Hell, he's probably safer in prison at this point. And so it's over for us, and I'm sure I'm the last person on his mind."

Leaning back into the bench, I can't sort the avalanche of thoughts, questions and feelings crashing through me. Through all the noise I keep hearing his proclamation, *I did what I had to do to protect you and Sasha.*

Protecting Sasha has been my top priority since the accident, and so this is an idea I need to sit with and process. The world Ramon is attached to from his past could've destroyed us, yet he chose protecting us over his own needs. That has to mean something.

I take a deep breath and shake my head.

He reaches over and takes his phone from my hands. I give it up willingly.

"Are you okay?" he asks.

I try to formulate an answer and finally I share the only answer I have so far. "I don't know. I need to process all of this."

"I understand," he responds in a sad voice. "And please know how much I regret that my mistakes from the past, ended up being a threat to you and Sasha. I'd have given anything to be able to take all of that back."

"But you can't," I agree mournfully.

He sighs. "No."

"But I can see you made choices based on what you thought would keep us safe. That says a lot."

"I did." He gives me a hopeful look. "So I know you need time, but can you consider if we can at least be friends again?"

"Maybe. Hey, and watch the excess drinking. You get really nasty."

He covers his face with his hands and groans. "I'm done with that. I really wish you hadn't seen me in that condition."

"Me too."

When I rise to standing, Ramon gets off the bench too.

"I'm going to get going. I think I'll go home and just hang with Sasha. I'm not going to tell her about this. Not yet, anyway. But I need to be there."

"I understand," Ramon murmurs. "She must hate me since I broke up with you so horribly."

I shrug. "I didn't tell her much about that night. I'm pretty sure she would've come after you."

"Ramon glances over at me. "I'm going to give you time, but maybe in a week or so we can get together and just hang out or something."

"Maybe. I'll call you if I decide that's what I want."

THE NEXT WEEK I'M TRYING to focus on my job during the day and working on my app at night, but I keep thinking about Ramon with thoughts that shift from avoidance, anticipation, anger, to possibilities, and back again with as many quick turns and nose-dives as a rollercoaster. There's no question that we've had a rocky start to whatever our relationship will be, but I can't seem to be willing to let him go. With the idea of him overtaking my thoughts, it's a miracle I can focus on any projects at all.

Finally on the following Monday I agree to meet him for coffee after work and I'm relieved to see that he still seems grounded. As we talk about our weeks he doesn't push me to see him again. He's just attentive and interested in me like he always was. It feels good to be listened to.

I promised myself not to linger, so when it's time to leave he gives me a hug and thanks me for coming, and says he'd love to meet up again whenever I'd want to. I surprise him by suggesting dinner, and Ramon being assertive, asks if I'm free tonight. I tell him I can do it the next night instead if he can get the night off. We agree to meet at his place.

"One last thing, Charlie," he says before I get in my car.

"What's that?" I ask.

"Tomorrow night can we start over?"

"Start over?"

"Like this is something brand new?"

I think back to all that we've experienced so far: from that first lap dance in the club, to him trying to find me a boyfriend, then the night our friendship ended, and drunk groping . . . we've not had an easy go of anything. Maybe a fresh start is just what we need.

"Okay. So tomorrow is our first date—yes?"

His smile lights up his face. "Yes! Our first!"

I may be crazy to start all this up again, but I can't help it. No one has ever affected me like Ramon has. What I've learned is that love isn't about being practical and safe. Sometimes you just have to jump off a cliff and hope you fly.

WEDNESDAY, THE ENTIRE TIME I drive to meet him I try to

picture Ramon's apartment to take my mind of my nerves.

He's such a dichotomy. The child of immigrants, who as a first-generation student was a linebacker on a college football team and a closeted gay, who then got caught up with the scene in Miami, then found himself again with help from his gay older lover, tried to open a club, only to be screwed by the mafia, his lover dying tragically, and then he ends up stripping in L.A. His life sounds like a made-for-TV movie. In contrast, I sound so boring . . . well, of course not the accident part and how that turned my life upside down, but in every other way I've been completely predictable and steady.

Parking is dicey in this part of Hollywood, so I circle the street twice before something opens up near the corner. Approaching his building, I glance up at the eclectic three-story Spanish-style apartment building that appears to be built around a courtyard. There are treats for the eyes everywhere you look, from Juliet balconies with wrought iron decorative railings, to French doors and random stained glass little windows. The entrance has a grand gate of an intricate metal design, framed under an arch draped in a violet bougainvillea. In the middle of the arch, hand-forged letters spell out *Jardín del Paraíso*, which translates to Garden of Paradise. At the gate, they've added a modern security box so that only the residents can allow you in.

When I press the code for Ramon's he responds right away. "Charlie? I'll buzz you in. I'm in 2F upstairs in the back of the second floor."

"Okay," I reply so he knows I'm not a random person trying to get into the building. After all, he didn't check to confirm it was me . . . as if he was that confident I'd show up. Well, the flip side is that it suddenly hits me how ready and happy he sounded that I'd arrived. Maybe tonight will set us on a new track. I hope so.

The center of the courtyard features an old stone fountain with several levels where the water delicately drips from one basin to the next. The sound is very soothing, helping me calm my nerves. There are rose bushes scattered about; they look like they've been here forever, but they boast bright roses of brilliant fuchsia, powder pink, and blood-red delicate blossoms so full they are drooping, heavy on their stems. Right before the walkway ends there's a bench to sit on and observe all the wonder.

As instructed, I take the back-right staircase and find myself behind a carved oak door at the end of the narrow hallway. His door swings open. "You're here!" he says as if he almost can't believe it.

My hands are awkwardly shoved in my pockets as I give him a crooked grin. "Guess I'm showing you how it's done."

"Well done, then," he replies as he holds out his arms and pulls me into a warm hug.

It already feels like things are off to a good start, and a wave of optimism flows through me.

He holds his arm open. "Come in. Let me show you my humble abode.

As I step inside it hits me that his place couldn't be more different than mine and Sasha's. Where our condo is all modern clean lines and shades of gray, turquoise, and silver, Ramon's is warm color and unrestrained passion. The living room walls are a creamy tan, almost ochre, and a large abstract, colorful painting hangs above the rococo burgundy velvet couch.

"That's interesting," I comment.

"A friend of mine from Miami painted it. He's starting to get a lot of attention in the art world."

"What's his name?" I ask.

"Ermano Acosta. He's Cuban."

"I like it."

"I've got one in the bedroom, too. He's very talented."

In the bedroom? "Was he a lover in Miami . . . like before you met Luis?"

He presses his lips together as if to suppress a laugh. "Are you jealous?"

I tip my head as I study the painting. "Maybe. I guess thinking of all the men before me that you must have had in your bed."

"Hmm, in my bed? I can count on one hand how many men I even brought home, and I assure you, Ermano wasn't one of them. He's straight. I worked with his wife, Mirana, at the club and we became friends."

Relief surging through me, I look back at the painting hoping he doesn't notice my red cheeks. "I guess I should feel special then that you've invited me here."

"Definitely. From the day I met you you've been the exception to my rules."

"How's that?" I ask.

"I hadn't found anyone interesting in quite a while, so I was taking an extended break. Then out of the blue I found myself really attracted to a serious, geeky guy who spends a lot of time figuring out algorithms."

"Hmmm, geeky?"

"Well he wears those sexy black frame glasses that I'd imagine scientists in the fifties wore."

"Anything like these?" I ask as I tap the frame of my glasses.

"Well, what do you know . . . exactly like those." He gives me a sexy smile.

I've never been flirted with like this and it's doing weird stuff inside of me, like making my heart feel . . . I don't know, kind of tender. I think I'm liking our 'first date' idea.

"So this place looks big," I comment. I note an arched doorway leading to a hallway that looks long for an apartment.

"It's a two bedroom so there's a place for my family to come stay whenever they want. My sisters, Rosa and Ruby, were here for a week in April, and I'm trying to convince Mom to let me fly her out for a long weekend. She doesn't like to be away from home that much."

"Then what does she like to do when she's in L.A.?"

"Oh, I've taken her to the touristy stuff like Grauman's Theater to put her hands in the celebrity footprints, and down to Olvera Street because it reminds her a tiny bit of where she grew up, but really she loves to cook for me and hang out."

"Have you ever brought her to the club?"

"No way, although I've told her about it and my bartending there. After I explained how it works she kept worrying that dancers get cold when they take their shirts and pants off."

"Oh man, I like your mom already," I chuckle. "This place is cool, but it must cost a fortune."

"Ah, that's where you're wrong. This place is actually a steal. But it's all thanks to our eccentric landlady. Her name is Gabriella Fontanoy, although we usually refer to her as Madame Fontanoy. She was an actress in her early years and married to some big Hollywood producer and studio head. Now she likes to entertain, holding parlor parties with artists, musicians, and other creative types. She loves to dance with me . . . especially to tango."

"Oh, I'd love to see that," I say.

"Anyway, she seems to have a lot of money, so she only charges each of us what she thinks we can afford. What matters to her is that each tenant be someone she'd invite to her gatherings."

"I can see why she'd love you."

"Really? And why's that?"

"Well to start with you can be charming."

"Can be? Go on," he says with an arched brow.

"And I suppose you're handsome, too," I tease.

"Says the man who looks like Cary Grant," he murmurs as he slides his hand under my elbow and leads me to the small balcony.

"You like old movies?" I ask. Sasha will love that if it's true. My parents used to have old movie night ever Sunday after supper.

"Oh, Ramon, darling . . ." a voice calls out from somewhere above.

I tilt my head until my gaze falls on a very attractive older woman in a flowing caftan. Her arm is looped through a man's arm. He's tall, dark, and handsome, wearing what looks like a linen suit.

"Do you remember Roberto?" she calls as the man nods his head in greeting.

"Yes, hello," Ramon calls out and waves to the man like this is perfectly normal to be shouting across a courtyard.

The sun is almost set now and the building feels like it's coming alive. I can see lit candles and someone in the kitchen in the apartment below Madame Fontanoy's. In another apartment on the ground floor someone is playing a grand piano and a Cole Porter song is drifting up to us.

"Is that your new beau, darling?"

"I want him to be," he answers. "This is Charlie."

She appraises me. "Charles, dear, please be good to my boy. He has a fragile heart."

Ramon has a fragile heart? "I'll be good to him," I assure her.

"Thank you, Charles," she replies. "He's quite lovely, Ramon. I approve. Would you two like to join us? Roberto brought some fabulous champagne and oysters on the half shell from Cape Seafood Market."

"Actually, we're about to leave for dinner. Can we take a raincheck?"

"Of course, my dear!" She waves her arm dramatically. "Now be off with you!"

Ramon waves good-bye and leads me back inside. "We better get going."

He holds my hand all the way down the stairs, through the courtyard, and down the three blocks of Franklin until we reach the café. I've never publicly been shown this kind of affection before from another guy, and this is a neighborhood where it's actually welcomed. It's a powerful feeling that I can be myself without fear. I feel a surge like maybe I can be exactly who I'm meant to be. Why did I waste all these years denying myself this vibrant life?

Ramon steps inside the café's door and the owner, a short man with a very expressive face, greets us like old friends and sits us at a choice table outside. Once we're seated, Ramon takes my hand again.

"How am I doing so far?" he asks with a boyish grin.

"Pretty flawlessly," I reply, looking down at where our hands are linked. "And you call me a romantic."

He sighs with a smile. "Something about you brings that out of me. This is new to me, too, you know."

"What about when you were with Luis?"

He shrugs. "He was more private about affection . . . maybe being older and raised in a conservative family. Our relationship wasn't a romantic one, maybe because in some ways he was fatherly toward me. But of course, not in bed."

I really don't want to think about Ramon in bed with Luis so I change the subject.

"Speaking of family . . . how is your mom about you being gay?"

He arches his brow. "The only son in a Catholic family?"

"That bad?" I ask, my breath catching.

"She always says I'm her baby. And it was an idea she had to adjust to. But she never made me feel less loved, and now it's a non-issue."

I wind my fingers through his. "I'm glad to hear that."

"I think she'd like you," he says with a soft expression.

For a moment, I wonder what my mom would've thought of Ramon. I'm not sure how she'd feel about the dancing thing. But she would admire that he has a master's degree and bigger goals. And if he charmed her like he did Sasha at first, well then . . .

The waiter brings over the bottle of pinot noir Ramon carefully picked out, and we lock gazes while he slowly opens it. I wish I could climb inside his head and know what he's really thinking right now.

Once the waiter leaves he lifts his glass. "Here's to you. For showing up tonight and giving me a chance to prove who I can be when it's just you and me, without my past rearing its ugly head."

I nod as we clink glasses. "I'll drink to that."

The feast of food soon follows: baked scallops, coq au vin, ratatouille, and salad. I notice he doesn't finish his glass of wine, but I have a second one. Before our cheese and fruit plate for dessert, which I don't consider a dessert in any way, shape, or form, he asks me about our childhood.

"My parents owned a vineyard in Paso Robles. It belonged to my grandfather originally. Actually, that's how my mom and dad met. He was working there one summer and she helped out in the tasting room. He always said it was love at first sight."

"So that's where you get your romantic side from," he muses.

"I guess so. But it was a fun place to grow up. Sasha and I were always running around the property getting into trouble."

"Do you still have the vineyard?"

My stomach flips over. My guilt for selling the property still haunts me. I look up at Ramon. "Actually, no. We sold it, but definitely with regrets. My great-grandfather purchased most of the land, and it was always intended to stay in the family. Sasha and I agonized over the decision but we couldn't bear the idea of returning there. My parent's lifeblood was in that vineyard, and with them gone . . . now, it's a reminder of everything we've lost."

"I'm sorry, I can imagine how rough that was." He squeezes my hand gently and I let out a long sigh. "I don't know anything about vineyards. Was it hard to sell?"

"Actually, we had a bidding war. The amount of land we had was unprecedented. So at least now Sasha never has to worry about money. She'll always be taken care of."

He gazes at me intently. "You're a really good brother, Charlie."

His tender gaze makes me feel like he sees something really special in me. The idea of it takes my breath away.

I've never been treated like this by another man . . . like I'm desirable and worth all the effort he's putting into this evening. I think I have craved this so much that I've been able to push the rough stuff we went through out of my mind and just focus on tonight.

This is all new for me. With Leo, we were awkward and figuring things out. Ramon has lived enough to know exactly what he wants, and with every moment passing he's making me believe he wants me. And the best part of it is how much I want him, too.

13. He's a Keeper

WHEN WE'RE DONE WITH DINNER, I'm filled with uncertainty as we start walking back to his place. *What's he expecting now? What am I?* There's nothing I've dreamt of more than being intimate with Ramon, but I'm worried that we're not on solid enough ground yet to weather it if things don't go well. Maybe I'm still haunted by the skanky storeroom sex at the Abbey. I need to know that the magic that's been around us tonight will still be there in the morning. As we pass the corner of his building he turns to me.

"What would you like to do now?" He pauses and caresses the top of my hand with his thumb like he isn't ready to let go of me. "Would you like to come upstairs? We could have a drink or some tea or something?"

I can tell he's being careful with me, but as nervous as I am, I don't want to be treated with kid gloves; I need to feel wanted. "Not more?" I ask, hearing the vulnerability in my voice.

"More?"

"You know, like making out," I say, realizing I sound like a twelve year old.

Reaching up, he cups my jaw with his hand and then trails his fingers down my neck until his hand is resting on my chest. "Well, if you'd like, we could do that." His eyes narrow into a sultry stare, and when he bites his lip it makes me want his lips against mine.

Looking up, I realize that we're already in front of his gate. He must sense my nerves because his voice is more soothing with his next words.

"How about we start with me giving you a goodnight kiss and

we'll see where that goes?"

"I'd like that."

Pulling us inside the gate and into the courtyard, he leads me to the fountain area where it's quieter and no one is around. Under the golden glow of the lantern lights and silver shine of the moon my breath catches. In this magical moment Ramon is resplendent. He's truly the most beautiful man I've ever seen. I step closer to him, all but telling him that I'm ready for my kiss.

He rests a hand on either side of my face and studies me.

"Thank you for tonight," I whisper.

He skims his lips along my cheek before he gently kisses it. "You're welcome."

"I'd really like for us to have our second date," I admit.

He runs his nose along my hairline, breathing me in. "I'm off Sunday night," he says suggestively.

"I'm not sure I can wait that long to see you again."

I see his eyes spark, the dark brown of his eyes seeming lighter. "I can't make plans for tomorrow, but do you ever go out for lunch during the work week? I could meet you near your office. How about Thursday?"

"Thursday's no good . . . I have a team meeting lunch. I can do Friday."

"Great," he says. "And I promise I'll be there right on time." He slides his hand down until he's pressing it into my lower back, pulling me closer.

When he kisses me every part of me lights up like an amped-up circuit board. A small groan escapes my lips, encouraging him to kiss me again, each pass of his tongue and nip of my lips claiming me as his. I'm so wrapped up in him that it doesn't compute that we're outside in his courtyard and he's cupped my ass and used the resulting leverage to press tight against me.

I'm achingly hard from the idea of *more* with Ramon. I always thought my sexual experiences would be with guys as awkward as me. So nothing surprises me more that this amazing sexual and erotic being takes pleasure in me.

"Ramon," I whisper, as his hand wraps around the back of my neck possessively. Every slight roll of his hips sends lightning bolts through me.

"Oh, baby, you feel so damn good," he says, his palm skimming up my chest over my muscles.

"So do you," I groan as I rock my hips back to where he's pressed against me.

He suddenly eases me away, his eyes wild with lust.

"What?" I ask.

He shakes his head, his gaze falling to the ground. "I understand we need to go slow, but I don't think I can take much more of this without dragging you upstairs into my bed. I'm being honest, Charlie, because I can only hold back so much. I'm a man with an intense sex drive, and I think you know that."

I nod, feeling dizzy with desire. "I'm sorry I'm nervous but you have to know that I want you so much. It just needs to be different than last time." I feel bad having to say that. I wish he could understand how much I want to be what he wants.

"Can I kiss you again?" he asks, looking hopeful that we're making progress. I glance at the fountain, its gurgling water creating a soothing sound that's such a contrast to my burning heat. Deciding to be brave, this time I'm the one returning his kiss, and it's with more passion than I thought I had in me. I feel his hot hand sliding over my shoulder, every kind of need blinding me to anything but this man's desire.

"Come upstairs with me," he whispers. "You won't regret it. I promise."

"Upstairs?" I ask nonsensically. Honestly, I can't even see straight at this point. All I can see is his handsome face delicately outlined by the moonlight.

"I want to feel you skin against skin. Surely you know how much I want to be inside of you?"

"Oh, Jesus," I groan, as my nerves flair again, and I feel my whole body flush with heat.

"Would you like that?" he whispers.

My dick throbs in response. *Would I like Ramon to make love to me?* I picture it in my mind and his powerful, muscular body curled over me, his hips sharply thrusting . . . filling me, and it's hotter than anything I can imagine. "Yes, I want that, but—"

"You know, handsome," he groans, then whispers in my ear, "I'd make you feel good, but don't worry. I want you up on my couch so I can touch you everywhere and we'll go from there. Okay?"

"Okay."

My gaze runs over him, from his swollen lips and flushed cheeks, to the distinct outline of his thick cock in his jeans. I know without a doubt, I've never wanted anyone more.

"But if you really aren't sure, Charlie, you honestly should go now," he says, gesturing toward the gate. "Before the last thread of my restraint is gone."

I swallow thickly, our shared gaze so intense I feel like he's looking into my soul. "I'm sure."

He studies me—perhaps to make sure I'm serious. Finally, he nods his head, and takes my hand, leading to the staircase. Perhaps he doesn't want to give an opening for me to change my mind, because not another word is said as he guides me up the stairs and to his apartment. I can feel my heart thundering when he pulls out his keys and opens his front door. He gestures for me to go inside.

Once I'm in the foyer and he's shut the door, he presses me up against it. Next thing I know his teeth are scraping their way down my neck as his hands and hips claim me. His kiss is so intense I almost feel like I'm being consumed. I'm panting with raw lust by the time he pulls me over to the couch and assertively eases me down until the cushions.

"You know, I want to make you understand how I feel about you, to make you believe it was worth taking another chance on me."

"You are so worth it," I say solemnly.

"Good," he breathes out, his voice ragged with intensity. "In the beginning I assumed that you only wanted me for sex. Now I know differently. So whatever happens tonight know that yes, I want to take you to my bed and be your lover, but that's not all this is. It's an expression of who you are to me."

"Because I'm yours?"

He nods as he rests his hands my shoulders and squeezes them. "You are mine."

I watch his smoldering expression as he unbuttons my shirt in between kisses. I lie back for a moment to watch him and marvel how we're drunk on great food and conversation, and this electrified attraction between us that's like a drug I want to shoot into my veins.

I reach over to kiss him, and although I wanted to take things slow, the way he passionately kisses me back consumes me, leaving me wanting more. My self-control starts to slip through my fingers like grains of sand. There's a fireball of desire and emotion growing inside of me. I desperately want to feel his weight on me as we explore each other's bodies on his velvet couch.

Ramon carefully pulls off my glasses to set them on the coffee table, and then studies my face with a burning look, running his fingers over my cheekbones and then along my jaw until he pushes me so I'm lying down and lowers himself on top of me. He slowly rotates his hips so that our cocks pulse against each other, my resulting moan edged with desperation. The room suddenly feels hot and steamy like those precious moments of peace before a tropical storm.

"Jesus, Charlie," he pants.

"I know, I know," I say, in a tone edged with desperation.

After a passionate kiss he whispers, "I want you so fucking much."

I groan, plastering myself against his warm, perfect body.

Unzipping my fly, he checks for my reaction before he slips his hand into my jeans, wrapping his fingers around my erection. Slowly starting to stroke me, he leans into me and bites his way up my neck and then growls in my ear. "Damn, you're so hard for me."

"You get me so worked up," I gasp, taking a sharp breath. He's the flame to my spark. Reaching down, I press my hand over where he's straining against the denim of his jeans.

He closes his eyes for a minute and rocks his hips down against my hand. "Baby, what do you say? Do you want to go to my bedroom?"

Rising off the couch, he reaches his hand out to help me up. I hear his words echo in my head and a fear deep inside starts to unfurl. The last time I was this close to having full-on sex with someone a policeman showed up at our front door telling me my parents were dead. Trying as hard as I can to shove the beginning of my panic away, I accept his help and unsteadily rise. I try to stay focused on how much I want him, but when he pulls me forward, I stumble.

He glances over at me and narrows his eyes. "Hey, you okay?"

My whole body starts to stiffen awkwardly. "No," I mumble.

Placing his hands on my shoulders, he eases me a step backward and lowers me until I'm sitting back on the edge of the couch. "What's going on?" he asks as he sits on the couch next to me and slides his arm over my shoulders.

"The last time I was this close to making love to my boyfriend, was the night my parents died."

"Oh damn," he whispers, the idea of my trauma apparently taking shape in his mind.

"Is that why you haven't—"

"Yes," I say abruptly, cutting him off. "I can't seem to separate the two ideas."

He slowly rubs his hand over my back. "I'm so sorry. Look, we don't have to do anything, okay?"

"But I want to . . . so badly."

He sits silently for a long moment, deep in thought.

"Well, we were doing okay with doing other stuff? Would you still be good with that?"

"Yeah, really good with that," I reply, trying to lighten the mood, relieved that he still wants me after my confession.

I wonder about the *stuff* part and feel a ray of hope that this night hasn't gone completely to shit.

He starts out slow as we sit on the couch. He gently rubs my knees and then my thighs. When he senses I'm calming down, he skims his lips against mine.

Sighing, I reach out for him, needing more.

The low room light paints him with a golden glow. My heart is thundering as he begins to gently kiss me again. While the passion rebuilds, he slowly pushes my unbuttoned shirt off my shoulders and pulls it aside. Once my torso is bare, he kisses his way across my chest, moaning as his lips close over my nipple and suck. Everything he does to me reignites my raw lust for him.

I moan hungrily, my fear falling away. I trust Ramon and the Universe not to let me down tonight.

His fingers are digging into my shoulders as he keeps kissing and biting his way across my chest. "You're so hot, Charlie."

"Can we take your shirt off, too?" I want to feel his skin against mine.

His hands grasp the hem, and it's tugged off in one fluid gesture and flung to the floor. A moment later he's straddling me on the couch to kiss me, and the feeling of his bare chest against mine almost makes me lose it before we've really begun.

He skims his fingertips across my skin while watching me with dark eyes. I can imagine how flushed I am considering how wild he's making me feel. His next kiss is intense as he pulls my hair and ravages my mouth. I moan loudly, electrified by the way he's slowly grinding his crotch over my lap.

"You like that, don't you?" he asks breathlessly, his hips rocking over me, making me desperate as I imagine him fucking me.

When my moans get louder, he slides back so he has room to free my erection that's still trapped inside my unzipped jeans. Leaning over to lick the edge of my ear, while stroking my hard cock, he whispers, "I want you in my mouth. Not like the other night . . . I promise, I'll make you feel so good you'll never want me to stop."

My dick pulses in response. "Oh God, yes," I moan. Shifting up enough to slide my jeans and boxer briefs down low, I watch a sexy smile spread across his face.

"Damn, Charlie," he moans as his gaze takes me in and he slowly edges my legs open.

I'm sure I'm in a dream state, with one Ramon fantasy after another playing out in front of me. It all begins with his hand wrapping around my cock with a reverent look in his eyes. "You're fucking perfect," he groans. At first he slowly strokes me, glancing up at me as if he wants to be sure he's giving me what I need. Damn, if he only knew.

His gaze is dark, his eyes half-mast. "I going to suck you now."

"Please," I beg.

When his lips slide over the head of my cock, my hips jerk reflexively, and I can feel his mouth curl into a satisfied smile as he slides down my shaft and back up. I close my eyes, lost in the feeling of his tongue running up and down while circling my girth in sensuous strokes. I want to cry he's making me feel so amazingly turned on beyond anything I've ever known.

"Oh fuck," I cry out when he takes me extra deep and my hips buck out of reflex. He is making me feel so worked up that I'm pretty sure I'm going to lose my mind.

"That's right, fuck my mouth," he groans.

Good God, this is so much hotter than any gay porn I've ever watched.

I take a sharp breath as I look down and see him gazing up at me through his thick eyelashes with a drunken expression. This is everything that our Abbey experience wasn't. He's focused on taking care of me, reacting to every response I have.

What surprises me is that he seems as turned on as I am, his moans getting deeper in his chest, his moves more urgent. I glance down and see his erection straining against his jeans right before he deftly undoes his fly and pulls his engorged cock out. The sight of him as he starts to jerk himself off while he blows me, is tearing me apart in the best way.

"I'm not going to last long," I warn him.

He moans with his mouth full of me, and nods like he's almost there, too.

The sensations are building with intensity and heat as he sucks me, while his fist works the base of my cock, causing stars to explode in my head. Meanwhile, his other hand working his cock is a blur.

"Ramon," I moan before he takes me in even deeper, pushing me past the point of return.

"Let go, Charlie . . ."

I don't even recognize the noises coming out of me as he takes me in the deepest yet, my body sizzling with the most intense pleasure. "Ahhh . . ." I chant breathlessly as my climax explodes, my head jerking back and his hooded, dark eyes revealing his victory in the intensity of my release. He presses his eyes shut tightly while his cries join mine as he comes.

A minute later, I collapse back into the couch, my chest rising and falling with each ragged breath. He joins me, pulling me against him, slowly stroking my back.

"Charlie?" he whispers, his swollen lips dark red and his gaze heavy with satisfaction. "Are you okay?"

"Okay?" I ask, completely both satiated and flustered. "Do you know how many times I've imagined you doing that to me?"

He looks pleased. "Once or twice?" he guesses in a teasing voice.

"Ha!" I sputter.

"Well, whatever number I can promise it's not as many times as I jerked off imagining giving that to you," he replies.

His words and the picture of him jerking while imagining his mouth on me make me sizzle, and stirs up my desire to give him the same pleasure. "Will you show me next time?"

"Show you?" he asks, his eyebrows arched.

"I want you to tell me what you like best." I can feel my cheeks burn. "Next time I want to go down on you."

His eyes grow wide. "I'd really like that," he whispers.

"I really want to. I've fantasized about it, too," I admit, happy not to be embarrassed to share that with him. He makes me feel like I can tell him things without being judged.

"I'm so into you, Charlie, and to watch you pleasure me . . . well, that would be about the hottest thing I can imagine."

I want to believe him, and it's hard not to with how supremely happy he looks.

He pulls me into his arms. "Being with you fulfills the fantasy I'd had about the two of us. You're a keeper, Charlie Morgan."

"Good," I say with a sigh. "Because this is exactly where I want to be."

14. A Future Investment

THE NEXT EARLY EVENING, WHEN I open the front door of our condo after running errands, I hear a burst of laughter. I grin remembering that Emily was coming over to watch a movie with Sasha and they were ordering pizza.

I glance over at them and Sasha waves. "Hey Charlie!"

Emily turns toward me and echoes her response.

"Hey girls. What movie is that?" I notice that they're drinking beer. It's good to see Sasha cutting loose.

"*Bad Moms* . . . it's so friggin' funny!" Emily says. "Hey, Sasha, let's be badass like them when we get old."

Sasha laughs. "They're not that old, Emily. But yeah, being badass is a good plan. Hey, you want to join us?" Sasha says to me pointing to the boxes stacked on the coffee table. "We saved some pizza for you. It's cold but you can nuke it."

I walk over and open the box to make sure they didn't get any of that freaky Hawaiian pizza with pineapple. Luckily, it's pepperoni with black olives, so I grab a slice with one hand and the box with the other, and head to the kitchen for a beer. A minute later Sasha rolls into join me since Emily has some messages she needs to check and respond to.

"No movie?" she asks.

"No thanks. I've still got some work to do, and I'm anxious to get it done so I can chill. Was your day okay? Lucia said you complained a little about not feeling great."

She rolls her eyes. "I told the woman not to bother you!"

"And I told her I'd fire her if she was worried about something and she didn't tell me right away." I fold my arms over my chest.

"You did not! That's cruel to make them fear for their jobs."

"Your care is very important to me. If you're getting another bladder infection then something isn't being taken care of properly."

"Shhh," she warns. "Emily doesn't need to hear about my peeing issues. Besides, Lucia gave me something and I'm feeling better already, Mr. Bossy."

"Well good!" Reaching over, I squeeze her shoulder gently.

"Besides I talked to Dr. Phillips and my therapist, Victoria, and we've agreed that I'm ready for more independence."

I set the pizza down as I try to sort in my head what she is suggesting. "Independence in what regard?"

"You're getting out more finally, and I feel like I'm doing well, and I can imagine that in a few years we wouldn't be living together anymore. I need to prove to myself that I can take care of myself with more minimal help from the caregivers, and eventually maybe even have a boyfriend." She grins at me and I can't help but feel delight in how her whole face lights up.

"Is that what you want?" I ask.

"Yes, I do. It's not fair that I depend on you so much. You've given up on a fuller life to make sure that I'm okay. I think it's time for you to focus on yourself and what makes you happy."

"When you're happy, I'm happy, Sasha."

She waves her hand at me. "See! This is exactly what I'm talking about. You deserve a big life, Charlie. I want to hear that you've come home from work with tickets to Paris, and you sweep your boyfriend into your arms before telling him to pack for your morning flight."

"Seriously? Can you imagine me doing that?"

"I can!" she replies with a big grin. "I can see you up in the Eiffel Tower arm in arm, living your big life."

"Where did all this *big* life stuff come from?"

She shrugs. "I don't know . . . maybe a Ted Talk, or video from Brene Brown. Or maybe it was the blissful expression on your face this morning when you told me about you and Ramon getting a fresh start. I loved hearing about your date and how special he made you feel."

"Ramon or no Ramon, I'm always going to look out for you, Sis."

"And I'm always going to look out for you. So give me some space to do that. Okay?"

I study her, marveling in her determination, her spirit that makes me believe she could do anything. I nod slowly. "Okay, I'll back off, as long as you promise to share all your ups and downs with me."

She gives me a warm smile. "Deal." She studies my face.

"So you and Ramon are back on? And you really like him, don't you?"

"I do, Sasha. Will you give him another chance? I really think he likes me. He's meeting me for lunch Friday at work because neither of us are willing to wait until our real date on Sunday—his day off." It's like a love-struck, starry-eyed romantic has inhabited my body, and I don't mind the feeling one damn bit.

"Okay then. I'll give him another chance, but it's conditional. This special treatment needs to continue." She reaches over and cups her hand on my jaw. "But if he continues to make you look this happy, I'll be his biggest fan."

I let out the breath I've been holding. "Thanks. You know how important your support is to me."

She nods. "I do. I think Emily is done, so I'm going to get back to our movie now. Okay?"

I wink at her. "Okay."

FRIDAY, RAMON TEXTS EXACTLY AT twelve-fifteen, *I'm here outside by the entrance.*

My heart flips around in my chest, and I press my hands together to still their trembling. The whole way down the elevator ride I remember my workout this morning at the gym. Every time I flexed a muscle to lift a weight or stretch I imagined Ramon's hands on my straining biceps, or my defined calves as he parts my legs open for him.

I was so distracted in my thoughts that it's amazing I didn't drop a barbell on my foot. During my shower, I rubbed the body wash into my slick skin, noting the definition in my abs and chest, grateful that I've kept up my workouts through it all.

As I got dressed at the gym, I felt a thrill when I thought about the steps I'm finally taking out of the closet, and I'm seeing my crush at lunch and Sunday, too. Actually, Sunday I'm not only going to see him but I'll be kissing his beautiful face and touching his gorgeous body again. I'm getting jazzed thinking about all the ways I want to be with him. Maybe with our fresh start my life can be more now—not just better than adequately productive . . . maybe it can be great. After all, we got through a dark time that would crush most new couples, and knowing that makes me believe we're meant to be. It's like I feel complete for the first time in forever. Somehow, I put that missing period at the end of my most significant sentence, or placed that final piece into my jigsaw puzzle and suddenly everything feels right in the world.

So as the elevator finally hits the ground floor at lunchtime, and the doors part, I'm the first out, determinedly focused on spotting Ramon as soon as I pass through the main entrance. My gaze scans the front area of the building until my eyes settle on Ramon casually leaning against the polished wall of glass to my far left. His lazy pose, accentuated by his white T-shirt and worn jeans, renders him hotter than any Calvin Klein ad I've ever seen. I feel a thrill at the sight of him.

I purposely jam my hands in my back pockets as I approach him so I don't reach out and grab him. Nothing has ever been as tempting. In the bright sunlight I can see that his hair is still damp, and he has the stubble of a beard that's blatantly sexy.

I grin as I step up to him. "So was your intent to look like a su-permodel today?"

The right side of his mouth curves up. "Are you attracted to supermodels? If so, then yes, that was part of my master plan today."

Digging my hands deeper into my pockets, I try not to blush. "Oh, I'm attracted to you all right." I gesture toward Wilshire Blvd. "Hungry?"

His gaze starts at my mouth and moves its way down my chest; it lingers below my belt and then trails down my thighs. He licks his lips slowly. "Famished."

I grin at him, so inspired by his blatant lustful gaze, that I can't help but tease him. "Subtlety is not your strong suit."

He shrugs. "Why bother being subtle when you can be direct and ask for what you want. Like right now I want to kiss you, but I suppose that would be awkward with your co-workers milling about."

I nod. "Much too awkward. Come on. There's a place called Prospect down the block that is a little pricey for lunch for most of this crowd. We should have our privacy there."

He steps away from the building. "Okay, lead the way."

Once we're settled into our corner booth near the back of the restaurant, he reaches under the table and takes my hand, winding our fingers together until they're intertwined. I don't even bother scanning the restaurant for my co-workers because frankly, I don't give a damn. It's not like we're lip-locked in front of the building for everyone to gawk at.

"Would you believe me if I told you that I've missed you?" Ramon asks quietly, as he leans into me. I can smell his aftershave, woodsy and crisp. It makes me want to wrap myself around him.

"Yes," I reply, squeezing his fingers. "I've thought about you a lot."

His grin is infectious. "How so?"

I shake my head with a shudder. "How much I like you. Sometimes I can't believe you want me with all the men you can choose from in this city," I admit.

He playfully pushes me. "Stop. You're exactly what I want. I love that you're incredibly smart and a very determined man. Plus, you've got class."

"Really? What makes you think that?"

"Well for one thing you don't grab at my junk every possible opportunity. As a matter of fact, for a moment the other night I was worried you might walk away without even a kiss, and me desperately wanting you."

"If I'd walked away I would've had serious regrets."

"And I'm so glad you didn't walk away. Seriously, you're so much classier with me than the women at the club. Last night the bad behavior hit an all-time low in that category."

I arch my brow. "The women got wild?"

"It was a particularly rowdy crowd. This one large bachelorette party was out of hand and they egged each other on."

"So they took advantage of the situation?" I know I shouldn't be jealous of women man-handling him, but I'm jealous of anyone other than me touching him.

"You'd think when I shook my head, and peeled their hands off my ass and package they'd back off, but they just got more wound up. I finally gave up and snuck backstage to get away from it."

"Whoa." I let out a long, frustrated breath, feeling protective of him.

"Right? I only want you touching me." Ramon's warm gaze and those brown eyes melt me.

"Well, at least I wait for a sign that tells me it's what you want."

He grins and winks at me. "That's appreciated, you know?"

Feeling bold, I share with him, "I'd be lying if I didn't admit that I wish you weren't dancing anymore. I guess I'm greedy and want that part of you just for me."

"Honestly, I feel the same. I'm really over this scene anyway. I want to get my club open . . . like yesterday. And at this point I've got years of work ahead of me. I'm not sure what kind of extra work I can do to bring in more money than the tips and overtime salary I can get at Wild Nights. Gene has been generous with me, and I still have some of what Luis left me, but it's not enough. I've even thought about going back to Miami to see if there's a chance I can get my money back, or at least my piece of the club if it's been built."

A wave of fear rolls up my spine. "Miami?" I ask after clearing my throat to hopefully keep my voice steady. "How could you think about that after what just happened with Marcus? Wouldn't that be dangerous?"

He shakes his head. "I can understand your reaction but I promise this is a different situation. I have friends there who were like family, and would look out for me. It's a different group of people than who Marcus was dealing with. Besides, a lot of time has passed since I was forced to leave. Everything could've changed." Reaching out, he takes my hand. "Don't worry, Charlie, I'm just going to check things out. I won't do anything stupid . . . especially now when I've got you in my life."

I wish I could believe him. I've already seen some unpredictable behavior with Ramon and that worries me. And although I'm still shaken by his cavalier announcement, I decide to take another angle as how to show him how he can make his club happen faster than he is thinking. Maybe that will keep him off the "go back to Miami" idea.

I sit up straighter and pull my hand out of his to take a drink of water, and then set my hands on the table to make the moment more weighted. "I'd like to talk about another approach to this issue. When I came to see you at the club last I was bringing you some figures I had worked up about your club idea."

His expression brightens. "Was that the white envelope you were holding?"

I nod. "It was."

"Damn, and I saw you trash it on your way out. I should've followed my gut and pulled it out of the bin."

"Don't worry, I saved the information on my hard drive. I think with legitimate investors, not mafia crooks, you could be open within two years, possibly less, if we find the right location and property."

He looks incredulous. "We?"

"Excuse me?" I ask, puzzled.

"You said 'we' Charlie. What did you mean by that?"

"I want to help you . . . and yes, I could be an investor if you are willing to try that route again. I promise I'm not a mafia warlord with an army of thugs to threaten you."

He leans back, a stunned expression on his face. "You'd be willing to do that? But we haven't even known each other that long."

I nod. "You're right, we haven't, but I think I have a pretty good sense of you now."

He twists his napkin nervously in his hands as he considers for a minute what I've said. "But, Charlie, I'm really falling for you, and the last thing I would want is for a business relationship to ruin the potential we have. No amount of money or business opportunity is worth trading in what we could be together."

I study Ramon's tormented countenance; it's like he's in pain. In that moment, I realize that his reluctance brings me comfort. This was my idea, not his, and now that he's resisting it for the good of us, it makes me feel even better about the idea and more impressed with him. My heart speeds up in my chest. He's a genuine man to his core. It would be so easy for him to play me, use me to get what he needs, but he isn't.

"You sound pretty resolute about this," I say with a serious tone.

"I am. But you know what?" He turns to me, looking animated like he has a great idea. "If you're willing, I would really appreciate your advice. Everything I've learned about you tells me that you're brilliant and strategic. I think we have different strengths regarding business so there's a lot I could learn from you."

"I agree about our different strengths. For one thing, you are way more personable than I'll ever be and that is key for running a club. And then something you don't know about me is that investing is one of my 'passions', for lack of a better word. Right now, it's only in the stock market, but eventually I'll expand into other areas. So, we can learn together."

From the way the luminescent grin spreads across his face I can tell that my response has more than satisfied him, and yes, for now he can think I'm only helping him strategically. *The rest will come later,* I think to myself. If we continue on this new path as a couple I'm willing to invest more than my heart with Ramon, and I'll have to slowly show him that we can make it work. We can be even more than what we've imagined.

I barely taste my lunch I'm so focused on Ramon and our conversation. He even manages to be charismatic when talking about business. I have to focus hard on his words when all I want to do is gaze into those big, brown eyes and feel his full lips against mine. He has completely enchanted me. When the check comes, he reaches for his wallet and I shake my head. "It's my turn."

"How about we split it?"

"Nope." I hold up the small tray as the waiter passes, and he grabs it before Ramon can protest any more. "So what's your afternoon like?"

He pats his stomach. "As soon as lunch settles, I'll be putting in a couple of hours at the gym."

"Are you dancing tonight? There must be a lot of pressure to always look ripped."

He shrugs. "As of now I'm not dancing tonight, but that's not what's motivating me lately. I want to look hot for you." He winks as we start to slide out of the booth. Before we head up front for the walk to WTS, he faces me and places his hand on my shoulder. "Thanks for lunch, Charlie."

"Thanks for coming to my side of town," I say with a grin before we head out the Prospect's front door.

He doesn't take my hand while we walk back to my building, but I can still feel the sizzle between us. We're passing the driveway of an empty storefront for lease when he takes me by the elbow, and steers me to the right. "I want to show you something," he explains. He leads us partway down the driveway and into an inset in the building for what must have been a delivery entrance, complete with a low-hanging awning. Next thing I know he has me pressed against the brick wall of the building as he kisses me, one hand cupping the back of my neck, the other running up my chest.

"I couldn't let you go back to work without something to remember me by."

Blinking at him, I place my hands on my cheeks since they feel like they're burning. How does he do this to me . . . getting me instantly flustered and worked up? "There's no way I could ever forget you, Ramon."

"Good," he groans before skimming the edge of his teeth along my jawline, and following with a mind-bending kiss.

We finally part to take a breath. He's pressing his hips into me and

I'm getting so aroused that I can't imagine how I'll be able to return to work, let alone focus on a damn thing the rest of the afternoon.

"Come home with me," he whispers. "I want to do things to you." He slips his hand down and lightly brushes over my erection jutting against my slacks.

"Can't . . . got a client meeting at two," I mumble almost incoherently, noticing that everything is hazy.

Taking my hand, he presses it over the prominent bulge in his jeans. "You're going to make me wait until Sunday, aren't you?" he asks.

I swallow a gulp of air. "Believe me, I'd so much rather go home with you than deal with the difficult client I'll be meeting with soon."

Ramon steps away and folds his arms over his muscular chest defiantly, but then takes a deep breath and winks. "Okay, I'll back off. But with great reluctance." He glances down below my belt and shakes his head. "We're both going to have to think about global warming or something before we face the public with our obvious *problem*."

I clear my throat. "Did you know that sea levels will rise seven to twenty-three inches in the next century due to global warming? Or that the last two decades have been the warmest in four hundred years?"

Ramon looks at me with wide eyes before leaning forward and kissing me one last time.

"You're one of a kind, Charlie," he murmurs, stepping away. Even though his kiss doesn't linger, it's perfect nonetheless. I'll be remembering the kiss and wanting more reasons to be in his arms all afternoon.

15. The Fine Art of Love

I RARELY GO TO THE gym on the weekends, but take a run instead if I feel like working off some stress. But this weekend, I'm motivated knowing I have a date with Ramon Sunday, so both days I'm out of the house before Sasha is even up. I put in long workouts both days, and then run errands after.

Saturday night Sasha is pretty quiet, and after picking at her dinner she tells me she's going to watch Netflix in her room.

"You okay?" I ask, the concern clear in my tone.

"I am. I overdid it this week and snacked too much this afternoon.

"You need to pace yourself. Remember what the doctor always says," I warn her.

She lets out a long sigh. "I know, I know." But her big grin that follows lightens the serious mood.

I'm trying to learn to trust her ability to read herself and know when things are too much.

WHEN RAMON SUGGESTED WE SPEND Sunday afternoon in downtown L.A., I thought it was a weird idea. Downtown never held any interest for me, but he assures me that there's been a renaissance in the area and I'll be impressed. He tells me he's bought tickets for the Broad Museum at four so we agree that I'll pick him up since he's close to the freeway we'll be traveling on. He's made dinner res- ervations, too, at a place called Church and State. I'm intrigued, and frankly I really like this assertive side of him making plans for us. I never thought it'd feel amazing to be so well taken care of.

I go to check on Sasha before I leave but she's in the bathroom. I knock on the door.

"Hey, Sash, I'm leaving to get Ramon. You sure you don't need anything until Lucia comes?"

She has the sink running so her voice is dimmed. "No, I'm fine. Have fun."

"I will, thanks."

It's a clear, mild day, so I lower the roof on the Audi. I rarely make use of the convertible feature but everything feels new and I'm guessing Ramon will enjoy it. When I pull into the loading zone in front of his apartment building, I take out my phone and text him that I'm outside. I hear my name called out. I look up to see Ramon's eccentric landlord exiting the gate. She steps up to the car.

"Hello, Madame Fontanoy," I say.

"Charles, darling. Please call me Gabriella. Ramon tells me he's taking you to the Broad and then out to dine."

"He is. I haven't been. I had no idea that downtown L.A. had become so interesting."

"Well, then, it's a good thing you're in Ramon's capable hands now. He knows what's happening and downtown is *the* place. So many chic restaurants, and my dear friend Mirabelle has a fabulous art studio in the Arts District with a terrace perfect for late night tête-à-têtes."

She pushes her sunglasses on top of her head and in the bright light her eyes appear violet. She waves her arm as she continues talking.

"At the Broad make sure you take note of the Barbara Kruger's they've recently brought out again—so provocative and relevant in these politically unsettling times. I say, dear boy, I'm back on Xanax to manage my anxiety over it all."

Wow. Madame has left me speechless, confused as to what topic I should address first, although definitely not the Xanax. Thankfully Ramon steps out of the gate and loops his arm over Gabriella's shoulder.

"You're late, darling," she admonishes Ramon. "You know what

Emily Post would say about that."

He grins. "Actually I don't, but I'm sure you'll tell me. Keep in mind that I'm not late, Charlie is early."

She turns back to me with a mock shocked expression. "Is this true, Charles?"

"It is, but it's a good thing I was since I was fortunate to see you."

Releasing a happy sigh, she turns to Ramon and rests her hand on his cheek. "Oh, if you don't marry this darling man, Ramon, I may have to."

He shakes his head. "Don't throw down that gauntlet, Madame, for surely I'll win. I suspect Charlie already is quite smitten with me."

Smitten? I bite back a laugh.

"So where are you off to now, Gabriella? Can we drop you off somewhere?" I ask to stop them from mock fighting over me. Besides, I like that I've fit into this conversation with Gabriella so naturally.

"Oh, I'm taking my midday walk to the bakery. I prefer my scones for afternoon tea fresh out of the oven. But thank you kindly anyway."

She waves and strolls off, wearing red slacks and a tunic of some exotic pattern, her silver hair swept into a sleek ponytail.

Ramon slides into the passenger seat and leans over to kiss me, before we take off. "Well, you've certainly won her over."

"I think she's awesome. She's like a character in those nineteen-forties black and white movies our parents showed us."

"Indeed," he agrees as he takes my free hand, while my other hand steers us onto the 101 Freeway.

Twenty minutes later we're downtown, and when we turn onto Grand Avenue I'm soon treated to the sculptures pretending to be buildings also known as the Broad Art Museum and the Walt Disney Concert Hall. The Broad is a box-shaped building with cut angles, and dramatic texturing that resembles white concrete scales of a fish where the Disney Hall is a symphony of curved metal, silver planes stacked like an abstract wedding cake of many layers and sharp edges. It's an abstract sculpture that defies the idea that inside it houses an amazing concert hall.

"Wow!" I say, quite taken with the dramatic buildings.

Ramon glances over me with a grin. "Right? So cool!"

I nod, already realizing how different downtown is from what I remember when we first moved here.

Once inside the ultra-modern museum space of the Broad, we wander from section to section, lingering at the Warhols, Rauchenbergs, and of course, Gabriella's recommendation, Barbara Krueger.

Ramon squeezes my hand when we approach the first of the Basquiats. "I love his stuff," he whispers. "So primitive." The images don't do much for me but I appreciate how Ramon lingers with wide eyes, taking in every detail. He has a similar reaction to Takashi Murakami's work. I wonder if I'm getting a peek into the playful, organic side of Ramon, as my preference for Warhol and Edward Ruscha speaks to the linear, over-thinking side of me. When I pause in front of Ruscha's painting, a simple black canvas with white block letters saying "Hollywood is a Verb," Ramon steps behind me and holds me to his chest while he presses his lips onto my neck. Every sensation in my body is on fire and I feel completely alive.

We've circled the galleries twice when Ramon tugs on my hand. "Are you ready for an amazing meal?"

I nod enthusiastically. When he grins, I feel a heat wave sizzling through me. The feeling is what I imagine falling in love feels like. What if it is?

Ramon navigates while I drive through industrial streets east of the museum until we finally arrive at the vibrant Arts District. Despite the old, converted brick buildings, and distant landscape of blue-collar bars, and nondescript factories, the streets are clean and hold promise that a new time has come. The abandoned industrial buildings lining up along these streets are now hot galleries, hip restaurants, and artist working studios. It's still a tenuous rebirth, but I'm inclined to believe it all will take hold.

We hand a guy in a zip-up nylon jacket and baseball hat a ten to park in the lot of an art print studio closed for the evening. As we approach the restaurant, Church and State, the warm lighting and jazzy music spills out into the street.

"Have you eaten here before?" I ask Ramon, who is pulling me along.

"Once, but I'm more happy to be here with you."

The hostess settles us into a corner table in the lively room, and Ramon hands me the wine list. "You pick and I'll have a glass."

"Are you sure?" I ask.

He nods. "I'm with you, so I know it's okay."

By the time we've surveyed the menu decisions have been made. "Definitely no frog's legs," I say.

"Agreed," Ramon replies. "How about the warm goat-cheese salad and the mussels to start?"

"Done."

By the time I'm on my second glass of wine, my ankle is hooked under Ramon's and our fingers are wound together. Our waitress even comments, "You two are like the perfect couple."

Ramon looks over at me. "What do you think, Charlie? Could I be perfect . . . for you?"

I grin at him. "Maybe so."

For a moment, I reflect on the fact that this is only our third official 'date' and so it's much too early to put us on the relationship pedestal after all the shit that went down between us, but I appreciate that she sees something special between us.

Ramon looks over at me with a serious gaze. "What do you think of Downtown L.A. so far?"

"You were right. It's really come a long way. I think it's very cool. If it weren't for Sasha, I think I'd even like to try living down here."

He nods at my assessment. "I'm glad you see it that way. One of the reasons I brought you down here is that I think it could be smart to have a club down in this area."

I'm really surprised by his idea. I assumed he'd been thinking West Hollywood, or Hollywood, which I'm good with. But I'm open to the downtown idea . . . especially since it's not Miami. "Would downtown attract enough of the demographics that you aspire to be your customers?" I ask.

"There's already a lot of young, working professionals down here, artist and creative types in the arts district, senior and graduate students from USC, and if the club is cool and unique enough people will come in from all over."

He must notice that my expression reflects my confusion. "But aren't you talking about a gay club? That's why I assumed a location like West Hollywood."

"I want it to be a new concept. Yes, a place where gays want to be, but not only that community. It could be a place of different interests and ideas."

As he continues to discuss ideas like art installations and using the latest music, video, and lighting technology, my thoughts swing from thinking this concept could be an enormous risk, or edgy enough that it could be ahead of its time and take off. What is clear to me is how much passion Ramon has for the idea and that he'd be willing to work night and day to make it a success.

When it's time to leave the restaurant, it's clear I can't drive and Ramon looks pleased about it when I hand him the car keys. He lowers the car top again before we pull out of the lot.

Once on the freeway I lean back in my seat, appreciating his confident driving style. There's something in his demeanor that would make anyone believe this is his car. I try not to stare as he keeps his focus straight ahead, but it's irresistible when everything about him seems to excite me on some level.

It's a full moon tonight, hanging low in the sky like a drunken sailor struggling to rise. The evening air is warm as it skims over us. Ramon's playlist is rocking out of the Audi's sound system, his fingers subtly keeping the rhythm of the beat on the steering wheel.

When we turn off Franklin, he deftly swings into a free parking spot, and then activates the coupé hardtop and it slides open and settles over us. He's out of the car as soon as it locks into place. Coming around to my side of the car, he reaches for my hand as soon as I step out, then walks us toward his building. This time I have no hesitation as I follow him through the courtyard.

"I'm glad you liked downtown," he says once we're near the fountain.

"I really did."

"I wanted to show you some places I love that perhaps you'd never been to."

I reach for his hand, and once we're joined I can feel the energy pulse between us. "I wish you could understand how you make me feel when you say things like that."

"Isn't that part of what being together is about? I want to show you what this can be."

In his apartment, I'm enveloped with this overwhelming feeling that has built up since I got my first glance of him tonight, a passionate hunger that won't be satiated until I'm lying stripped of my clothes and stretched out across his four-poster bed with him in my arms.

As he leads me into the bedroom, I take a sharp breath realizing that I'm going to surrender to Ramon completely tonight, to go wherever he leads me, and to be everything he needs. Judging from how the air is crackling between us, I figure he's decided the same. He will own me with every word spoken, every touch that pulls us closer together.

Only a foot away from the bed, he turns and faces me. "Do you trust me, Charlie?" he asks in a hopeful voice, his gaze heavy with desire.

I nod without even considering the question. I do trust him. My instincts tell me that despite my fears around consummating our relationship, Ramon will make it good. He's proven how much he genuinely cares about me.

He skims his fingers across my chest. "The key here is to relax and enjoy how I'm going to make you feel."

"Okay," I whisper.

Placing a hand on either side of my face, he gazes at me intently. "My handsome man." He grazes my lips with the pad of his thumb and slowly trails his touch along my neck and across my chest.

I glance down as he begins to slowly unbutton my shirt. My breathing is already ragged because with every movement and item of clothing removed, he caresses me, trailing tender kisses across my bare skin.

When he starts unbuckling my belt, his gaze is locked with mine. My breath catches as he eases my jeans down, my erection jutting against my boxer briefs. He wraps his fingers around my dick and it throbs in response. A moment later my boxer briefs join my jeans in a pile on the floor.

"I want you on my bed. Don't cover up any part of your perfect body. I need you lying there imagining how good I'm going to make you feel."

Oh God. This is really going to finally happen.

I ease myself onto the mattress and scoot back, while remaining lifted up, resting on my elbows so I can watch him. Ramon walks over to his bedside table and eases the top-drawer open. Grabbing a bottle of lube and a condom, he tosses them on the bed.

I blink repeatedly when Ramon pauses, his legs spread hip-width apart. As he leans against the bed, his searing gaze roams over my body, my thick erection rising off my belly in response to his hungry stare.

He clears his throat. "You have to tell me what you like, what you need. Okay?"

"I will," I whisper. I can feel my face get hot. My one worry is how long can I last with the way he's looking and talking to me. I feel like if he stroked my cock once or twice I'd lose it completely. I tell myself internally to calm the hell down, but my focus is laser sharp as he begins to peel off his T-shirt and undo his jeans.

How is it that he makes every move and gesture sensuous and sexy? His swagger is off the charts, and watching him undress amps up, the surge of my lust for him burning over me. My cock is rock hard as I desperately crave his touch. This moment of seeing him completely naked, his impressive erection, the flush of color over his chest, the hungry look in his eyes, undoes me.

Joining me on the bed, he skims his fingertips over my chest, carefully watching my reaction as his hand trails to my abs. When I bite my lip, he leans closer and kisses his way up my neck while grazing his fingers over my nipples. Everything is soft and slow, which is making me crazy in the best way. I want to pull him on top of me for the sheer friction, but I resist and let him lead.

I moan as he covers my mouth with his. I've never been kissed like this, like I'm the best thing he's ever tasted and he can't get enough. His body undulates over me, but he's torturing me, too, because every time I rock my hips up suggestively he slows down.

"More," I moan. "I need more . . ."

He smiles with satisfaction like he was waiting for those words, and he lifts up to his knees and backs away. "Spread your legs for me, baby," he says in a husky voice.

"Are y-you going t-to . . ." I stutter.

"I'm going to get you ready," he responds as he coats his fingers with lube. He starts slowly, gently coaxing me as I gradually open for him. "So good," he praises when I take two fingers and then three, but he's being so attentive that all my fear has fallen away. He's stroking my thigh with his free hand, and he leans over to kiss my chest. It's hot the way he's taking care of me.

"Please, Ramon," I groan, needing more.

"Tell me you want me." His eyes are dark and hooded, as lust-filled as I've ever seen him.

"So much," I say. Running my fingers over the sheet, I feel the condom packet and hold it up. I need him to hurry up and put it on.

I watch him carefully roll it on, and when he's fully sheathed he lifts himself over me to give me a heart-seizing kiss. I spread my legs, and bend my knees open farther, and take his cock in my grasp, sliding it down between my ass cheeks.

In that moment, where he's pressed right against me, I'm suddenly overtaken by emotion. My heart is thundering as I feel the truth surge through me. This is about so much more than fucking. This is about us becoming one.

"Ramon?" I whisper anxiously as he begins to press against where I'm open for him.

"Yes?" he asks, lifting himself off of me so our gazes meet.

"I have to tell you . . . I mean, I think it's important for you to know."

"Okay," he says with a look that's patient but also makes me think he can't hold back much longer.

"It's just that. . . . you . . . this . . . really matters a lot, it's a big deal and it means more to me than you may know."

"Oh, baby. I know," he reassures me.

His look gives me the courage to say what I feel most of all. "The thing is, you need to know that I'm falling in love with you."

His sex-god expression shifts to a soft, tender gaze, almost as if I can see right into his heart. "Well, you better hurry and catch up with me. I'm already there."

"You're in love with me?" My voice catches because those words are so good that they hurt in the best way.

"Shhhh," he whispers, running his fingertips along my jaw. "Yes, I am. Now let me show you how much." And with that he slowly begins to ease inside of me.

I'm vaguely aware that my mouth has dropped open from the brief pain that has morphed into a pleasure so intense I want to cry. I can feel his body vibrate over me with his overwhelming pleasure, too. I remind myself that he's waited patiently for me and from the way he's moving and the intensity of his gaze, it was worth the wait.

He works me until I'm full of him, and the feeling of our connection as he slowly fucks me is everything I never thought I'd have.

He is everything, and we're in love, and life is so much more than I ever thought my little world could contain.

16. My Person

I HAVE NO IDEA HOW much time has passed, but we're lying in his bed wrapped around each other and supremely content when there's a sharp knock on the front door. I feel Ramon tense up, and with the second round of rapping he sits up, now absolutely alert. The sound becomes more like a pounding and we can faintly hear what sounds like Madame Fontanoy's voice calling out for him as if something's horribly wrong. For a moment, I'm totally confused. *Weren't we just making love? Is the universe really going to fuck with me again?*

What the hell?

Jumping off the bed, he wraps a blanket around his waist and rushes to the front door. I awkwardly hurry to follow him, wrapping myself in his sheet. As I charge down the hall I see that Ramon already has the door open, and Gabriella has a distraught expression. I finally find my glasses on the coffee table and hurriedly put them on.

"Charles, is with you, yes?" she asks Ramon insistently before she notices me.

"Yes, why?" I call out, trying not to be horrified that she's seeing us in this state but she seems not to care, or be the slightest bit surprised.

"Charles, there's a man downstairs who says he's 'Lucia's brother,' and they've been trying to reach you."

I feel all the blood rush out of my head and panic overtakes me. I suddenly remember that we turned our phones off in the museum and in my selfishness I not only forgot to turn it back on, but I haven't checked on Sasha for several hours.

Ramon glances at me and immediately registers that this is gravely serious and likely something about my sister. "Oh no. Did he say what's wrong?"

"They had an ambulance take his sister to Cedars-Sinai . . . something about an infection that spiraled out of control."

I let out a gasp, and start to collapse forward before catching myself by grabbing onto my knees. I glance around, frantically trying to remember where my clothes are. I have to get there immediately.

"To the hospital? That must be serious," Ramon says, the concern clear in his voice.

"Dear boy, you must get Charles to the hospital right away. Apparently, Lucia is quite undone."

I slam my fists down onto my thighs. "I should've been there!" I cry out.

I can see the worry in Gabriella's expression, but I can't tell if it's about Sasha, or also for me by the concerned way she's staring at me.

"I have to go. Where are my clothes?" I don't even recognize my voice.

"In the bedroom," Ramon replies.

"Thank you for finding us," I say to Gabriella. "Thank you, my God, thank you."

Ramon asks one more thing of Gabriella. "If that man is still downstairs can you tell him that Charlie is on his way to the hospital?"

She and Ramon share a knowing glance before I turn and rush down the hallway.

Seconds later Ramon is pulling on his clothes as fast as he can and I don't even stop to ask why. He barely exists for me right now, all I can think of is Sasha in the Emergency Room and my panic grows exponentially.

"Where are my fucking car keys?" I growl as I dig through my pockets fruitlessly.

"I have them, but you aren't driving," Ramon states firmly, slipping on a pair of black boots and quickly tying them before grabbing a leather jacket.

"What the hell are you talking about? Of course I'm driving. I should've been the one to take her there."

Ramon's expression registers all the deeper meaning behind

my words and his demeanor gets more stern. "I'm taking you to the hospital, Charlie, and that's all there is to it."

"I don't think it's a good idea for you to be there." I see him flinch but his determined expression overrides everything else.

"Okay. But I'm still going to get you there nonetheless. It's not safe for you to drive in this state."

I start to protest but he cuts me off. "Do you know how bad traffic is through Hollywood right now? That street fair has blocked off a bunch of streets and the surrounding streets are jammed. If I take you on my bike we'll get there twice as fast."

I picture it all in my head, and can't argue with the facts about the traffic. "You're right. Okay, let's go."

Grabbing two helmets out of the hall closet, he hands me one, and then waits while I turn my phone on. It's another punch in the gut when it explodes with all the missed call prompts. As we rush down to the parking garage, I try calling Lucia but the call goes to voicemail. I shove my phone in my pocket. There's no time to spare.

Watching Ramon approach his bike, I'm amazed that I had no idea he rides a motorcycle. I have a brief moment where I'm distracted from my upset as he swings up his leg, and straddles the seat. In his fitted leather jacket, boots, with his muscular thighs tight with tension, he's never looked hotter.

As he fires up his silver Yamaha, I'm stunned back into reality and scramble my way onto the bike.

He turns to me. "Hold onto me really tight, Charlie. I'm going to go fast, and do some crazy moves. All right?"

I nod. "The faster the better."

We pull on our helmets, and Ramon stays true to his word. He weaves his way through the traffic at a crazy speed. He's risking his own safety to get me there, and the tension and aggression in his body as I cling to him would have me hard as hell, if I wasn't so distraught about Sasha.

The most terrifying part of the ride is his race down Highland Avenue, which is packed with cars due to the street fair overspill. He rides at breakneck speed along the center left-turn lane, swerving out of the way from cars that actually enter the lane to make a legitimate turn. It's a miracle we don't get hit.

By the time he tears in the Cedars-Sinai Emergency Entrance I figure he cut the travel time down by two-thirds. He stares straight ahead as he waits for me to get off the bike. I'm not sure how to read that, but when I hand him my helmet and gaze in his eyes they are dark with worry, or hurt, or both.

"Please let me know how she's doing. Please," he implores.

I nod my head, then pause for a moment as we share weighted gazes. "Thank you for getting me here."

He nods. "Of course. Go on now."

Turning, I run toward the entrance, my terror-induced adrenaline pushing me forward.

Thankfully I know this hospital like the back of my hand, and one of the ER nurses recognizes me. "Follow me," she says softly.

The reality of it all is sinking in, and my heart is pounding so hard it feels like it's going to burst out of my chest. I see Sasha first, lost under a plethora of tubes, and an oxygen mask strapped to her face. Her eyes are closed and it's quiet other than the beeps from the machines monitoring her. I suddenly realize that Lucia is to the right of me. Appearing distraught, she holds up her phone.

"I tried, Charlie. I called over and over, and then I got scared and called for the ambulance. She was declining too fast. Please don't be mad at me." Her eyes are glazed and full of fear.

Resting my hand on her forearm, I reassure her, "You did the right thing, Lucia. Absolutely. And I thank you for it." I feel another wave of regret run through me. "I'm so sorry I had shut my phone off in the museum and forgot to turn it back on."

She nods silently. She knows me well enough to know that I won't be forgiving myself for this mistake.

"She's been asleep for an hour or so," she explains.

"Who's the attending physician?"

"It's a woman doctor named Ohadi, and I've also contacted Dr. Phillips but I got his answering service. I'm waiting to hear back."

"Good. I'm going to go find Dr. Ohadi. I'll be right back. You'll stay here, yes?"

"Yes, of course."

"And my phone is on now and will not be shut off again."

One of the nurses finds Doctor Ohadi for me. I immediately feel calmer in her presence. She has a kind demeanor and looks at me sympathetically when I explain that I'm Sasha's brother and guardian.

"I'm glad you're here," she says as she closes a chart she'd been looking at. "Sasha had a bladder infection that spread to her kidneys very quickly, and due to her other issues, it progressed rapidly. It's good her caretaker called emergency. We've administered the first rounds of powerful antibiotics, which are very effective in cases like this, and we've made progress getting her fever down. I'm optimistic that we have thwarted any further issues, and am hopeful the drugs will take care of this infection as fast as possible."

I let out the breath I've been holding. "Thank God."

"The caretaker said your sister lives with you and that you're very close."

"It's just Sasha and I, and she means the world to me."

The doctor gives me a warm smile.

"Doctor Ohadi, thank you for the care you're giving her."

"Of course. I don't know if you've had a chance to talk to Lucia yet, but apparently there's been a problem with the morning caregiver which contributed to Sasha becoming ill. Lucia shared with me that when she arrived for work today your sister admitted that the morning caregiver had missed the last three days of work due to her mother being ill. Sasha didn't tell Lucia about the other caregiver's absence and by then it was too late, she was already ill and progressively getting worse. For some reason Sasha hadn't shared this with Lucia, and I assume you as well . . . perhaps to protect the woman's job."

My hands curl into fists and I can l feel my face flush with fury. "She didn't show up for three days and didn't call me?"

Doctor Ohadi shakes her head soberly.

"I'm going to fire her ass and then strangle her," I curse nonsensically.

"Well, you surely know my opinion of the strangling idea. I

think you'll be far more help to Sasha if you aren't in prison. But yes, clearly, this is a serious issue with the caregiver, family emergency or not. Not calling is a horrible breach of her duties. I'd report her to the agency as well."

I rub my hands over my face in frustration. "Sasha loves her. I'm sure she was protecting her, and trying her best to take care of herself so as not to draw attention to her absence. I'm assuming the infection issue was around the catheter."

"Yes, a common and critical issue to keep an eye on for paraplegics. And if bowel care isn't handled carefully it is common in these situations that the bacteria can spread, causing this type of infection."

When I return to Sasha's room, I guide Lucia into the hall to talk about what happened with Estella. She assures me that she was a little concerned when Sasha wasn't as clean as usual when they did her care yesterday evening, but before that she hadn't seen anything suspicious. Her countenance clouds over. "The doctor told me that I did the right things before the ambulance came." She brushes a tear away.

Reaching over, I give her a hug. I'm moved by how worried and diligent she's been tonight to make sure Sasha is okay. "You were great. And I appreciate it so much. Thank you."

When we part I can tell that she appreciates my reassurances and gratitude. "Why don't you head home? I can call you an Uber."

She seems relieved. "Thank you. My brother usually picks me up, but he's at work now."

"Will you thank him for coming to find me? I'm so appreciative."

"Of course."

Pulling out my phone, I order the Uber, and leave a message for the driver that my friend Lucia will be standing on the edge of the Emergency Room entrance for her pick-up. Before we part I assure her I'll call tomorrow with an update.

I step back into Sasha's room and approach her bed. Resting my hand on her forehead, I notice she's too warm but not burning up, so the fever must have subsided some. I take her limp hand in mine and close my eyes, trying to process all my emotions and self-loathing that's pulsing through me. Gently running my thumb over her fingers, I whisper, "I'm so sorry that I wasn't with you, Sash. But I'm here now and I'm not going anywhere."

I stare at her intently, and then finally decide to take a seat for the long night ahead. After a few minutes of self-chastising, I pick up my phone to see what my call and message lists look like. Scrolling down from the top there are at least two dozen calls from Lucia, but when I get near the bottom of the list I see there's a call from Sasha that was made soon after I left to pick up Ramon. My fingers tighten over the phone as I stare dumbly at the screen. I'm pretty sure that it's going to break me to know that Sasha reached out to me first and I wasn't there for her. I start to hyperventilate and feel my chest get tight.

Leaning forward, I try to focus. Me freaking out isn't going to help anything right now. I take deep breaths as I grab my knees and close my eyes. When I finally have gathered myself, I'm calm enough to remember that when I tried to check on Sasha right before I left she said she was fine. Surely she didn't change her mind right after I left. It's at that moment that I decide to listen to her voicemail.

Her voice is weak so I press the phone to my ear even tighter so I can hear everything.

"Hey, Charlie. I was thinking about your date with Ramon and how he's made all these plans to take you downtown to cool, special places. And it made me think that it's really clear how much he likes you. So that made me think about you guys, and I know you really like him. And realizing all of this has made me so happy. Because you know what? You deserve all the good things. You're such a good man, and you deserve love, and a boyfriend who will really care about you. And I'm hoping now that Ramon is that man."

There's a pause, while she takes some ragged breaths and then coughs. I freeze until she starts talking again.

"So please, please, will you give him a chance? Promise me, okay? I love you and I can't wait to hear about your date."

I blink rapidly and then listen to it two more times, until there are tears running down my face. I love my sister so much, but I don't deserve to be loved back after the bad choices I've made. Doesn't she know this?

Rising, I walk to her window and stare out at the desolate side street that runs the inside length of the complex. Everything feels so vast and empty. For some reason, it causes me to remember how forlorn Ramon looked before he took off on his bike, and that makes me recall his request to hear about how Sasha is doing.

With a weary sigh, I step out into the hall and call him.

"Charlie," he says when he picks up after the first ring. "How is she?"

"She's asleep but they've stabilized her. I like this doctor who's overseeing her."

"Well that's good, right?" he asks uncertainly.

"Definitely. But I'm furious at myself for not paying more attention to how she was feeling this week, and to top it off I find out that her morning caregiver hasn't shown up the last three days and didn't call me, which led to her getting an infection that's now spread to her kidneys."

"Damn," Ramon says. "Are you firing her?"

"I sure as hell plan to."

"Do you know how much longer Sasha has to be in the hospital?"

"We'll know more about that in the morning. I've got to call my boss next so they know I'm not coming in tomorrow."

"How much later will you be there tonight?"

"Oh, I'm not going home tonight. I'm not going anywhere until I know she's well on her way to being better."

Ramon is silent for a moment and then speaks up. "Well, you let me know if you need anything . . . if there's anything I can do."

"There isn't anything," I respond, not even feeling guilty for being an asshole. My fury and concern about Sasha has rendered me powerless to be polite or civil.

After hanging up, I settle back into the room's guest chair and go into a zone, preparing mentally for the long night ahead. About thirty minutes later my eyelids are getting droopy when my phone text prompt goes off. It's Ramon.

I'm downstairs by the ER entrance. I brought your car.

Slamming my phone down onto my thigh, I feel my temper flair. I didn't ask Ramon to bring my car, and he shouldn't have shown up here. My car is my furthest concern right now. It also occurs to me that more than anything I'm not ready to face him right now.

As I ride down the elevator this horrible realization comes over me that Ramon is who I want in my life, but tonight showed me that I can never be with him the way I want to. I was a foolish dreamer to ever think I could, and it's going to rip me up knowing that when I have to face him.

He's walking toward me as I step through the automatic glass doors that open to the street. There's something about his handsome face and build of his body as he's still wearing the boots and leather jacket that guts me. Seeing him like this reminds me of how powerfully drawn I am to him. The sensation sharply twists my knife of regret into my heart.

As compelling as he is, a look of apprehension is etched all over his face. I jam my hands down into my pockets.

"What are you doing here?" I ask. There's a definite edge to my voice and he flinches a little.

"Hey," he says gently as he approaches, handing me my car keys and ticket stub for the parking, "I figured I'd bring you your car."

"I could've gotten it later," I reply.

He shrugs. "Well there are two problems with that idea. One is that where we parked your car will be towed in the morning if you don't move it. And two, and more importantly, did you forget that I still had all your keys? After I drove you to the hospital I forgot to give them back to you. I thought you might need something at your apartment, and you said it's near here."

"Damn, that's right," I curse.

"I know you needed to stay with Sasha, so now it's parked in the guest lot." He turns and points to a lot on the right side of the ER building.

"Okay, I feel shitty though that I made you come all the way over twice tonight. How are you going to get home?"

"I can Uber, but I thought I could stay with you for support."

"That's not necessary," I reply.

"I know that, but I want to help, Charlie." His eyebrows knit together like he's trying to figure me out. He holds up a canvas bag I hadn't noticed. "I brought you a jacket, blanket, pillow, and water. Oh, and my portable phone battery recharger. I've spent a lot of time sitting in hospital rooms."

I realize he's referring to his love, Luis, while he was dying, and I swallow the pain the image renders in my mind.

"What can I do to help you and Sasha?"

"Nothing." I let my gaze fall to the floor. It hurts to look at him.

"You really want me to leave?" I can hear the disappointment in his voice like he senses that I seriously don't want him here, and I don't have the energy to deal with it.

I nod as I feel all my emotions freeze inside of me until there isn't anything left to feel. "Yes."

"Surely there's something I can do," he argues. "You're very important to me. And anyone you're hurting over, I'm determined to be here for."

"That's very kind of you, but I've got to let you know that after what happened tonight everything is going to have to change. I don't think I'm going to be able to see you for a while."

He takes a step back, a stunned expression on his face. "What? Why? I thought things were—"

I cut him off. "Tonight I was reminded where my responsibility has to lie. It's my fault she's lying in that hospital bed right now."

"No it's not," he argues.

"Yes it is," I reply angrily. "And she could've died."

"I understand how upset you are, but I really think you're overstating this."

"Overstating?" I ask in a frustrated voice. Who is he to accuse me of such a thing? Part of me wants to punch him in the face.

Instead I grab his wrist and yank on it. "You want to see for yourself if I'm exaggerating things?" Not waiting for an answer, I start pulling him toward the ER's entrance. He doesn't resist me, but instead allows himself to be dragged along. I silently march him past reception, into the hallway, and around two lengths of rooms before we get to Sasha's. Once we're in the room, I let go of him and point at my sister.

For a moment, I wonder how this scene looks through his eyes. Sasha looks comatose and pale as a ghost, or at least the part you can see not covered by the oxygen mask. The beeping monitors suddenly sound painfully loud in our silence. All of the tubes strung over her make her appear so helpless. "Her lungs get weak when she's sick," I say to explain the oxygen mask.

I glance back at Ramon and he's studying her carefully. Moving his gaze to me, he says, "She's asleep?"

I nod.

"And she's getting top notch care? It's good your caregiver got her to the hospital, yes?"

My frustration is building in me like a volcano about to erupt.

"Yes, she's got good care, but she shouldn't even be there. It's all my fault."

His eyebrows knit together. "No it isn't, Charlie."

"You aren't getting it," I insist.

"Well, then can you explain it to me?"

Grabbing his wrist again, I pull him out of the room and back down the hall until we are out of the building and enough out of the bright light of the entrance to be shadowed and hidden. My anxiety and fury has taken over me and I feel like my face is on fire.

Once I've stopped, he turns toward me. "Okay. I get that this is bad . . . really bad, and you feel responsible. And I've got to say that it makes me feel like shit that you are willing to give the idea of us up so easily so you can dedicate your entire life to your sister's care. But has it occurred to you that that's not what she wants to happen?"

My eyes narrow in a glare. "You don't know anything about her!"

"I have a pretty good sense of how much she loves you and wants the best for you. Is this the best for you? Is this what you want?"

"It doesn't matter what I want," I cry out pathetically.

"Of course it does. You matter!" Reaching out, Ramon grabs my shoulders and shakes them fiercely.

Something snaps in me, like the sharp break of a long stick you bend over your knee. The break is quick and clean, causing my emotions to well up to a point that they can no longer be contained.

"No!" I cry out before pressing my hands over my face and stumbling forward until Ramon catches me. The sob that tears out of me wracks my body with my deeply felt regret. "It's my fault," I whisper into his shoulder.

Wrapping his arms around me, he runs his fingers through my hair and down my back. "No, it isn't your fault."

"I didn't even see her this morning. I was at the gym early so I'd look good for you. How fucking selfish is that?"

"It's not selfish. You were taking care of yourself," he murmurs gently, his hand never stopping his soothing strokes.

"And she was in the bathroom when I left to meet you. Why didn't I wait to make sure she was okay, rather than ask through the door?" I sob again, and it's so fierce that I almost choke.

"What did she say when you asked her through the door?" Ramon questions calmly.

"She said she was fine." I can feel that I've made his shoulder wet with my tears.

"So she told you she was fine, and you are blaming yourself for this?"

I try to pull away from him but he tightens his hold and pulls me tighter.

"Stop trying to change how I feel. It won't work!"

He ignores this and proceeds. "And what about her caregiver who didn't show up. Why aren't you blaming her?"

"Because I hired her!" For a brief second I realize how insane I'm sounding, but then I continue on. "And if I hadn't lied about Leo and my science project in high school so we could have our weekend of sex, I would've been on that trip with my family and my parents would be alive and Sasha would be dancing."

"Oh, Charlie," Ramon says gently as he pulls me tighter still. One hand cradles my head, the other is resting over my heart, undoubtedly feeling how it's thundering. "You can't blame yourself for that. That's not how life works. Besides, if you'd been with them you'd be dead, too . . . not all of you alive."

"It's complicated," I cry.

"Well I'm sorry, but it's wrong and I'm not going to let you believe that. Is it my fault Luis got cancer and died?"

"No, but those are two completely different things."

"Yes, and no. You know life is random. If we could control what happens in our lives, everything about our existence would change. And I have to ask you the most important question."

"What?" I sniffle, like some big stupid kid.

"If your parents knew that you'd lied and stayed home to have sex with Leo, do you think they would've blamed you for their deaths? Do you think Sasha would?"

I think about that one long and hard while he keeps cradling and soothing me. It feels so damn good that it's distracting and calming me when I want to scream in fury instead.

"No, they'd probably say it was an accident and I can't blame myself for any of it."

"And what would they say about Leo?" he asks.

"I guess they'd be happy I cared about Leo enough to be true to who I was, and that I'd taken a step toward opening my heart to a good person like him."

I see a flash of what could be jealousy in his eyes but then he blinks the look away. "And what happened with you and Leo after the accident?"

"I ended it. I couldn't handle seeing him because of my guilt."

"Oh, you lost everything that night," he says with such sadness I start sobbing again.

"I did. And I reached out to him after you blew me off and he was happy to hear from me, and told me he's married to a great guy and doing well."

"Wow. And I think I've had a rough time. Jesus, I wish you'd told me all this."

"Why?" I say as my sobs slow down again.

"Because I'd have known how tender you are."

"You probably would have avoided me like the plague if you'd known all my baggage," I groan. "I never would have gotten the lap dance that changed my life."

I can feel him skim his lips across my neck, and then he pulls away far enough so our gazes meet. "We'll never know that. All I know is that apparently we were destined to meet. Look at us . . . two broken men . . . what if we can help each other put our pieces back together?"

"I don't want you trying to fix me. I'm fucking pathetic."

"Oh stop with that crap. You're brilliant and amazing in so many ways. Accept that I'm not giving up on you, and you aren't going to be allowed to avoid me. You're mine now, and I'm yours. And I will help you with Sasha but we have to be a team."

"A team?" I ask, trying to imagine what this picture is he's painted of us.

Turning, he takes my hand then leads me back to the front door. "There's a *Coffee Bean and Tea Leaf* a couple of blocks away. Since we're going to be here all night I want some good coffee, and I'll get you some, too."

I start to protest and he holds his hand up.

"The only thing you can open your mouth up for is to tell me if you want a single or a double."

I drop my head in frustration, but it's also dawning on me that this man is turning out to truly be *my* person, the one who's flawed but just right for me. He heard all of my garbage, the worst things I've ever done, and he still wants to be by my side and help me. The love that I've been feeling for him takes a gigantic leap in my heart to something beyond anything I could've imagined.

I let out a long sigh, realizing that surrendering to him is the smartest thing I could do. "A double vanilla latte please," I say.

My head is still dropped forward, so when he steps forward he places a kiss on my head. "Double vanilla latte it is."

I rise back up to watch him as he walks away, his hands in the pockets of his jacket, and a purposefulness in his step. He's tired and wrung out, and he must be battered emotionally from my rejections but he's soldiering on. A weird thought settles over me. *Did my parents have a hand in bringing Ramon into my life? Was I sent a hero capable of saving me in this beautiful, stubborn, loving man?*

I look up into the night sky, wanting with all my heart to believe they did. I've fallen in love with Ramon and tonight he has brought me out of one the darkest places I've been in six years.

"Thank you," I whisper to the stars before heading back in the building and to my sister's side.

17. Never Let Go

I SENSE THAT THE ROOM light is bright through my closed eyes. As I wake I slowly start to realize that I'm sitting up, leaning awkwardly against Ramon with my head on his shoulder. Somewhere close I hear whispering.

"How long have you guys been here?" the voice asks. It starts to occur to me that the voice sounds like Sasha's, but edged with exhaustion and not as much inflection as she usually has.

"I brought Charlie here about seven hours ago. I had taken him downtown and we shut our phones off when we were in the museum. He was so upset when he realized that he'd been unreachable when you needed him. I feel bad about it, Sasha."

"Please stop that," she says quietly. "I was happy you guys had a date."

I start to stir, and Ramon reacts by rubbing my thigh to my knee and back.

"Hey, wake up, Charlie. Sasha is awake."

Suddenly alert, I sit up and lean forward. "Sasha," I say with my next breath.

She reaches out her hand and I lift off the chair and move toward her. Winding my fingers through hers, I study her face without the oxygen mask. "You look better."

"I feel better. Believe me. Sorry about all of this."

I can't hide the distress in my expression remembering last night. "You're sorry? Don't talk crazy. I'm the one who's sorry since you guys couldn't get a hold of me yesterday. That will never happen again. I promise."

"Don't promise that. I was watching you two together until Ramon woke up."

"What were we doing?" I ask, trying to hide the embarrassment in my tone.

"Holding onto each other," she says with a weak smile. "It made me happy."

I squeeze her hand. "You're such a romantic."

She nods. "Guilty as charged." Dropping her head back on the pillow, she closes her eyes as if this little bit of discussion has completely worn her out.

I glance back at Ramon and he gives me a hopeful smile. "She sounds good considering. Don't you think?"

Nodding, I let out a breath of relief. "Definitely." I look back at her and gently run my fingers over her forehead that now feels like a normal temperature.

Her eyes flutter open for a second, and then she whispers, "I'm so tired."

"Rest, Sash. You can entertain us later."

She closes her eyes again as the edges of her mouth curl up. "I will. Tell Ramon I like him again. Maybe a lot."

Leaning down, I kiss her on the forehead. "I'll tell him," I assure her since she's apparently forgotten or she's pretending that he isn't sitting only feet away.

"You two are so cute together. I swear, you have no idea how cute," she murmurs sleepily.

I hear Ramon chuckle and I glance back at him. "We're cute!" he whispers.

I shrug. "I'd rather be handsome, but I'll take it."

We're interrupted by a nurse who comes to check on my sister. "Boys, would you give us a few minutes. I need to do some attending to Sasha."

We both scramble out of our seats. "Of course," I reply. "Sasha, we're going down to the cafeteria to get some breakfast. We'll be back, okay?"

Her eyes open halfway. "If they have any blueberry pancakes can you bring me some?"

The nurse shakes her head but I give Sasha a wink. A moment later her eyes drift shut like she has no energy left to speak.

We're halfway down the hall when Ramon asks, "This hospital is pretty fancy. Do you think they have an omelet bar?"

"Undoubtedly," I respond with an eye roll. "And you can wash yours down with a few mimosas."

"Are you getting snappy with me?"

"I suppose. I promise to be better once I get my morning coffee."

He winds his fingers through mine and we walk hand-in-hand down to the cafeteria, preparing for what certainly won't be the kind of meal we're hoping for but knowing that's okay because at least we'll be together.

Sasha sleeps on and off the rest of the day. Ramon stays by my side, only leaving around noon to pick up decent sandwiches for our lunch from the deli on Beverly Boulevard.

Dr. Ohadi won't be in until the next day, so in the late afternoon I'm directed to talk to Dr. Schulman who informs me that if Sasha keeps progressing as she's been, that she could go home by tomorrow after the morning rounds as long as her caregivers are with her. He's also heard from her primary physician, Doctor Phillips, and they've gone over everything. The conversation reminds me that I need to call the agency and find a replacement for Estella. I haven't even officially fired her yet. When Dr. Schulman and I are done, I step into the hall, thinking about making that call, but something stops me. Estella was always so amazing with Sasha and she was a total professional. This breach of protocol was so unlike her.

I pause in her doorway, trying to figure out the best way to share the news about Sasha's possible release from the hospital, when I realize that I'm interrupting a moment between her and Ramon. Her eyes are closed with an expression of supreme pleasure on her face while Ramon gives her what appears to be a hand massage. I try to recall if I told him how much she loves to have her hands massaged and I can't remember talking to him about it.

Sasha suddenly speaks up. "The thing about love, Ramon, is that it can hit you when you least expect it."

"Damn right," I softly murmur to myself. I notice that she sounds stronger than she was this morning, and I relax with relief. It's clear her recovery is headed the right direction.

"Is that what happens in the romance books you read?" he asks in a serious tone like he's not teasing her.

"Sometimes. There's no one *right* way. Is there?"

"No, I suppose not," he answers thoughtfully as he gently pulls on her lotion-soaked fingers one at a time.

As I watch from the hall I'm stunned that Sasha is being so direct and open with Ramon. She's treating him like he's already family.

"I have to tell you something and I want you to listen. Okay?" she insists.

He chuckles. "Okay. Frankly, I don't think I have too much choice with this considering where I am right now." She peeks up at him and he nods, his eyes still downward cast where he's adeptly working lotion into Sasha's palm.

"The thing is, Charlie is a very special guy. There aren't that many guys out there like him."

I consider stepping into the room and stopping her lecture, but Ramon breathes out, "You can say that again," and it stops me in my tracks.

"He is fiercely loyal, and he has the biggest heart. But what you need to know is that he's a problem solver and doesn't suffer fools gladly. If he didn't see something really special in you, he would never have opened his heart to you. So you can't toy with him like not showing up when he's fixed you a special dinner. That was a horrible thing to do to Charlie, and he never told me about the other time you met after you blew him off. All I know is that he was completely heartbroken."

I've noticed that Ramon has stopped massaging Sasha's hand and is instead holding onto it. "I've gotten myself in some really stupid situations, and I really regret all of it. Sometimes I still get down on myself, and I think he deserves better."

She shakes her head. "That's for Charlie to decide and he's crazy about you. Next time you start feeling that way, still show up for dinner and talk to him about it. He's a terrific talker-outer."

"Talker-outer? And look at you looking out for your brother. Has anyone ever told you how adorable you are?" Ramon asks.

"Yes, I get that all the time," she says with a wink. "So, tell me . . . how did you know Charlie was the one for you?"

"The one?" he asks, his expression hard to read.

"Oh, don't pussy foot around with me. It's clear you two are made for each other."

I can see his cheeks getting red. "It was the time I took him to a club to find the right kind of man for him and I dragged him out onto the dance floor."

"And . . ." she says, urging him on.

"Well, first of all, I got really jealous when the first guy he met that night was blatantly flirty with him, even though I was the one who encouraged it. Then when we were alone for a few minutes, I took Charlie out to the dance floor and damn! When he dances this whole other side of him comes out and I was mesmerized. I was already crushing on him, and knew to appreciate what he's about, but something clicked. You know?"

Her eyes shine bright. "Yes, I do."

I'm amazed they haven't noticed me yet, but they're so focused on each other and I've stepped back so I'm only in the doorway enough to see and hear them.

"You can thank me for your big moment," she says proudly. "I was the one who taught Charlie to dance when we were teenagers."

"Did you now?" Ramon asks with a grin. I already told him the story but he's encouraging her to tell it anyway.

"I had always danced . . . you know ballet, tap, hip-hop as a kid. And in high school I started to watch one of those dance competition TV shows and became convinced we could win it. Charlie thought I was nuts but he went along, because he's just like that. He didn't want to let me down. And once we got going, I realized he was a natural."

"He's very sexy when he dances," Ramon says with a sigh full of longing.

"Well, I think I'll stay clear of that comment."

"I think it's great that you and Charlie are so close. My two sisters and I were always close and I really miss living nearby so we can see each other often."

"Charlie told me you have sisters. And while we're on that subject, I want to make something clear."

"Okay," Ramon says. It's obvious he's already mastered how to make Sasha feel validated.

"Charlie and I aren't a package deal. If you guys get serious, I don't want you to think that you're responsible for me, like Charlie feels. I'm really working on learning to be more independent because I want to have my own life, and I want Charlie to have his, too. I know I screwed up this week by not telling Charlie right away that Estella couldn't come in while she's dealing with her mom's illness, but I know what to do better next time."

My fingers clench over the doorframe as I step center into the doorway. "What do you mean you didn't tell me about Estella? What were you thinking?"

Ramon sits back with a shocked expression, and Sasha's gaze casts downward. "Shit," she mutters.

"Sasha!" Walking over, I grab the metal frame at the foot of her bed.

"I'm sorry, Charlie. I screwed up. So is this a good time to tell you that you can't fire Estella because I made the wrong choice withholding information? But I promise you I won't do this again. I learned my lesson."

I shake my head, too angry to respond. She glances over at Ramon with wide eyes. "I'm in trouble now," she warns him.

"Well, that was wrong, Sasha. Like you said earlier, Charlie is a problem solver, and if you want to have more independence I'm sure there's smaller steps that could be taken."

"Baby steps?" she asks.

I growl, still furious.

Ramon ignores me, apparently intent on changing the subject. "You know, there's a guy in my building named Emmett. He's super-cool, a songwriter and a novelist. You should hear him play the piano. He's performed professionally."

Ramon has clearly distracted me because I wonder out loud, "Was that the guy playing Cole Porter the first time I came to your place?"

"Yes, he was. But Emmett is going through a really rough time because he has a degenerative disease that will eventually leave him deaf. Right now, he only has partial hearing. There was hope that the processor's transmission from a Cochlear implant surgery would create the sense of sound for him when hearing aids no longer were effective, but the specifics of his issue prevented it from working. I'd really like you to meet him. We're all worried about him, and I think you could inspire him."

For a moment, I'm mad at Ramon for suggesting such a thing—using Sasha's disability to cheer up a depressed guy she doesn't know—but her expression is that she's delighted by the idea. "I'd like that."

I settle down in the guest chair, the emotional exhaustion of this conversation overtaking me.

Ramon glances back at me. "You okay, Charlie?"

I study both of their steady gazes and the way they are still holding hands, and the well of emotion I feel surprises me even though I know my exhaustion is intensifying it. I have to push back tears so I don't make this scene even more dramatic than it is.

Ramon loves me and he clearly, honestly cares about Sasha. Despite all this stress and drama, I'm so full of hope that I can't even stay mad at my sister. Ramon stands up, and releases Sasha's hand so he can brush her hair off her forehead. Then he walks over to me and squeezes my shoulder.

"I love you guys," I say, probably the most random yet heartfelt truth I've ever blurted out.

"We love you, too," Sasha replies with a big grin.

Leaning over, Ramon kisses the top of my head. "So much," he states softly.

And now it's my turn to grab his hand and hold it like I'll never let go.

18. A Working Man's Compensation

THE NEXT TWO MONTHS FLY by, and our very different lives start to meld into each other, slowly taking shape into something we never could've expected. Despite our work hours being pretty much opposite, we carve out time for each other whenever we can.

It's almost too good to believe, as if I'm always waiting for the other shoe to drop, a semi to crash off a freeway overpass, and the sky to fall in. It's hard to live always fearing the worst, but Ramon is so eternally optimistic that I try to have faith that we'll make it.

Thursday afternoon, we've finished a meeting at work when Ramon calls to let me know he'll have to cancel our dinner plans. Taking a deep breath, I remind myself to have faith and not immediately think something's wrong. As it turns out, he explains that he's agreed to fill in for one of the guys who'd hurt his back at the gym and was scheduled to dance tonight. Ramon has been taking on extra work lately to see if he can save more money toward his nightclub dream. I'm normally supportive of his plans, but today the news is more disappointing since I'm feeling an extra strong need to be with him.

It's been five days since we've been together, and I don't just miss his company, I'm pent up with sexual tension. I could've never imagined that sex could be so mind-blowing, but the downside is that my desire for him grows stronger over time until I start to go a little crazy when we haven't slept together.

I'm distracted at dinner to the point that Sasha notices.

"You okay?" she asks, concern in her expression.

"I'm missing Ramon," I say with a sigh.

"He's working again?"

I nod, but then get an irrational thought, and I can't let go of it. "I think I'm going to go by the club to see him dance."

Her brows knit together. "Are you sure that's a good idea? If he's dancing aren't you worried you'll get jealous watching him dance for other people?"

I shrug. "No. I know where we stand. And I know he's not into women, so I'll be fine."

She purses her lips together and then sighs. "Okay, if you're sure."

Before I leave for the club, I change out of my work clothes and into my fitted jeans and navy sweater. I smile remembering how Ramon complimented me last time I wore this outfit. Smoothing my hands over my chest, I imagine it's him touching me. I'm thrilled at the thought of his hands on me, as I shake my head with a smile. *I've got it so bad for him.*

Feeling myself get even more worked up as I think of him undressing me, I take a sharp breath to calm down.

When I approach the club's entrance the big bouncer, who I now know is named Louis, nods at me.

"Hey, Ramon told me you're his guy," he says with a wry grin.

"That's right," I reply proudly.

"You know he's dancing tonight, right?" he asks as he studies me, as if he's also making sure I'm okay with it.

"Yeah, I know. Thanks."

He nods and waves me in.

It's been a while since I've been in Wild Nights, and almost every seat is full and the music is pumping. The air is charged with excitement, and the room dark, other than the stage and the beams of colored lights scanning the crowd. The show is already going full throttle, and everyone is focused on the performers so I'm able to slide into a chair near the back without much attention. Scanning the dancers for Ramon, my heart jumps when I see him on the far left of the stage, rolling his hips slowly in sync with the music. The caramel-colored skin of his muscular arms, thighs, and chest glow in the warm stage light. He's so damn beautiful.

After observing for a few minutes, it's clear that the place is full of screamers tonight, and it's a particularly loud and amped up crowd, with wadded up dollars and random pairs of panties being tossed on stage. I roll my eyes. These women really need to tone it down. I know this atmosphere encourages decadent behavior, but they're acting like drunken harlots.

Ramon has my full attention as his gaze scans the crowd. Focusing on one woman at a time, he flashes his sexy grin for each of them. A prickle of irritation starts working up my chest and throat until I have to swallow it down. Random women are now approaching the edge of the stage waving money toward particular performers, and the men respond by dancing toward them and getting close enough for the women to stuff money into their briefs.

My agitation is especially getting fired up because I realize that Ramon seems to be getting the most reaction from the audience. He's so charming and charismatic with them that it's no wonder they all want his smile and sexy stare focused on them alone.

If I was honest with myself, I'm feeling exactly the same as the rest of the audience. I should feel great, even proud that my man is the most desirable of them all. Dancing across the stage, the various men, who are far too handsome and sexy for their own good, are weaving between each other in a pattern, stopping at key points in the music to thrust their hips toward the howling women, or turning to shake their tight asses their way. Shouldn't I be thrilled that among the pack of desirable men, Ramon stands out like a shining star?

But my emotions twist into a darker feeling. I'm realizing that sharing Ramon, even when it's for a performance, is a hard-limit my needy heart can't make peace with. Why did I have to come and sit in the audience and watch women touch him to come to this conclusion?

Apparently, I'm not the Sherlock Holmes of solving the mysteries around my deep-seated emotions.

My fingers curl into tight fists and I take a sharp breath, trying to remind myself that this is a job to him, nothing else. He's a performer. So even though it looks like he's having the time of his life, it's really all for show.

Or is it? my devious mind asks, taunting me. It occurs to me that Sasha was right—it probably wasn't a good idea for me to come here.

I step out of my seat and head to the bar where I proceed to throw back a shot of Jameson. Glancing back at the stage where Ramon is now positioned front and center, I order another shot and throw it back, with my teeth gritted.

The clock next to the cash register indicates that the show will be wrapping up soon. *Thank fucking God.* I'm not sure how much more I can take of watching Ramon tease these horny women into a frenzy.

Slowing walking back to my seat, I decide instead to lean up against a pillar so I have a clearer view of the performers as they dance their way off the stage and into the pit full of worked-up women ready to devour them.

A few of the patrons had pre-paid for lap dances and it's their time now to have their dreams fulfilled. Naturally Ramon was one of the lucky dancers picked for this debauchery, and a particularly flirty blonde, with her tits practically falling out of her low-cut top, looks more than ready for him. If my eyes aren't playing tricks on me, the wicked creature actually licks her lips as he dances toward her and straddles her thighs.

It's unfortunate for me that I have a side view of them, so I can clearly watch Ramon thrust his crotch toward her with a sultry gaze as she takes liberties by running her hands up and down his thighs.

I fold my arms across my chest so tightly that I can barely breathe. For a moment, I imagine approaching the scene from behind and jerking her chair backwards until she gracelessly tumbles to the floor. But I know that wouldn't go over well with Ramon, and especially not with his manager, Gene, watching. I have enough sense left to know that I can't risk provoking Gene who has been incredibly kind and generous with Ramon.

When I focus back on my man's moves, I notice the blonde's hands run up over his chest and to my horror she actually pinches his nipples, and he throws his head back theatrically like she's turning him on. *What the hell?*

Part of me needs to march out of the damn place, but the other part needs to follow this absolute mind-fuck out to the bitter end.

Finally, after what feels like a lifetime, the music starts to wind down and the grabby-hands whore tries to cling to Ramon, but he grins and pulls his way out of her grasp, winking at her before backing away. Obviously she's used to getting what she wants, because she stands and approaches him with a fistful of bills, which she one by one slips into his briefs. Finally, in the final act to verify her intentions, she takes a scrap of some kind of paper, perhaps a business card, and holds it up to Ramon and says something before sliding down his happy trail and into his briefs. A moment later her hand cups his bulge.

My resulting rage feels as if my head has burst into flames. I'm about to storm forward but Ramon shakes his head sternly and backs away from her, wagging his finger at her like she was a badly behaved little girl.

The various dancers are now working their way off the floor, and right as Ramon looks up to see the best route to escape, his gaze meets mine. His eyes widen and the corners of his mouth turn up. He changes directions and moves toward me.

"Charlie! What are you doing—"

But before he can finish I bark at him, "What was that paper that last whore slipped into your briefs?"

He narrows his eyes and glances around. "Whore? You better calm down, Charlie."

"What was it?" I ask louder.

Grabbing my wrist, he pulls me toward the empty hallway behind the bar.

"What's gotten into you?" A flush works its way across his chest. "It was her phone number."

"Are you going to call her?"

His eyes bug out and his mouth drops open like something from a weird cartoon. "Are you serious with this shit? Am I going to call her? What are you doing here anyway?"

"Well are you?" I growl.

Several dancers start down the hall. One nods to Ramon, but when they see my furious expression they quickly walk past. Ramon follows after them, only to turn and speak to the guy who let me into one of the private rooms several months back.

The guy nods and gives him a key. "Number one is open."

Ramon thanks him, grabs my wrist again, and pushes me in the room. The way he snaps the lock shut makes me both worried and turned on at the same time. He pivots around to face me.

"What the hell is going on, Charlie?" The charismatic smile he shared with all those women is long gone.

I suddenly feel awkward and ridiculous. "Well, I've missed you. So I thought I'd come see you."

He lets out an exasperated breath. "You knew I was dancing tonight. What exactly were you expecting?"

It's a valid question, but my focus swerves back to my original issue that set me off. "I want that phone number that girl gave you."

Everything about his expression reveals disbelief. "You want her number? Sure, dude, it's all yours." He drags his briefs down as low as they can go on his hips so green bills flutter toward the floor like dirty snow. Grabbing her business card, he thrusts it toward me. "Here you go. Have at it." Then he reaches around and plucks a few other scraps of paper free.

"And look, here's a few more for you. You can have you own harem with this bunch."

I crush the scraps in my fist. "All these women gave you their number?"

His eyes are dark with fury. "What exactly do you think goes on here? When the lights go off, do you think we all go roast marshmallows together and sing Kumbaya by a campfire, after making these women think we want to fuck them? This is part of their fantasy. They want to think that *they* are the one girl in this club that I'll call because I couldn't resist them. They leave with hope . . . and when we don't call, they come back to try again."

"That's fucked up," I grumble.

"Well, you didn't mind when it was you, as I recall," he replies with a scowl.

Adrenaline shoots through me like a rocket, and I take him off guard by pushing his shoulders until his back is against the wall. Then I step closer to him, and press my body tightly against his. "Don't treat me like I'm one of them."

"How about you stop being an asshole?" His jaw is tight and there's fire in his eyes, which only turns me on more.

"Did she make you hard when she touched you? Did she excite you?" I ask. Yet when I grind my hard dick against him I can tell he isn't aroused, nor was he when he first approached me—after he walked away from that woman I made sure that I checked.

"No, Charlie, she didn't excite me. But considering how hard you are, should I conclude that she excited you? Or are you trying to tell me that you want a threesome?"

I growl in response like I'm a wild animal. I'm still growling when it dawns on me that I'm grinding harder against him with my hot breath against his neck. It's as if I'm going to explode with the storm of emotions taking over my twisted heart and fired-up libido. Whatever shards of sanity I still maintain around Ramon have apparently gone on vacation, leaving me completely unhinged.

"Can you feel how much I want you?" I ask, my voice edged with desperation. I take his hand and push it down, tightening his fingers over where I'm aroused for him. He tries to pull his hand away, but I hold it right where I need to feel his grip.

"Damn, Charlie," he groans. "What the fuck is going on?"

"I've missed you," I lamely reply.

"I've missed you, too . . . but this is not okay."

"But can't you see . . . I need you."

"And . . ." he asks, still not understanding.

"You're mine, not theirs."

"Charlie, you know I don't want those women. This is my job, damn it!"

"All mine." I slide my hand down between us and curl my fingers around his cock, tightening my grip and stroking him as he grows harder.

"You should know by now that I don't want anyone but you," he groans.

Even if I wasn't stroking the evidence of his arousal, I'd be able to feel his desire flaring in the heat he's projecting. Knowing he's so turned on emboldens me.

I narrow my eyes. "No one can fuck you but me."

Did I really just say that? Never mind the fact that women don't have the body parts to fuck him. I'm not making any sense, and my cheeks flush with embarrassment, but I can't look away.

"What are you saying? You want to fuck me? Here? Now?" he asks, his eyes wide and his voice breathless.

I swallow and shut my eyes tightly as I nod. My overwhelming desire for him will be my undoing. "I *need* to fuck you."

Have I lost my mind?

Taking a deep breath, he glances over at the double-wide leather bench in the middle of the room, and he grabs a towel off the side table and spreads it over the surface. "Take off your clothes," he instructs as he pushes down his briefs and the last of the money falls out.

I have a moment of doubt that he's serious, but then I'm relieved to see his cock is now fully hard, confirming he really wants this. If I wasn't so worked up I'd be questioning everything. But instead I stare at his dick, my gaze half-mast with desire.

He approaches the bench and lies down across it, then spreads his legs wide. "So possessive," he whispers. He strokes himself, giving me a sultry stare. "You want me? Come on then, take me," he taunts in a smoky voice.

Suddenly my heart is racing to realize that this is really going to happen. I've always bottomed for him and never thought it would be different. I have to know what it's like now that he's laid out before me.

"Condom?" I ask as he points at the table near us, and warns me to use plenty of lube.

He shakes his head. "No, bareback. You need to feel everything so you can understand completely what I'm giving you."

Nodding nervously, I approach the table to slick my cock generously. I carefully crawl onto the edge of the bench and glance down at him. He appears almost high on some erotic drug that's side effect is bringing out my alpha boyfriend's submissive side in bed. It's sexy as hell even if it seems unlike Ramon.

Yet all I can focus on is his beautiful body and the way he's spread open for me. It's the most glorious image I've ever seen. I clear my throat. "Tell me what will make you feel good. Do I prep you? What should I do?"

His intense gaze meets mine. "I want you to fuck me until you have all your answers."

I swallow hard, but the whiskey keeps me from understanding his undertones. Has my suddenly showing up at his work, becoming fueled by jealousy, acting out and flipping the table, and then demanding sex . . . upset him? All I can think of is how much I need him, and how desperately I want to fill him and claim him knowing he's only mine. When I press the head of my cock against his entrance, he nods.

"Come on. Fuck me," he whispers.

My lungs suddenly fill with something akin to hot desert air, and I freeze. Can I do this even half as magnificently as he makes love to me?

"I need it . . ." His anxious tone is demanding.

I have to fight every instinct not to bear down and take him hard. Instead, I push into him slowly, my body practically shaking with relief to know the ecstasy of how it feels to fill him. I know I'm big, and his eyes widen as I penetrate him, but he bites back a groan, making me want him all the more.

"Oh God, oh God," I moan as he clenches around me. "So damn good."

He reaches up and presses one hand on my lower back, drawing me closer, and the other hand cups the back of my neck. "This is for you, Charlie. I'm only yours to fuck. I always was."

And with those words I lose myself inside of him. I growl and thrust slow and deep, gasping at how perfect he feels. With each minute passing I go deeper and deeper with more intensity until I wonder if I'll break him in two. But his moans of pleasure, and the fire in his gaze, tells me what I need to know. I'm amped up because he's loving how I'm making him feel, and how I've taken control. I put my weight on his thighs, opening him wider for me, as my thrusts build into something more powerful than I thought possible.

"Damn, Charlie," he moans with a deep yearning, arching his body as our rhythm builds. His eyes roll back, and his legs begin to tense around me. He's gorgeous in his surrender—flushed cheeks, a clenched jaw, and his broad chest rising and falling to the rhythm of my thrusts.

I never understood that this feeling of taking him would mean everything to me—to claim my mate with such intensity and to give him equal pleasure as what I'm taking from him. Ramon is giving himself to me completely, and he's so much stronger, loving, and solid than any man I've ever known.

He's folded open with legs bent, and my passion is burning through us as we make love. I lean down with my full weight and begin kissing him, bruising his lips as I consume his breath. "Are you okay?"

"Perfect," he groans as his hands grab my ass and pull me back into him.

I sense his climax building and I angle his hips up like he's done with me, and thrust deeper. "I want you to come," I moan into his ear before licking the edge of it and along his jaw.

"Oh fuck . . . that's it . . . right there," he stutters, letting me know I've hit the spot that makes him wild, and then after a series of short gasps, he lets go. Watching him climax makes me wild with pleasure and pride because he cries out and comes like he's never been so satisfied, so perfectly worked up to his greatest release.

I've held back because I needed to see him come first, and only a moment later I'm electrified, my entire body arcing back, wave after wave of hot pleasure working through me before I collapse onto him. "Oh . . . Ramon," I moan with a ragged breath.

We're silent for several minutes, as we catch up with both our breathing and our emotions. I'm resting my head on his chest, but trying to keep my full body weight off of him, while he gently runs his fingers through my hair.

"Are you okay?" I whisper.

"Are you?" he replies, with the corners of his mouth turning up.

I consider all of the complicated emotions that exploded out of me tonight, and I nod my head. "I'm more than okay. I was needing you so much."

"I know," he murmurs.

"And you gave me a part of yourself . . . more than I deserved. I hope you don't regret it."

"Of course I don't. It's what I wanted, too. You need to understand how much I want you, even when you're a hot mess."

I smile and angle my head so I can kiss his chest before resting back down on him.

Our weird position on the bench is getting awkward, so I lift myself off Ramon and bring over the box of tissues to clean him up. He watches me take care of him with a tender expression.

When I'm done, we slowly get up and get dressed, then sit back down on the bench to put our shoes on.

Laughing, he shakes his head. "Damn that was hot, but from now on you're going to really try not to show up at my job and create a scene, right?"

I know I'm blushing because my whole face feels hot. "It's so hard sometimes for me. I don't want to share you."

"But this is how I'm saving money right now. We have to work this out. Do you know none of the straight guys who work here can maintain relationships? At some point the jealously with their girl-friends breaks them down."

"I can see that. What about the gay dancers?"

"It's not as much of an issue, one because our audience is made up of women, and their boyfriends don't come watch them being man-handled."

"Sasha warned me not to come," I say with a sigh.

"Did she now? Damn, I love her. She's so protective of you."

"She is," I admit as I stand up and smooth down my jeans.

He nods back to the bench with an expression like he's remembering me on top of him. "So you liked that?" he asks.

"Being inside of you? It was amazing." Rising, I extend my hand to him to lift him up until he's standing, too.

"Good, then maybe I'll let you do it again sometime." He gives me a playful wink and for a moment my breath catches as it hits me again how extraordinary Ramon is. He handles my rough times like a pro, and makes me calm again. How the hell did I ever end up with someone as amazing as him? I can't ever allow myself to take him for granted.

"Thank you for putting up with me," I murmur, pulling him into a tight hug.

He shrugs. "You're not so bad."

I take his face in my hands. "I don't know about that. But even when I'm bad, you make me want to be good again."

He smiles quietly at me.

"So what now?" I ask.

"Call Sasha. I need you with me tonight." His expression suddenly appears vulnerable, and I take it seriously.

"Okay. As soon as we get outside I'll call her."

Leading me into the hallway, he asks me to wait a minute so he can put on his street clothes.

When he returns, he reaches out and takes my hand, and as we step outside the door, through the dark hallway, and outside where the neon and billboard lights shine brightly, I pull out my phone. I know I made a mistake coming to the club, but Ramon understood my struggle and we worked it out in our own way. Now I'm going home with my man.

TWO DAYS LATER I GET an unexpected phone call from Madame Fontanoy.

"Charles, dear, I was hoping you could join me for a drink tonight before Ramon gets home."

"That's not too late for you?" I ask, trying to be low-key to cover up my intrigue and concern as to why she wants to see me.

"Sleeping is so dull and overrated. Regardless, I'm a night owl."

"Then sure. I'd like that. Can I bring anything?"

"Just your handsome self. Let's say nine-ish."

"I'll be there."

As I end the call I really start to wonder what this meeting is about. Knowing Gabriella, it could be anything, so I decide it'd be best for me not to let my mind worry about it. I'll find out soon enough.

I've never been inside of her apartment, and my anticipation is rewarded once I pass through her doorway by a feast of the senses: jewel tone colors shimmering under the flickering lights—the spice-scented candles burning on every surface despite the fact that it was a warm day.

Wearing an intricately embroidered Chinese jacket over silky pants, Gabriella is as glamorous as ever. I wonder what her closet must look like since I've never seen her in the same outfit twice.

When Ramon and I talked about this mysterious meeting earlier, he told me that this is the ritual of being brought into her inner circle, and that I should be flattered. He also shared that her suite was created by combining several apartments into one, and not to be surprised how grand and eclectic it is. I assured him that I fully expected as much.

When I arrive, I note that the 'sitting room' as she refers to what I'd call the living room, features a grand fireplace with an intricately carved mantle. Above the mantle is an oil painting of a gorgeous woman in a vintage styled dress. I'm about to ask the origin of the painting until I realize it is Gabriella from when she was much younger, and what she's wearing must have been the current style. When I ask about it she rolls her eyes.

"What I remember best when I look at that artwork is the endless posing for hours with the artist as he painted. My husband, Clarence, had flown him in from Italy, and he worked in the old school style with oils and patient subjects. That was not me. I begged Clarence to instead do a George Hurrell photographic study, or to work with famed fashion photographer, Horst, but he balked at the idea. He said a painting is permanent and my portrait would likely end up in a museum." She lets out a sigh. "He was such a dear, yet I provoked him. I pointed out that a painting will last forever unless our house burns down, and that besides—without heirs, it would likely end up in a thrift shop. Oh my, did I have a way of getting on his nerves." She fans herself. "But he always insisted he'd take a spirited girl like me anytime over a boring one."

Inviting me to sit down, she gestures toward the tray in front of me that offers an open bottle of wine, assorted cheeses, grapes, and chocolates.

"Wine, my dear, or would you prefer whiskey? I have some good vodka as well since many of my young friends do vodka and soda for some new diet trend." She sighs. "Why must we restrict ourselves of some of life's greatest pleasures? I'll take a bit of Swiss chocolate and a fine glass of Cabernet over anything that dull any day."

I nod and pour us both a glass of wine, which she accepts with a smile.

I glance back up at the painting. "Were you married to Mister Randolph long?"

"Sadly, no. He passed twelve years after we met. But I can proudly say that despite being Clarence's third wife, I was the one who lasted the longest."

I raise my glass to her. "Well, that says a lot. What was your secret, if you don't mind my asking?"

"I always treated him like he was more important than all the other distractions in my life."

"*Distractions?* Like being a movie star?" I love how she always underplays what a sensation she was. I Googled her a few weeks after Ramon and I got involved, and I was amazed at the career she had. I normally don't follow up on celebrities, and I hadn't realized that she was in some of the movies my parents had shown Sasha and I.

"Yes. And that is not easily accomplished, Charles. I must say I navigated that minefield with the utmost care. Especially since he was a producer and head of the studio I had at one time been under contract with. And, of course, there was one other more critical secret to our success."

"Which was . . ."

"I remained faithful and kept him so happy that he remained faithful, too. Jealously and mistrust will destroy a relationship."

I nod and swallow hard, as I remember how jealous I got watching Ramon dance only a few days ago. I start wondering if this is why I was invited over here.

"So how did you accomplish that? I know you co-starred with some really handsome and popular leading men."

"I picked my roles not only for the parts, but I had enough options that I could pick to work with co-stars who were happily married, or secretly with men, of which was true with more than you would've believed."

"Wow. You were never tempted?"

"Oh, I'm human, dear boy. Of course I was. But I knew what was at stake so I was vigilant. There's only one man who I may have broken my vows for, but the moment I realized it, he did the honorable thing and left me. He was a true gentleman." She lets out a sad sigh. "I often wonder what became of Kingsley."

"Was he one of your leading men?"

"No. He was my bodyguard, and he left me right after the night he saved my life."

"Wow," I reply.

"Some night when Ramon is here, we will drink a bottle or two and I will share that story of my brave Kingsley. But not tonight."

I twist my hands together and try to gather my courage. "Gabriella, did Ramon telling you about my jealous rage the other night?"

She focuses her large, green eyes on her wine glass before glancing back up at me. "He did. He came to me for advice."

My chest hurts suddenly imagining what it took for Ramon to share our conflict with her.

"What did you advise him?"

"Well, other than imploring him not to work so much overtime,

I told him that I thought he handled the situation as best he could. And then I told him I was going to talk to you."

I'm so horrified that I press my hands over my cheeks as they flush. "Talk to me because I was an asshole, right? I know I was."

"Let's say you were rather dramatic. You know how I spoke of choosing my co-stars? In the same spirit, you need to avoid watching Ramon dance for the patrons. Nothing good can come out of that."

Except hot sex in a private room, I think. But then I correct myself. The scenario would not play out like that a second time.

Reaching over, she places her hand over mine. "Charles, I want you to know that Ramon has confided in me that he truly, madly, passionately loves you. Over time he has shared much of his life story with me, and so I know how significant you are to him. As long as you stay centered and make your love and devotion known, he is yours completely."

"I should've never gone to the club. Those women are so aggressive."

"By all means, stay away from there, unless he's dancing just for you. Can you tell me why he's working so much extra overtime lately? And is that what provoked you?"

I nod, sorrowfully. "It is. He's been trying to save money to buy his own club, and he hit a wall of frustration that things weren't moving fast enough so he took on a lot of overtime. Meanwhile, I've been missing my time with him so much."

Shaking her head, she huffs. "That boy is so proud. I have offered to invest a number of times and he turns me down . . . something about not risking our friendship. How does he think empires have been built? He needs to work his connections!"

"That's what I always tell him. He won't let me invest either."

"Okay, good to know. I'm not going to allow this to continue. He and I will be having another talk. Meanwhile, watch yourself, Charles. The last thing you want to do is push Ramon away."

"No. I can't," I reply anxiously. "I love him, Gabriella. I've never loved anyone like I love him"

"Good," she says with a satisfied smile. "Then we are compatriots fighting for the same cause. True love is a treasure to be protected at all costs with a noble and fierce intent." She raises her glass. "To you and Ramon . . . may true love prevail."

19. If You Were Mine

RAMON AND I FIND OUR rhythm again and everything seems to have settled until I share with him some unexpected news. It didn't occur to me that Ramon wouldn't take it well.

We agree to have a drink that night after his show. So we meet at the bar at The Hollywood Roosevelt Hotel where one of Ramon's friends from work had started bartending.

"Are you okay?" Ramon asked, reaching out to stroke my arm. "You look really tense."

I make a face. "Well, it was a strange day, and I'm not sure what to do about the situation."

"Tell me about it. Maybe I can help," Ramon encourages.

I swirl my whiskey around in the glass. "I got promoted today."

Ramon leans back in his chair with a surprised expression, then tips his head to the side. "You say that like it's a bad thing. Promoted to what?"

"I'm now officially a Senior Team Director. I got a raise and everything, but there's a big problem."

"Which is?" Ramon asks.

"That I don't want the job."

Ramon appears increasingly perplexed. "Why not? What do you want?"

"My old job?" I say more as a question than an answer. "Actually, what I want is a career change. Corporate programing has really lost its appeal."

"And you don't think the new position will challenge you and make it interesting again?"

"I hate the idea of being a manager. I'd much rather be the person doing the work. I have no idea why the hell they thought I was suited for this."

Ramon leans back in his chair and I can see that every muscle in his body is tense. Several expressions move over his countenance until he settles on a big smile that doesn't feel genuine. "Well, despite your reservations, maybe it won't be as bad as you think. I'd say congratulations are in order, Charlie."

He tries looking happy for me but I can tell he isn't feeling it, and I'm not either.

"You know what I'd really like to do?"

Ramon shakes his head, but his expression tells me his mind is somewhere else.

Reaching over, I take his hand. "I want to help you run the club."

He scowls and glances down at the table. "What club? At the rate I'm going, taking my clothes off so I can stash away tip money, it's a joke. Do you know how much insurance costs for nightclubs, let alone the crazy top-dollar terms the building owners in this town want on their leases? As I research everything and the weeks and months pass, my dream seems to keep falling out of reach. Now I'm starting to wonder if I should give it all up."

I sit up straighter and lean forward to try to keep him focused on what I have to say. "You can't give up. I know you're overwhelmed right now and it's a lot, but why won't you let me help you? I already told you I'd really like to invest in your club and work with you on it."

"We've already talked about this, Charlie. Look what happened the first time I teamed with investors. I'm not doing that again. And furthermore, you're too important to me to risk our relationship over."

Ramon finishes off his wine in a large swallow and surprises me by gesturing to the waiter to bring another. "I've got to say, sometimes I wonder what you're doing with me. You're a successful businessman and what am I? A stripper with big dreams. What a fucking joke."

I wish I'd anticipated what telling him about my promotion would do to him. I'm an idiot and I have no idea how to fix this. I need to say something to stop his spiral into self-deprecation.

"You're not a joke, Ramon. Don't ever say that."

He shrugs with a bitter expression. "Whether I say it aloud or not, it's the truth. Only an idiot would make the mistakes I've made. I wanted it so bad . . ."

I edge my chair closer to him and rest my hand on his knee. "We all make mistakes, Ramon. You've learned from yours, and so you can't give up. Still fighting for your dream is what matters." I wrap my arm around him and he leans his head on my shoulder for a long moment and sighs. I can feel his shoulders relax a bit under my arm.

"Thanks, Charlie," he murmurs.

I'm relieved to sense that he seems a little calmer and not as defeated.

"Promise me you'll think about letting me work with you."

He nods.

"And I believe in you, Ramon, so together we'll figure this out. Okay?"

He gives me a weak smile, but I'll take it.

"Okay," he whispers. "I won't give up."

I THINK THINGS HAVE LEVELED off with Ramon's disappointment and downturn, and my new position hasn't started yet, so things feel somewhat back to normal. But that Friday morning, when I call to confirm that he's working at the club that evening, I find his responses evasive and that troubles me.

"Um . . . actually, I took the night off."

"Really, why?" I ask. Ramon has always seemed diligent about his work schedule. Besides, he's been working more hours lately, not less.

There's a silent pause, and then he clears his throat. "I'm really tired, so I thought I'd stay home and work on my business plan."

"Your business plan?" I ask. *He has the whole day to work on that, why is he really blowing off work?*

"I guess I'm feeling inspired." I can hear him lightly humming and my curiosity is now really piqued.

"Well, I was going to take Sasha to dinner, but why don't I come over after and help you?"

"Oh, you don't have to do that. Enjoy your night with Sasha."

When I end the call, I can't shake the feeling that something is going on. I talk to Sasha about it over dinner and she points out that things have been solid between us and she's sure I'm reading into things that I shouldn't.

"Charlie, Ramon surprised you with a day trip to Santa Barbara for your two-month anniversary last weekend and you said it was wonderful. And didn't he buy symphony tickets at the Disney Concert Hall for next month when you'd had a horrible day at work the week before that?"

I nod, my cheeks getting hot with embarrassment for sounding like a fool.

"Why don't you bring him flowers after dinner and tell him you couldn't wait to see him?" She grins widely.

"You're such a softie."

"Nothing wrong with a little romance," she insists.

So, despite my apprehension, I pick up an impressive bouquet of sunflowers at the florist at Gelson's market before they close, and head to Ramon's. My heart is pounding when I head up the stairs. I'm freaked out about what I may find. Why am I being like this? Ramon hasn't given me any reason to question him. The worst he's ever done was not show up for dinner, and we're way past that early screw-up in our relationship.

When I approach his apartment, I realize that the front door is cracked open and dance music is playing loudly. I push the door open wider and peek inside. At the front of the hall off the living room Ramon is turned with his back to me, but his hands are suspended on the opposing walls of the hallway. Rocking his hips to the beat, he's completely lost in the music.

For a brief second I panic that he may have someone else in his apartment—after all, he's never acted like he did this morning on the phone with me—but after watching him sway, sink low, and shimmy back up several times, I'm pretty sure this is Ramon alone in his own space, dancing because it's a way he expresses himself. It reminds me of the first time I watched him dance at the club and how he owned me by the time our special dance was over. A wide smile breaks across my face.

I push the door open a little more, and when he spins and lifts his arms as he starts to dance forward, his gaze meets mine. Expecting him to stop and blush with embarrassment, instead he keeps dancing, slowly sashaying his way to me. I can't avoid the sexual desire that charges through me. When Ramon moves like this it's the most erotic thing I can imagine.

Once he's before me, he reaches out and grabs my wrist then pulls me inside and snaps the door shut behind me. I hold out his flowers and he takes them in one hand, and brushes his fingers across my cheek with the other. He carefully sets the flowers down on his coffee table and then steps right up to me. Sliding his hands up my neck until he links his fingers together, he rocks his hips into me. As our gazes meet, he nods his head in encouragement. "Dance with me, Charlie," he says, his smoldering gaze seducing me.

I love seeing this confident, sexy side of him again. As much as I want to do a helluva lot more than dance, I begin to move, my hips now in sync with his.

Damn. My early uncontrollable lust for him when we first met hasn't faded, but instead has gotten richer and more intense, like the aging of a fine wine whose flavor is now intoxicating and irresistible.

I want to kiss him so badly, but before I try he turns so now his back is to my front, resulting in his ass grinding against me. This is almost more than I can take.

"Ramon," I groan.

"Charlie," he responds before stepping away and dancing around me, rolling his shoulders back as he rocks his hips. He grazes my arms, my ass, and my hips with his fingers until my heart is pounding wildly.

"What are you trying to do to me?" I ask as I struggle to focus on anything but him.

He winks at me suggestively. "I want you worked up."

How do you respond to that when your boyfriend is aroused and looking at you like he needs to rip your clothes off? Far be it from me to question anything when I'm about to get naked with this man. And he's not just *my* man, but a dancing god among mere mortals.

Feeling unusually assertive, I lead him to the bedroom. He makes us pause to adjust the iPod to Billy Holiday with one hand, while he tries to unbuckle my belt with the other. I push his hands away.

Who is this frenzied Ramon, and what happened to the cool, calm, collected one?

His lips are on me as soon as we're through the door, and then he deftly unbuttons my shirt, but I reach up and stop him.

"What's going on?" I ask.

"I'm going to make love to you, baby," he says, in his sexiest voice. He's so matter-of-fact about it that it takes a moment for me to get my mind clear to respond.

"We're not doing anything until I know what has you acting like this. I was worried when you were so strange and distant on the phone this morning, and then I show up here to find your door standing open and music blasting. I actually had a moment where I wondered if you had another man in here."

His brows knit together and his eyes narrow. "But why would I do that when I'm with you?"

"Exactly. That's what I wondered until I realized you were danc-ing alone."

"But you're here, and I'm not alone anymore. I'm glad you dropped by . . . it's the perfect surprise. Besides, I wouldn't cheat on you, Charlie," he says earnestly. "I belong to you."

"Good, because you know I want all of you . . . no less."

"Well, I feel the same about you, so can you relax?"

He attempts to unbutton my shirt one last time and I stop him. Instead, I start dragging the edge of his T-shirt up his chest and over his head. Then I push his wandering hands away and unfasten his jeans and jerk them down his thighs so he can step out of them. The entire time he studies me with a wide-eyed stare.

I can feel my blood boiling with this weird possessive sensation. It makes me think of things he's done with me in the past. "Get on the bed," I say, trying to sound commanding as I loosely gesture to the tangle of sheets and blankets. "I want to look at you while I undress."

"Fuck, Charlie. This is hot." His eyes light up like he's won the lottery.

I undress slowly to provoke him, and he fists himself anxiously. "Hurry up," he groans.

"Be patient." When my slacks and briefs are off he's staring where I'm hard for him. "See how worked up you got me?"

He nods and swallows. I watch his hand move and how his cock throbs in his grip. "Please come here," he whispers. His eyes are as dark as the night and his face is flushed with desire.

I approach the nightstand and pull his bottle of lube out of the drawer. My gaze passes the open drawer where I notice an open duffle bag and grooming kit on the floor surrounded by piles of clothes. I'm overcome with curiosity.

I point to the duffle bag. "So what's that? Are you going somewhere?" I ask, despite the fact that it's challenging to think about anything but Ramon being inside of me.

He lifts up and glances at the bag and then back up at me. He's suddenly bewildered. Clearly he hadn't planned on me seeing that. "Oh, I'm taking a short trip tomorrow."

"To see your family in Texas?"

He seems nervous. "No. Actually, Florida."

My body tenses up. Suddenly sex isn't at the forefront of my mind. "Florida? When were you going to mention that?"

"When I recovered from our hot sex," he replies with an uneasy grin.

"But I came here looking for you, Ramon. You brushed off seeing me tonight. When were you going to tell me?"

"Look, this whole thing has come together fast and I'm overwhelmed. Please believe I would have told you. Of course I would have." He shakes his head at me like he can't believe I'd think other-wise. "Besides, I knew you wouldn't like me going and that you'd try to talk me out of it."

His declaration pisses me off even more. "What's so damn im-portant in Florida that you have to rush out of here with almost no notice? Was this about the club?"

"I got a call from Javier."

"Javier? I've never heard you mention that name. Who is he?"

Ramon's expression is sheepish, which makes me nervous.

"A friend from Miami," Ramon says quietly.

"A friend?"

"Well, we were lovers for a while, but that ended right before I met Luis. He's my friend Mirana's cousin and he was involved with the club plans."

"So this Javier person calls you and you jet off to Florida on the drop of a hat? Who does that?"

"It's because the main asshole, Ernesto, the criminal who screwed me over, has been missing since last week. He was the kingpin of the group. Javier's pretty sure he's a goner and so he's saying he can help me get my money back, or claim my stake in our club, *Fusion*. Don't you see, Charlie? That would take the pressure off my plan of getting a club open here knowing that I was so far off from having enough funds. I could finally realize the dream Luis and I had."

I'm starting to wonder about this naïve side of Ramon. I know he grew up underprivileged with the stigma of being an immigrant kid, but he's smart and educated and should know better by now. Maybe it's the dreamer part of him wanting to believe that the right thing will happen. I'm going to be his reality check. "How do you know you're not being baited?"

"Why would Javier do that to me? I was good to him. He'd have no reason."

I decide to change my tactics, and I wonder if I should follow him there to keep an eye out so he isn't in danger. "How long will you be gone?"

He hesitates and his gaze doesn't meet mine when he finally

answers. "I'm not sure. The club is partially finished. I told Gene I may need to be there a few days this trip to sort everything out."

"Why is this all coming together now when you left several years ago?"

"I'm not sure," he replies. "But I'll find out. There could be a lot of reasons."

"If the club is well on its way to finally being finished, are you thinking this could be a permanent move?" I ask, my fingers curling up tight with tension.

"Maybe, until the club opens and I sell my part in it. But I wouldn't do anything without us figuring things out first."

I'd like to believe that he means that, but so far he seems like he's forging ahead without considering how I fit into his puzzle.

He rubs his hand over his chin. "Have you ever been to Miami? It's a very cool city . . . such a unique place. I had the impression you weren't so invested in L.A. So maybe then if things work out even better than I've imagined, you could move there, too."

I can feel my eyes bug out. "Wow. So that's what you think, that it's that simple. And what about Sasha?"

"Well, you could bring her!"

Is he fucking serious? Has he not paid attention to her relationships with her caregivers and medical team? And never mind my job and career. He thinks we'd uproot our lives so we could support him opening up a gangster-riddled club?

An anxious wave of nausea rolls over me. I finally know how it feels to have a devoted lover, and now he may be taken away from me over a bad business deal?

I glance down next to the bed and fish my clothes off the floor.

"Where are you going?" he asks apprehensively.

"Home." I realize after I've buttoned my shirt that it's off kilter, but I don't even care. I yank my jeans on and quickly zip them up. Spotting my shoes under the bed, I grab them and slide them on without bothering to do the ties. My anxiety is making me feel like I can't breathe and I need to get out of here before I pass out or have a full-on panic attack. Not to mention that I'm pretty sure I'll say something I regret if I don't walk away now and calm down before we discuss this again.

He hurries off the bed and pulls on his jeans. "I'm not moving to Miami, Charlie . . . not without you."

"But you've thought about it," I respond.

"Please don't go. Not like this," he asks, fear in his expression.

"Like what?" I ask as I pull out my car keys.

"I can tell you're upset."

I feel dizzy for a second so I reach for the edge of the dresser. "Look, I love you, so yes, of course I'm upset you were running off to Miami without letting me know before you booked the flight and started packing. And seriously, after what you told me about what went down there, who knows what could happen to you? Look what happened with Marcus, and here you are being so cavalier about going. As a result, I'm not feeling at all well, so I need to go before I feel worse."

Not looking back at him, I walk down the hall and into the living room. Billie Holiday is crooning "If You Were Mine" from the iPod dock.

If you were mine
I could be a ruler of kings
And if you were mine
I could do such wonderful things . . .

I pause as the lyrics settle over me. What if Ramon isn't *mine* after all? Maybe Florida was always destined to call him back, and if it does all the 'wonderful things' will tumble out of my life until I'm left empty once again.

Feeling his hand on my shoulder, I shiver at his unexpected touch.

"Charlie," he whispers.

I shake my head, my gaze fixed on the floor. I feel like I'm about to sink down through the floorboards.

"Please don't be this way. We'll figure this out. I need you to understand I can't pass this opportunity up, my last chance to take back what was taken from me. It wasn't just the money . . . it was my dreams, and my chance to validate how Luis believed in me."

"What if it's a trap? I could lose you."

"I don't think Javier would do that to me."

"You are so trusting. When was the last time you talked to him? What if he's changed? That's not an impossibility."

He considers what I'm saying. "No, I suppose there's always a chance, even if it's a small one."

"Isn't there anyone else who can corroborate his story?"

"Well, I could call Mirana. Even though she was against me getting involved with them in the first place. She's family, so she must know something."

"Call her. Do it for me."

"What, you mean now? It's really late there and my flight is tomorrow morning. I can call her when I get there."

My gut instincts are sharp and I'm relying on them completely right now. "No, I need you to call her now, and give her my number if she doesn't answer."

His expression is confused but maybe he senses it's the only thing that will placate me. Picking up his phone, he flips through his contacts until he locates her number. After he prompts the call, I hear a phone ringing, but the call goes to voicemail.

"Hey Mirana. It's Ramon. It's been a long time and I hope you're good. Anyway, the reason I'm calling is Javier called me and said I needed to return to Miami. He told me Ernesto is missing and he can help me take back my claim in the club. It'd be really good to see you and catch up. I'm flying to Miami in the morning and he's meeting me at the airport, so let me know if you and Ermano are free for dinner tomorrow night."

As he starts to wrap it up I point at myself, reminding him to give her my number and he does. When he ends the call, he looks up at me with a somber gaze. "I wish you believed in me."

"I'm completely in love with you, Ramon. I do believe in you, but I'm starting to wonder if you chasing your dream back to Miami will be the end of us. As we both know, not every love story has a happy ending."

Pulling me into his arms, he holds on tight. "Don't say that, baby.

Please don't give up on me . . . on us. We deserve a happy ending."

I breathe him in before I shrug out of his hold and step away. "As much as I want to insist you don't get on that plane tomorrow, I know you're going to. What time is your flight?"

"Ten. So with the rush hour traffic I'll be leaving for LAX around seven-thirty."

I nod. "Okay, I guess that's it then. Will you let me know when you arrive?"

"Yes, I will."

I turn and walk toward his door. *What if this is the last time I see Ramon?* It feels like this forty-foot wave of emotion is about to hit me and flatten me to the ground. My eyes are tearing up and I have to leave his place before I lose it completely. I pause for a moment after I've pulled open the door. What if I stay and refuse to let him go?

You're such a fool, I think to myself. In my gut, I know this trip is going to change everything and there's not a damn thing I can do about it when it obviously means everything to him and it has since I met him.

"Charlie!" he calls out. I don't turn around but I wait to hear what he has to say.

"I love you, Charlie."

My heart shatters into tiny fragments, causing fissions that will keep splintering until my whole world cracks apart. Stepping outside, I quietly close the door behind me. I'm a mechanical man, yet apparently poorly constructed for this kind of heartbreak. The tears trail down my face as I stumble down the stairs, through the courtyard, and out the gate of this magical place that opened up my world.

I glance up at the sign, *Jardín del Paraiso,* and sigh. Without Ramon, the idea of paradise has never felt so bleak.

20. Weirdest Day Ever

THE NEXT MORNING, I WAKE up with a start, and focus on trying to push my nightmares, which taunted me all night long, out of my mind. Evidently my subconscious had a field day with the news that Ramon is possibly leaving me to open his club in Miami. Every time I think about it, this sick feeling spasms through me. Why would this happen so soon after we found each other? We'd realized not only how easily we fit together, but how powerful and all-consuming our love and lust were for each other.

Splashing water on my face after using the bathroom, I'm trying to think about my schedule for today to distract me, but I can't shake the ominous feeling creeping up my spine that Ramon won't come back from Florida. I check my phone but there's no word from him, only the realization that he must be on his way to the airport.

When it's time to head to work, Estella and Sasha head down to the parking garage with me since they've decided to run their errands early. I've put on a good face pretending it's just another day. "Where are you off to?" I ask.

"We're going to pick up my prescriptions at the drug store, and guess where after that?"

"Oh gee, I don't know . . . the bookstore?" I tease.

"How did you ever guess?" she replies with a grin.

"Keep her out of trouble," I warn Estella.

She gives me a warm smile. I wonder sometimes what she would think about knowing I was so close to wrongly firing her, but luckily we never had to find out.

I'm about to get in my car when my phone rings with a number

I don't recognize, but my mind flashes to Ramon's call to Mirana last night, and I anxiously answer it.

"Hello. Is this Charlie, Ramon's friend?" the unsteady female voice asks.

"Yes, is this Mirana?"

"It is. I'm so glad I reached you. Is Ramon with you? I've left him three messages and he hasn't returned my call. It's critical that I speak with him before he goes to the airport."

I feel a lump form in my throat. "He's probably almost to the airport already," I reply. I notice that Estella and Sasha are watching me with worried expressions.

"No! Why won't he answer his phone? He needs to stay as far away from Miami as he can."

"Why?" I ask, my heart already pounding.

"I can't get into it now, but things are going down and it's going to be bad. Ernesto isn't missing . . . he's dead. So you see, you have to stop Ramon."

I feel like I've been punched in the gut. "Stop him? I don't even know what airline he's flying there with."

"I'm pretty sure it's American. They have non-stops, and I know that's who he flew when he moved to L.A. because I helped him book it."

I realize I've been holding my breath so I inhale sharply. And even if I rush to the airport, they won't let me into the passenger gates without a ticket. "Mirana, let me try calling him."

"Yes, but before you do there is one other thing and it's very critical, Charlie. Ramon needs to meet us briefly at the airport in Las Vegas."

Seriously? When did my life become a mystery adventure?

"Las Vegas? And by 'we' you mean . . ."

"My husband, Ermano. We have a painting of his that we want to give him before we leave the country."

"I understand that you're leaving the country, but can't you ship it to him?" I can't believe they expect him to fly to another state for a friggin' painting. Or could they be using the painting as an excuse to talk to him face-to-face?

"No, no. He has to pick it up. It's too fragile to ship, and we really want to see him since we don't know when or if we will again."

Ever again? I'm speechless at the gravity of what she's said.

"Charlie, you have no idea how important this is to me. Promise me you will get him to Las Vegas. Our layover is from three to five thirty Vegas time."

"Today? But I don't know if I'll even reach him in time to stop boarding the Florida flight," I protest.

"Look, our flight is almost done boarding. We have to get on. But, Charlie, I can't stress this enough. He can't go to Miami, and if he meets us in Vegas, I know it will mean a lot to him to see us, and for us to see him."

"But . . ." I start to protest, but I hear a man's voice calling her.

"I've got to go. Godspeed, Charlie. I'll say a prayer for Ramon."

After she hangs up, I hold the phone away from me in shock.

"What is it, Charlie?" Sasha asks.

"I have to stop Ramon," I mumble, my fear building as the levity of the task hits me. I hit the call button. It rings three times and I'm doubtful he's going to answer but to my shock he picks up.

"Charlie?" he says, but the reception is crap and I can barely hear him.

"Where are you?" I ask.

"In the security line, but my phone is about to die. I forgot to charge it last night I was so freaked out. So it's been off but I had to turn it on again to show them by mobile boarding pass."

My adrenaline surges. "Ramon, listen to me . . . you can't get on the plane."

"What?" he asks, his voice crackling.

"You can't get on the plane!" I yell through the phone. I notice Estella bristling and Sasha's mouth drops open.

"But I told you last night that I had to do this. You need to . . ."

The line goes dead.

"Fuck!" I yell out, wanting to hurl my phone to the ground. I turn back frantically to the girls. "His phone died. I have to stop him."

"What's going on, Charlie?" Sasha asks, her eyes full of fear.

"I need to get to the airport, and I'll have to buy tickets to get to the gates. I'll have to go to Vegas with him. It's the only way I'll know it will happen," I mumble to myself.

"What are you talking about?" Sasha's intense gaze is alarmed.

I signal off my alarm and yank the door open.

"Wait!" she calls out. "You can't drive and book plane tickets. Besides, if we take the van you can do the carpool lane. That's gold during rush hour."

Estella is already lowering the ramp to roll Sasha up inside the van. "And Estella can drive me back so you don't have to take the time to park. We can drop you off." Using her hand commands, she rolls her wheelchair into the van and before I can argue with them, Estella has her chair secured and the ramp is folding back into place. I jump into the front seat and Estella hands me the keys.

"Godspeed, indeed," I whisper as I pull out onto the street.

I'm so amped up that I barely remember what route I take to get on the freeway, only that I zig-zag across town until I'm on the 405 heading South. When I glance over at Estella, her knuckles are white where she's clinging to the door handle. She also lets out little groans when I run yellow lights that are actually red, and barge into the freeway carpool lane before it's my right to do so.

Meanwhile, Sasha—who is a wizard with her iPhone—has located what is probably Ramon's flight, an American non-stop set to depart at ten-0-five, and is now looking at flights to Vegas in the same terminal. "There's one arriving at three-fifteen," she informs me. She's impressive under pressure. I know she thrives on a challenge.

"Book it, using my information," I say, digging into my pocket and handing Estella my wallet. "Please take my Visa out and read her the number," I direct her.

"For the both of you? You're sure, Charlie?" she asks.

"I'm sure," I respond. This isn't the time to stand back and watch for the outcome. I need to be in the game, fighting for Ramon's future, for our future.

I slam my foot down on the gas pedal and weave my way through traffic like a character in a Bourne movie. When we get to LAX, I do a crazy maneuver that lands me in front of the American terminal. I've got our tickets to Vegas loaded on my phone and overwhelming terror that I won't find Ramon. I also know that even if I do get to him before his plane loads, I may not be able to convince him that his plans need to change.

"Go, Charlie!" Sasha cries out, as I unsnap my seatbelt and slam the van into park.

"Thanks for your help, I'll let you know what happens," I call out, before jumping out of the van. Moments later I'm pulling out my ID and running through the terminal. I have to fumble with my phone at the first stop to head into security, but I'm passed through. However, my heart sinks when I see how long the main security line is. I'll never get to Ramon in time.

For the first time in my life I feel like a bull fired up with enough rage to crash through whatever gate is holding me back. I boldly rush up to the front of the line. And hold up my wallet up to the security person checking tickets and IDs. Everyone behind me is grumbling, but I have to take this chance. I wave my phone, that's open to my ticket, and my ID, both in my other hand.

"Miss, my boyfriend dropped his wallet after he took out his ID and his plane is boarding. I have a flight, too, but I have no luggage to scan. Please let me through so I can get his wallet to him in time."

She narrows her eyes at me as she examines my ID and boarding pass, but to my surprise she waves me through and summons over the next traveler. I drop my phone, wallet, keys, and watch into the tray and walk through the scanner, and once I've retrieved my stuff I run full throttle down the corridor toward gate twenty-two. Thank God Sasha found the gate number online since I'm too freaked out to have to stop and figure that out. As I see the gate a hundred or so feet away, panic sets in when I realize that it looks empty of travelers. I glance at my phone; it's only nine-fifty. *Have they shut the doors already?* Then suddenly I notice a short line of ticket holders still moving through, and three from the end is Ramon. I almost cry I'm so relieved.

"Ramon!" I yell as I run toward him.

Startled, he looks around until our eyes meet. "Charlie! What are you doing here? I just texted you. I was charging my phone as long as I could before boarding."

He's only a few people back now from having his ticket checked before boarding.

"You can't go."

His face twists up in confusion. "What do you mean I *can't* go? I'm going!" He waves his boarding pass at me.

The woman behind him purses her lips, and arches her brow.

"I spoke with Mirana. She said you'll be in serious danger if you go."

"Are you making this up? Because that'd be really fucked up if you are."

"No, I swear."

He's one person back from check-in now and I wave the woman behind him to step ahead.

"I'm going," he insists, folding his arms over his chest.

Grabbing his arm, I yank him toward me. "You can't go. Ernesto isn't missing, Ramon . . . he's dead. And Mirana and her husband are already on their first flight, to leave the country as we speak."

"What? He's dead?" he asks, the color rushing from his face.

"Yes." I look up and see that only Ramon is left and the woman is waving him forward.

"We're about to close the door. Now or never," she warns.

Ramon's backpack straps slide off his slumped shoulder. And his duffle bag falls to the floor.

"He's not going," I say to the lady and Ramon is too stunned to argue.

Ramon shakes his head. "I couldn't sleep all night, I kept thinking about how upset you were. But maybe Luis was trying to tell me not to go, too."

Frankly, I'm a little tired about hearing how Luis always comes up in big moments like this, but right now I'll take whatever will convince Ramon that not going to Miami is the right decision.

Walking him over to the rows of chairs, I take his boarding pass and sit him down. "This will take a minute."

I go up to the counter and explain to the agent that Ramon just got devastating news and couldn't take the flight. The man glances over at him and then nods, before entering the information into his system. "He'll get an email as to what to do next if he's seeking a refund on the ticket."

"Thank you."

I realize that the door is being locked and the overwhelming sense of relief that I got to Ramon in time almost flattens me. Sliding down next to him in one of the blue plastic seats, I let out a long sigh. He's bent over with his face pressed into his hands. I rest my hand on his back.

"I'm sorry, Ramon."

"I can't believe this," he whispers, dragging his fist across his eyes to wipe tears away. "I thought this was it. I was finally going to be able to move forward with the club. And now it will never happen."

"It's going to happen."

"I may be an optimist, but I'm losing hope, Charlie."

"It will happen, and I'm going to help."

Gazing off in the distance, he shakes his head. "Damn! I can't believe all this crazy shit."

"Remind me how Ernesto was connected in all of this?" I ask, rubbing wide circles over his back.

He lets out a sigh. "He's Mirana's brother, and he's a fucking monster. She warned me against him at the beginning of all this."

"I noticed she didn't seem upset when she said he'd been killed," I reply.

"He treated her like shit. I wish Ernesto and my paths had never crossed. I can't say I'm sorry to hear he's gone."

"But something bigger must be behind him. Why else would she and her husband be leaving the country?"

He lifts his head up so our gazes meet.

"Marcus told me that Ernesto was in deep with some major dealers. Mirana and Ermano must be at risk for some reason. Damn, I hope they'll be okay."

"Well, here's the next part of the drama."

"There's more?" his asks, his expression distraught.

"We'll be boarding a plane around 1:30 today for Las Vegas to meet up with Mirana and Ermano during their layover."

"I hope you're joking. You are, aren't you?"

I shake my head slowly and open up my phone to show him our boarding passes. "She insisted on it. They have a painting they want to give you."

His expression softens. "Wow, that's so nice. But how do they have time for thinking about things like that when they are fleeing the country? It doesn't make sense."

"Maybe they simply really want to see you. It could be the last time."

His gaze drops downward. "Yeah, that's true. That makes me really sad to think about. She was a true friend to me when Luis got sick and all that."

Taking his hand, I squeeze it.

"So we fly to Las Vegas and meet them, and then what?"

I shrug. "We fly back home."

He lets out a low whistle. "Weirdest day ever."

It all hits me and I bite back a smile. "I don't want to be as ass, but for me it's a good day."

"Are you nuts? Why is it a good day?"

"Because you aren't leaving me to live in Miami." I rest my hands on either side of his face and kiss him, not caring who might see us and that we're in a public place.

When we part, he brushes my hair back off my face. "You know I would've kidnapped you and Sasha so you'd be there with me. I wasn't going to let you go."

"Hmmm," I hum, giving him a cynical look. "I guess we'll never know about that, but for now I'll take your word for it." I lift up my phone to check the time. "What do you want to do now? We have three hours to wait."

"Sleep," he responds without even thinking about it. "But I'm so wound up I feel like I could crawl out of my skin. Maybe I need to try to meditate and calm myself down."

I point to the length of the bench of seats we are on. "Look, you can stretch out on this one. Why don't you put your head on my lap and close your eyes while you meditate."

"Will you rub my head?" he asks. "That really relaxes me."

"Sure. I'm a head-rubbing expert."

He does as I asked, and once he stretches out and I start rubbing his scalp, he passes out within minutes. Poor baby really was tired.

With my free hand I text Sasha with the latest. She texts back a picture that Estella took of her in the bookstore with a short stack of books on her lap and a big grin on her face. She's giving me the thumbs up, and I can't help but smile.

Next, I text Brittany at work to tell her I won't be in because I need to help my boyfriend with a crisis and I'll make up any lost work this weekend.

Your boyfriend? she asks in her reply text.

I love that I outed myself to my work colleagues like that. *Yes, his name is Ramon.*

Is Ramon okay? Is there anything we can do to help?

My finger pauses over the phone's keyboard as a warm feeling surges through me. To know not only was I not judged, but that Ramon and I were supported, is the most amazing feeling in the world. Next time I see Brittany I'm going to give her a big hug of thanks, and in the future if there is anything she needs, workwise or anything, I will be there for her, above and beyond—two hundred percent.

I think we've got it under control but thank you so much.

Of course. Let me know if anything changes. If not, I'll see you to-morrow, yes?

Absolutely. Thanks again.

For the next hour that Ramon sleeps I never stop soothing him with my touch. I'm trying to catch up with my emotions and my thoughts of all the things that have happened since yesterday. It's been so overwhelming.

I know Ramon is terribly disappointed that he won't get back what he lost after all, but we will figure out how to get his club open. We were already working on it before all this happened. And through this crazy experience we've proven that we can be there for each other.

21. Sin City

WHEN THE SEATS AROUND OUR gate start to fill up the noise gets progressively louder and Ramon wakes up. He blinks up at me as I stroke his forehead.

"Hello, sleepy head," I say softly.

"Hey. How long have I been out?"

"Over an hour. Are you hungry?"

He nods as he pulls himself up to a sitting position. "Famished. With everything that was going on I haven't eaten a meal since lunch yesterday. Are you up for a late breakfast?"

"Sure."

We get a table in the Wolfgang Puck café a few gates away and Ramon orders enough food for a family.

I eat a regular breakfast of bacon and eggs with hash browns and toast, then sip my coffee while I watch him tackle the main plate he ordered and then one side plate at a time. He's very methodical about it, which I'd never noticed before. I guess there's still a lot of things for me to learn about Ramon.

"I'm amazed," I say when he pushes the last empty plate away and leans back into the booth.

"After Dad died we never had enough to eat. But Mom always made sure on our birthdays, or a special occasion, like getting a great report card, that she'd make whatever dishes we loved and then we could eat as much of it as we wanted."

It's hard to hear they didn't have enough to eat when we always had more than enough and took it for granted. "So is today a special occasion?"

He takes my hand and holds it, rubbing his thumb over my knuckles. "It is. You went above and beyond to protect me, Charlie. I'll never forget it."

I consider telling him what I actually think of what he put us through, but I figure I'll wait until we get through all this craziness.

At one-thirty we head over to gate twenty-seven for our Vegas flight. I can tell that Ramon is humming with anticipation, where I'm ready to get this over with so we can get back to L.A. and head home. I call Sasha to fill her in on what happened earlier, and where we're headed now. She loves adventures, so she's thrilled to hear all about it.

"Why don't you stay in Vegas tonight and have a wild time?" she asks breathlessly. "I hear there are awesome restaurants and the most amazing clubs and shows there. Do it, Charlie! Do it!"

"Are you kidding? As soon as we're done with Ramon's friends, we're booking the next possible flight back to L.A."

"Awww, come on! You only live once and I want to do all the things! Will you take me to Vegas sometime? I'd love to see that big, fancy fountain show, and gamble recklessly in a red evening gown surrounded by dashing men."

I chuckle. "Anything else?"

"Yes, I want to stay in a suite that looks over the strip, bright with neon signs and sparkly lights. Can you imagine it?"

"I can since you've described it so vividly. Let's add it to next year's bucket list."

"Deal."

When we're settled on the plane Ramon falls quiet, his gaze fixed somewhere faraway as he stares out the small window of the plane.

"What are you thinking about?" I eventually ask.

"Remembering my life in Miami."

"Do you miss it?" I inquire, not sure I want to hear the answer.

"In ways. It was wild and crazy fun at times. I was finally able to be out in the world and true to who I was. All of that was fantastic. But after a while the shine started to dull." He turns to me. "But when

I think of my life now, and what I have with you, I'm truly happy. You see, you're the kind of man I one day hoped to be."

"And you're okay staying in L.A.?"

"Actually, I think L.A. is great. There's no place like it, but it didn't hold my loyalty because I hadn't met a good man there who'd be my partner. Yet here you are, and since I met you L.A. became full of promise."

"That's good to hear because I sure as hell don't want you running off to Miami like that on me again. That was shitty."

"I'm sorry. I wasn't trying to hurt you. When it comes to what happened to me there, I get irrational. I need to work on that."

"You do. Besides, you know what? When I used to get down my parents would say, 'Don't ever give up, Charlie, because the most amazing thing may be just around the corner.' I believe that and you should, too."

He nods, then looks back out the window. "I'll try to," he agrees.

We don't have to search far to find Mirana and Ermano at the bar they'd texted me about once we de-board at the Vegas airport. Ramon rushes over to them, pulls Mirana off her stool, and swings her around.

"Mi amiga!" he cries out. She kisses him on both cheeks, and then he sets her down to introduce me to his friends. Ermano is polite, but he appears to be nervous, which makes me uneasy. But I guess if I suddenly felt compelled to leave the country for our safety, I'd also be nervous.

I order a good bottle of wine and the stories flow as easily as the wine, the lingering taste bittersweet. When Mirana excuses herself to "freshen up", I take the opportunity to ask Ermano the timing of their next flight. So when he and Ramon continue talking about the pros and cons of Miami versus Los Angeles, I'm on my smart phone booking our flight home. As it turns out, we'll leave for our gate only minutes before Mirana and Ermano do. I can't help but feel a surge of relief at the idea of it.

A few minutes before we are to separate for not only different departure gates, but for different parts of the world, Mirana reaches behind where they're sitting and lifts up a carefully wrapped painting that's somewhere between small and medium-sized. She presses it against her chest protectively.

"We both agreed that we wanted you to have this Ramon."

Ermano nods. "It's called 'The Dreamer'."

He holds the painting up, and I study the image of a young boy running across a colorful field, his arms outstretched as if he's sure he'll take flight.

Ramon's eyes glaze with tears. "Oh, I love it. Thank you so much."

Mirana turns toward me. "Please be very careful hanging it. It has special instructions on the back of the piece.

I tip my head, trying to imagine what would be so complicated about hanging a relatively small painting, but I nod respectfully. "I'll be careful." Then I turn to Ermano. "You're a wonderful artist. All the best to both of you on your new adventure."

He gives me a wry look, because certainly trying to escape the country unnoticed is no small feat.

Ramon's expression suddenly turns somber and he's silent for a few moments while we wait for him to speak.

"This has been a roller coaster two days for me. My hopes were spurred on by Javier that I would be able to reclaim my stake in the club in some way, only to have those hopes dashed."

Ermano suddenly holds up his hands to silence him, then slides out of the booth, his gaze scanning all the booths and tables around us. When he slides back in, he gestures to everyone to lean forward and speak quietly.

I glance around, realizing now why he asked for the far corner booth. The concerned and fearful look in his eyes is haunting.

Before he continues, Ramon nods like he understands. He lowers his voice considerably. "Don't get me wrong, I'm so grateful for your warning. And I'm especially touched that you wanted to see me. Can I ask you . . . what should I make of Javier at this point?"

Mirana shakes her head. "I know he was your friend, Ramon, but

I'm sad to say he got pulled into the scene. He's an addict now, and from what I understand he owes them a lot of money."

"So he was framing me." Disappointment and hurt are etched across Ramon's face. "He knew I still had some of Luis' money left."

"I'm sorry," Mirana says.

I reach out for him under the table and rest my hand on his knee.

"I shouldn't have listened to him. I think in my gut I knew something was wrong, but I wanted to believe so much . . ."

"I know," she whispers.

Ramon twists his napkin up. "And I'm worried about you now. Why do you two have to leave? You always stayed clear of all that."

"We did, but I'm family. And even though Ernesto and I were always at odds, I'm still his sister and to them family is everything."

"Well, to all of us," Ramon says, and then glances at me.

"But you didn't have evil in your family. They know Ernesto had screwed over a lot of people on drug deals and other things and had hidden the money. When he finally took the wrong person and realized it too late, he tried to flee. He called me from the road to tell me where his safe was and the combination. He wanted the money moved so he'd be able receive the funds from me later and he offered me a kick-back for doing it. As if I'd do that for him!" She shakes her head with disgust.

"Wow," I say. "And now they are going to assume you have the money and will come after you?"

Ermano nods. "The minute we heard he'd been assassinated gang style we knew we had to leave. It would be a matter of days or hours before they'd come for us."

"Can we do anything to help you?" Ramon asks.

"I don't think so, but we appreciate the offer. I have to say that seeing you with a good man, and making a life in California makes me so happy. It makes meeting here today in this crazy airport extra special."

"I feel the same," he replies. "I'm so happy I got to see both of you again and introduce you to Charlie."

I nod, and then glance at my watch and show it to Ramon. "We've got to go." I slide out of the booth and everyone moves to do the same. "Like Ramon said, please let us know if there is anything we can do for you." I pick up his painting and hold it so Ramon can say his good-byes.

"Thank you," Ermano says as he shakes my hand and hugs Ramon. Mirana hugs us both and holds onto Ramon extra long, and then strokes his cheek when they part.

"You are going to do big things, Ramon. I'm so proud of you."

"I love you," he whispers. "Thank you for always being such a good friend."

She kisses him on the cheek, and I wish them well one more time.

22. When Dreams Come True

DESPITE MY WEARINESS, AN INCREDIBLE sense of peace settles over me as we let ourselves into the courtyard at *Jardín del Paraíso*. Ramon has his backpack and the painting, and I have his duffle bag along with the take-out dinner that I called in on the Uber ride from LAX.

I also called Sasha with an update, and she encouraged me to stay with Ramon tonight and I agreed. It's not only that I'm working hard to support her desire for independence, I really need to be with him tonight. I still can't shake the feeling that I could have lost him if it weren't for our angel, Mirana, calling with barely enough time for me to get to the airport, and stop him from getting on that plane.

We're almost to the staircase when we run across Madame Fontanoy, in the dim light of dusk gathering some roses for what I assume is an arrangement.

"My darling boys!" she exclaims.

"Hi Madame," Ramon replies.

"I saw you stealing out in the early morning, Ramon, and now I see travel bags. Whatever were you up to?"

"It was a business trip that fell through, but Charlie came to rescue me, and we picked up dinner on the way back from the airport. And he promised to take care of me tonight so I'm all good."

She pats my cheek. "Such a good boyfriend."

"I try my best," I assure her.

"Well, from what I can see you are doing a marvelous job." She waves her hand toward the stairs. "Now get on up there and eat before it gets cold."

Ramon takes a hot shower while I transfer the take-out to real plates and open a bottle of wine and pour us both glasses. He looks worlds better when he walks up to me after his shower, in his sweat pants, white T-shirt, and wet hair and gives me a hug.

"Thank you," he murmurs against my neck.

"For what?"

He glances over at where I've set the table for us. "For this . . . for being here . . . for being mine."

I respond by kissing him. I've wanted to kiss him since kissing him at our gate in the airport, and that was hours ago.

"Screw dinner, let's go to bed," he teases.

"Dinner first!" I demand.

He settles into his seat and puts his napkin in his lap. "I like this bossy side of you. It's hot."

"Good, I like it, too."

We're pretty quiet as we eat. I think all the emotions and exhaustion have caught up with us. I'm about to refill our wine glasses when an idea strikes me.

"Hey, why don't we hang up your painting? I think it should be unwrapped anyway . . . she said something about the canvas needing to breathe."

"Great idea. I was thinking it would look good over the desk in the living room."

We head to the living room and pull the desk away from the wall. After Ramon carefully unwraps the painting, I hold it up and Ramon gives me directions until it's in the right spot, and then he marks the wall with a pencil.

I gingerly lay the painting face down on the desk to measure how high the wire is mounted to determine where the nail should be hammered into the wall, and then adjust the pencil marking. I glance down and notice a note written on the backing.

Remove protective paper so the canvas can breathe.

"He sure has a thing about his canvases breathing," I joke.

"Yeah, Ermano's kind of a particular guy."

"I forgot to ask if you have nails with those frame hangars to hang it with."

Ramon shrugs. "I think I do. Let me go look and I'll get the hammer."

"Meanwhile, I'll tackle this paper backing." I start picking at the tape securing it on all four sides. When I've got enough of the top right corner lifted, I pinch it between my fingers and slowly pull it away, the paper tearing, yet leaving a wide enough piece to give me a good start. I pull it down lower and my gaze travels up to see what should now be the back of the painting but it's anything but that. My entire body freezes as my brain furiously computes what's before me.

I gasp, and continue pulling away the paper but now at a frantic pace. "Ramon!" I yell. "Holy hell, Ramon!"

I hear his footsteps slap across the kitchen floor as he runs across it. He's got a hammer in one hand and jar of what looks like nails in the other. "What's wrong?" He looks completely freaked and I'm sure my frantic expression isn't helping.

My hand is clasped over my mouth, and I lower it. "Oh my God, come here." I hold my other hand out toward him.

He slowly approaches me as if he's almost scared to see what I've found. As his gaze sinks down I pull away another strip of the brown backing paper. His eyes open impossibly wide and his mouth drops open. "Wha—" He sucks in a breath. "Is that . . ."

I nod frantically, ripping away more paper. Stacked in neat piles, from one end of the canvas bars to the other, are more green bills than I've ever seen in my life in one place.

My first reaction is terror knowing who this money was connected to, but I remember that we've gotten this far dealing with his past, so for every problem there is a solution and we'll certainly figure this out. It's too damn amazing not to celebrate.

"Cash money," I whisper, watching him take it all in, his eyes studying each pile as if he's looking at a mirage. I pick up one stack and fan through it. "They're all one hundred dollar bills."

I realize he's shaking and the color is draining from his face, so I lead him to the couch and sit him down. Returning to the painting, I carefully extract the stacks of bills and every time my hands are full I deposit them on the coffee table in front of Ramon. He appears to be in shock.

"Charlie!" he exclaims, pointing to the growing pile. "I think it's all of the money Ernesto took from me."

"I know, baby. I know."

The tears start streaming down his face. "And Mirana . . ."

"She wanted you to have this enough that she was willing to risk her own safety. Wow," I say softly.

As a sob comes out of him, I join him on the couch and pull him into my arms before he really falls apart. His entire body is wracked with sobs and nothing could have ever shown me more clearly what that loss had meant to him.

Minutes later, when he finally calms enough to speak, he asks me, "Do you think Luis knows I got the money back?"

And for the first time I realize that I'm not irritated that Luis has come up in another one of our big moments. After all, I've learned that he had a big hand in the man Ramon turned out to be, so if anything I should be thanking him every chance I get.

"I do. I bet he even had something to do with it happening."

Ramon sits up tall and wipes his eyes. "You do?" His eyes are as bright as ever. "I've never told you this, Charlie, but I think he sent me you."

"I've thought the same about my parents and you," I reply.

He presses his wet cheek against my neck. "I want to believe that's true. I know for sure Luis would have really liked you, and I hope your parents would have liked me."

"They would have for sure. Hey, that reminds me; remember that time I drove you up to the observatory?"

"The time you kissed me for the first time. Sure, how could I forget it?"

"Well you brought up Luis in our conversation after we kissed, and I sent a message to him . . . I mean a virtual message."

He pulls away from me, smiling. "Really? What kind of virtual message?"

"I promised that if you gave me a chance, I'd be good for you."

Cupping my chin, he gives me a tender kiss. "You're so good for me," he whispers before he kisses me again and again.

Moments later we're wrapped up in the velvet cocoon of his couch, kissing and touching each other like we need to prove to ourselves that all of this is real. I have no idea of how much time has passed when Ramon sits up, all red-cheeked and swollen lips and pure joy reflected in his eyes.

"Hey, I have a really good bottle of champagne in the fridge that Gene gave me for Christmas. I've been saving it for something special. Why don't we open it and celebrate?"

"Lets!" I agree, feeling victorious. "While you get that, do you have something you'd like me to put the money in until you get a safety deposit box or something?"

He goes to the hall closet and pulls out a small suitcase made of fine leather. "How about this?"

"Perfect." I carefully move the stacks of bills into the luggage in an organized pattern. It's almost like I'm playing with Monopoly money because I can't get it in my head that this is real money. I shake my head. "What a crazy day," I mutter to myself.

As I finish loading up the stacks from the coffee table, and then the back of the canvas to the suitcase, I find a folded note tucked under one of the final stacks of hundred dollar bills.

Your inheritance returned . . .
Now the dreamer can make his dream come true.
~We love you, Ramon. Stay strong.

I hold the note up higher and read it again. I'm breathless as I realize how much the people in Ramon's life love him, and he freely gives that love back. Could I have ever imagined that I would meet a man like him under the strangest circumstances? From that first seductive dance that he performed for me, until now, we were magnets set far apart by our contrasting lives and world. However, a force kept pulling us together. Now we have joined with a determination so fierce, that we will forever resist being pulled apart.

Algorithms programed to understand human nature are meaningless on a night like tonight when magic is in the air lifting our love and hopes for the future higher than we could've dreamed.

Since the accident six years ago, I'd been living in a box, searching for answers in codes, and living within formula's solutions that were black and white . . . and then I met Ramon.

As we fell in love, what I found instead was a world of color in my lover's arms, and the knowledge that quite often the best things in life make no logical sense at all.

I look up from the note as Ramon returns with the bottle of Dom Perignon and two champagne flutes.

I hold the piece of paper out to him. "This was in with the money."

Setting everything down, he reads it, then takes a sharp breath and presses the small square of parchment paper up against his heart.

"Wow," he whispers.

I nod at him. It's all so incredible.

Ramon reads the note one more time and places it on his mantle. Then he carefully tears the foil off the champagne bottle and gracefully goes to work opening it. He only pauses for a moment to wipe off new tears before continuing on. After the iconic *pop*, he fills our glasses, then tops them off when the bubbles subside.

He lifts his glass toward me and I do the same.

"You know, Charlie, earlier today when we got on the plane to Vegas you told me to believe that something amazing could be right around the corner."

Grinning, I hold out my hands. "I know! Pretty damn impressive how spot on I was, right?"

He shakes his head and laughs. "And to think I could have spared myself all that agony if I'd know how psychic you actually are. But seriously . . . all those months ago when I met my 'Prince' Charlie, you were like royalty to me, and I was merely a dancer flattered by your attention."

I shake my head at how wrong he is portraying us. He was *my* prince and I was the awkward guy who had no idea how to ask for what I wanted, what I needed.

He holds his hand up, not wanting to hear my protests. "I felt like a loser after what had happened in Miami and that I didn't deserve brilliant you, but you showed me over and over that I mattered. The funny thing is that now that I have the money back and the club will be a reality, I realize none of that plays into your love for me. You love *me* Charlie, ME. I *am* a dreamer and you always believed in me and believed in my dreams. I'll love you forever for that."

"I do believe in you. You opened up my life to so much more than I could've imagined," I reply solemnly before raising my glass higher. "So here's to big dreams and amazing things around all our corners, but most of all to you, the man who saw something in me that fateful night, as you danced your way into my heart."

Epilogue. Ramon

THERE'S A ROAR OF LAUGHTER from his sister's bedroom, followed by a sharp squeal from Sasha, and Charlie sits up with a look of concern. "What are they doing in there?" he asks.

I shrug. "Laughing . . . having *fun*." I raise my eyebrows suggestively.

Charlie springs off the couch and walks over to her bedroom door. He pauses, and then knocks softly on it, but doesn't wait for a reply. Instead he opens the door and pushes it open wide. My last view from the living room is him with his fists pressed into his hips and a stern expression on his face.

I get off the couch and follow him since I don't want to miss whatever's going to happen.

I have to admit, for both of their sakes I was hoping we'd find Emmett and Sasha in a compromising position having every bit of sexy fun that they deserve. When Sasha privately asked me to order a book for her called *Love, Sex, and Disability*, because she was afraid Charlie would flip out if it was delivered to their condo, I knew things were headed a certain direction with Emmett. But I was also pretty sure they wouldn't be doing it at their place while Charlie was home. He's overly protective of Sasha, but I'm sure if it were my sister I'd be the same.

Once I've joined them I see I was right. Instead of a love fest, Sasha and my neighbor, Emmett, are hunched over her laptop watching what appears to be a video. Emmett is wearing some kind of special earphones for the hearing impaired.

"Sasha!" Charlie calls out louder. "What are you doing?"

She glances up at him with a wide-eyed stare and pulls off her ear buds. "We're watching our favorite YouTube channel. Why?"

Charlie appears embarrassed for barging in on a situation that certainly didn't need intervention. "I don't know . . . your laughing was a little hysterical."

Narrowing her eyes, she arches her brow. "Hysterical?"

He nods awkwardly. "Um yeah, that's what I thought. So which one is this one?"

"*Fun Haus.*"

"The one that makes fun of video games?"

She nods and glares at him, but then focuses back on the screen when Emmett nudges her and points to the screen with a grin. She pops her ear buds back in and leans into him.

I have to bite back my smile when Charlie gives me an alarmed look. I gesture for him to follow me out of the room, and when he's still watching over Sasha to make sure nothing is happening, I take his arm and pull him out.

"Come on, Dad," I say. "Let them have their privacy."

He grumbles, "I'm not sure I like him. Are you sure he's a good guy?"

"Yes, I'm sure. He's a gentleman and I've never seen or heard of him doing anything inappropriate. He's not a party guy, and he's the first person Madame Fontanoy goes to when she needs help with anything. So I really think you can chill out."

About thirty minutes later Emmett emerges from Sasha's room looking a little sheepish. He sits down on the couch, picks up a *Time* magazine on the coffee table, flips through it, and sets it down again to stare out the window.

Charlie studies him for a minute, and then glances at me with raised brows.

I shrug, and then turn to face Emmett. "Hey, Emmett, what's up?"

He looks over at me and shakes his head, which I've learned means he didn't hear me.

"What's up?" I ask more loudly as he watches my lips move.

"Sasha's fixing herself up for Madame's party, so she sent me out here."

"Cool," I say and then go back to watching the TV.

A couple of minutes later Sasha emerges from her room with her hair brushed and fresh lipstick on. Emmett smiles widely when he sees her. *Oh this is a thing all right.* I can't help but grin with delight. For once, my efforts as matchmaker have paid off.

Charlie springs off the couch and approaches the pair. "Are you sure you can drive the van?" he asks Emmett, remembering to raise his voice.

Sasha sighs. "Charlie, he's already driven it a bunch of times. He's got this."

He turns back to Emmett. "You sure?"

Emmett nods. "Yes, I am. And I did a run-through on the old elevator at the back of the apartment building and it works fine. So all's good getting Sasha up to Madame's floor."

I can tell he's about to say something else but Sasha tugs on his arm. "Okay, guys, we'll see you over there."

Taking the cue, they both hurry out of the condo before Charlie's weirdness shows its face again. I turn to him. "So is this what it's going to be like when we have kids one day?"

His eyes grow wide. "You want to have kids with me?"

"Sure!"

Smiling, he shakes his head. "I'll probably be even worse."

"So I'll be the cool, fun dad?" I tease.

"Undoubtedly."

AT *JARDÍN DEL PARAÍSO*, MADAME Fontanoy has parties often, some with obscure themes, some dinner parties, some vintage movie screenings, or *Sound of Music* sing-a-longs. The cast of characters attending always varies, but the one sure thing is that the party will be festive. Tonight's party is to celebrate that Charlie and I have signed the lease on our club.

It was fortuitous that several months earlier we discovered that our soon-to-be building landlord for the club was a softie. I knew that Gene owned several properties in downtown L.A., yet it didn't occur to me that he owned one that fit our needs and was also available. It all came to light when I asked his advice about a building we were looking at near Temple and Third, and he crooked his head and his eyes lit up.

"What?" I asked, recognizing his *I've got a great idea* look.

"One of my properties downtown is vacant, and I've been thinking about converting it into residential lofts. But if you guys are interested you could take the project on. It's pretty much a shell now."

The most intense feeling came over me. I suddenly felt hot and my heart was pounding. I realized that was the moment that I knew the stars had finally aligned for my destiny.

The next day Charlie and I joined Gene's business manager downtown, and by the time we left the space we were both excited.

"I think it's the place, don't you?" he asked me.

"I do!" I said, almost afraid to believe it.

Worried about my past connections, my smart boyfriend had already taken steps to protect us by creating an investment group that buried our names as owners of the business. He also got regular updates from the private investigator he hired to keep tabs on Marcus and his goons who were still in prison, and what generally was happening in Miami with the people still there who'd been involved with Fusion, which still remained boarded up.

Gene was generous with us, agreeing to great terms as long as we agreed to make certain improvements to the property. The added bonus was that he owned the parking lot across the street and so we were able to work out a deal with him for evening use.

"So if he owns all this property why is he working at Wild Nights?" Charlie asked me a few nights later.

"Because he loves being around all the cute guys," I replied, matter-of-factly. "He always says it's what keeps him young."

I think Gene and his touchy-feely ways used to make Charlie

uneasy, like he thought Gene had a thing for me, but hopefully he came to understand that it's simply Gene's way.

I DEBATED FOR A LONG time about making a call I'd thought about since I started picturing my nightclub. The week after finding the ideal space, I finally summoned the nerve and after a Google search I dialed Sorentino, Whitley, and Associates in Seattle, Washington.

The receptionist asked where she should direct the call.

"To Jason Sorentino please," I replied. My nerves spiked up as the memories of those days in Salt Lake City came flooding back to me.

"May I tell him who's calling?"

"I'm a friend from college, Ramon Diaz."

"Seriously?" Jason said when he took the call. "I can't believe it's you. How've you been, man?"

I was relieved to know he was glad to hear from me. "Really good, thanks. And look at you guys with your own firm!"

"Crazy, right?"

"The best kind of crazy! And that's Dean, right . . . Whitley? So he's your partner?"

"He is. In every way."

I could hear the smile in his voice. "Good for you . . . both of you."

"So what are you up to these days? Did you ever make it to Miami?"

"I did, and it was a wild and crazy time. But I'm in L.A. now."

"West Coast like us, cool! What type of work do you do?"

"Well, that's why I'm calling. My boyfriend and I are opening a nightclub and we want to do something really cutting edge, and I was wondering if this could be a project you'd be willing to design? We've found the location and have the money to get it off the ground."

"Sounds interesting. Dean and I have been considering opening an L.A. office due to all the film industry work we've been contracted for, and we're heading down there for some meetings next week. I'll look at our schedule and let's see if we can figure out a time to meet.

Do you have the space secured yet?"

"We just signed the lease."

"Excellent. I'll hook you up with my assistant and she'll get it on the calendar."

"Great. Hey, thanks, Jason."

"Don't even think about it. I owe you. I probably wouldn't be sitting here today with Dean if it weren't for your encouragement to accept who I was."

"Glad it all worked out," I replied. I marveled as I signed off to realize how far we've come from those confusing, stilted days in Salt Lake City. There was a period when I could've seen myself in a serious relationship with Jason, but time proved that it was never meant to be. I got a warm feeling thinking about Charlie and how he turned out to be the perfect guy for me.

LATER THAT NIGHT I FOUND my boyfriend hunched over his laptop, staring at his screen with laser focus. What I'd learned about Charlie is that when he had an idea it was best to get the hell out of the way as he made it happen. It's one of the traits that I've loved most about him.

A minute later he suddenly yelled out, "Score!"

"I thought you didn't play video games," I remarked drolly as I left the kitchen where I've discovered that he'd planned chicken parmesan for dinner. I wanted to find out what he was so excited about.

"No. This isn't a game. I found him, Ramon! I found him!"

I gave him a stern look. My man better not have been finding my replacement. "Found who?" I inquired.

"Kingsley! I found Kingsley!"

"No way!" I yelled out, rushing over to his side. "Madame's old bodyguard she told us about?"

"The one and only!" Charlie gave me a wide grin. "And he's up in Oregon. He retired there after working in New York protecting the rich and famous."

"And why exactly were you trying to find him?"

"Well it started out as curiosity. But then I wondered what it would be like for them to see each other now . . . all these years later."

"Can you tell if he's married or single?"

"Well according to a news posting I dug up, his wife's memorial was about two years ago. It doesn't say what she passed from, but records show he stayed in Oregon. I see no records that he remarried."

"This is a little risky," I warned him. "Didn't she say it's been over thirty years since she saw or talked to him?"

Charlie pushed back his desk chair and swiveled toward me. "So where is your sense of romance? What if they saw each other again, now with no encumbrances, and they instantly fell madly in love?"

Reaching down, I picked up his glass and sniffed the clear liquid. "What have you been drinking?" I teased.

"Water!" he exclaimed. "Besides, you know as well as I do that Gabriella is always surrounded by those pretty young boys, but what she needs is a mature man to be her equal—a true partner who is solid and true. I think this could be the guy. Why don't we invite him to the party she's throwing us?"

"But he lives in Oregon, and what if she doesn't want a new relationship?"

He shrugged. "Everyone wants one, whether they admit it or not. And as for Oregon, that's what moving trucks are for. After all, he moved away once because he was in love with her and couldn't have her, maybe he can move back now that he can."

Walking over to him, I pulled him out of his chair and into my arms. *This man.* He was an analytic programmer with a brilliant mind, and a closet romantic with a big heart. Besides, the new cologne I bought him made him smell good enough to eat. My mind started wandering as to all the things I felt like doing to him instead of eating dinner. But then I remembered something I needed to tell him.

When I let him sit back down I nervously cleared my throat. "Hey, don't get mad at me, but I did an impetuous business move today."

He arched his brow. "And what was that?"

"I called my college crush, Jason, and asked if he and his boyfriend could work on our club space."

He scowled. "I don't like the sound of you working with your college crush. I wish you'd given me a heads up. You know my jealous tendencies."

Placing my hands on his tight shoulders, I started to rub them. "He's of no interest to me in that regard anymore—hasn't been for years, but their work is amazing and it's the kind of feel we've been talking about." I pointed at the screen of his computer. "Here, bring up their website *SorentinoWhitleyandAssoc.com.*"

Opening the website, he went to the gallery section of the page to look at their designs and photos of their finished projects. He silently clicked through each image, and I was feeling like I'd climb a wall if he didn't speak up soon.

"Well?" I finally asked.

He shrugged. "I guess they're okay," he murmured.

"What? Did you see how many design awards they've won?"

The corners of his mouth inched up as he turned toward me. "Okay, they're talented. Watch yourself around Jason if you don't want trouble from me."

"Deal."

I was happy his reaction was reasonable, so to reward him I teasingly ran my fingers along his jawline, down his chest, and then up his thighs.

"Besides, I don't want trouble, baby, I just want you."

He glanced at my fingers as I slid them back down his tense thighs. His lips were pursed, but I noticed the tops of his ears were turning red. I was getting to him—I knew it. Stepping back, I slowly pulled my T-shirt off, and once it dropped to the floor, I rubbed my hand across my chest. He swallowed hard, his gaze moving down as I spread my legs wider, then pulled on his arm rests until his chair slid between my legs.

"Are you going to dance for me?" he asked with a scorching fire reflected in his eyes.

"Maybe. Would you like me to?"

He nodded wordlessly.

Taking the handles, I pulled the chair closer, close enough so I was straddling him. I took his hands and placed them on my ass before I began rolling my hips.

He leaned his face into my crotch and moaned. "Damn, what you do to me."

"I make you feel good?" I whispered as I reached down and stroked him.

"So good," he replied, closing his eyes tightly as I wrapped my fingers around his hard shaft.

A moment later he was focused completely on the thick outline in my jeans. I lifted his chin up to face me. "I'm thinking about a hot shower before dinner. Care to join me?"

"Will we get dirty before we get clean?"

I rolled my hips and then settled myself over his hard-on. "Oh, baby. Can't you picture me in the shower on my knees in front of you . . . the water washing over us as I get you off?"

His cock pulsed against me in response. "Holy hell," he said as he lifted my hips off him and stood up. "Go on now . . . lead the way."

LESS THAN A WEEK LATER, we picked up Jason and Dean from the Chateau Marmont hotel where they were staying, and drove them downtown to see the future home of our club we'd decided to call Freedom.

When Charlie and I approached the two men as they walked out of the hotel, I was stunned to see how much more confident Jason appeared, and that he wore it well. Dean, on the other hand, was striking as always, and although he didn't exactly give off a gay vibe, anyone would be able to tell that he and Jason were closely connected. I could feel the electricity passing between them.

Hugging Jason, I made introductions, and I got the impression that Charlie wasn't the kind of guy they expected to see me with. That made me happy. Charlie, in his nice slacks, tailored shirt, and sharp glasses looked like someone to be taken seriously.

As we approached the car, Charlie joined Dean in the backseat and Jason sat with me in front, and by the time I drove up the Hollywood Freeway onramp toward downtown, I realized we'd been having completely separate conversations. In the backseat, Charlie, who had sent our building specs and the photos we had ahead of time, asked Dean a lot of questions about new construction versus renovation of an old building like ours, and Dean was completely engaged by Charlie's smart questions.

Meanwhile, Jason and I exchanged stories about leaving Salt Lake and how we were both happy that we'd ended up exactly where we wanted to be.

"How'd you meet Charlie?" he asked.

"In the club I'd been working at. We connected right away." I smiled to myself thinking about the first time I danced for Charlie. Of course I wasn't going to share that with Jason.

"What's it like working with your boyfriend?" I asked, explaining that Charlie would eventually be running the club with me. He didn't want to quit his job until we were ready to open.

"I like working with Dean," Jason said with a satisfied expression. "Don't get me wrong, there are times we really get on each other's nerves, but overall we love our business, we push hard to do our best, and we've figured out that we both have different strengths which made it work."

"I think Charlie and I will be like that. Our strengths are different, too."

Jason looked over his shoulder and noticed how intense Dean and Charlie's conversation had become and he turned back to me and nodded. "He seems like a really smart guy, Ramon. Is he good to you?"

"So good to me," I responded with a contented smile.

Jason sighed. "I'm glad. You deserve that."

SO HERE WE ARE THREE weeks later, with Charlie smoothing out my jacket lapels before we leave for our party. He steps back and gives me a once over.

"You're so handsome," he says in a straightforward way, like he's reciting an absolute fact.

"Thank you. Do you like my new suit?"

He narrows his eyes at me. "Your pants are too tight."

"But that's the style now. And look . . ." I turn and lift the back of my jacket up. "Doesn't my ass look great?"

"Too great," he replies with a scowl. "I know our meeting with Dean and Jason went well, but did you really have to invite them tonight and then wear tight pants?"

"Ah, so that's why my tight pants bother you? You know, I think yours are too loose. Besides, the guys are going to be living in L.A. part time. They need to start making friends."

"You are so damn nice." Charlie glances down at his watch. "Hey, we better go. We have to go get Kingsley at the hotel before we pick them up."

It didn't take much for Charlie to convince Kingsley to fly to L.A. to be reunited, at least for one evening, with the woman he'd at one time protected. We booked him a room at the Andaz hotel on Sunset Boulevard, and I think he's relieved when he sees us pull up and immediately recognizes that we're respectable people.

Charlie notices him first, and waves as we walk toward him. Wearing a tailored dark gray suit, handsome Kingsley is tall and fit, despite being in his late fifties or so. He has a thick head of silver hair and striking blue eyes.

"I hope you're right about this," Kingsley says after introductions, and settling into the backseat. "Gabriella was never one for surprises."

"When was the last time you saw her?" I ask.

"Thirty years ago," he states quietly, and then turns to gaze out the window. He looks deep in thought like he's remembering the last time he saw her.

"She told us about you. She held you in such high regard."

He sighs. "She was a magnificent woman. Absolutely one of a

kind."

Charlie glances over at me with raised brows, and a grin, before directing his gaze back at Kingsley. "She still is," he responds.

He runs his fingers through his silver hair. "How much longer until we get to her place?"

"We're picking up our two friends on the way and then it will be less than fifteen minutes," I assure him.

He takes a deep breath, rolls his shoulders back, and nods stoically.

Dean and Jason are waiting in the driveway at the Chateau Marmont when we pull up, so they jump in the backseat with Kingsley. There's some idle talk on the way, Dean explaining to Kingsley that they're from Seattle but have decided to live in L.A. part time. Dean mentions that they've already located an office space in a co-op that will work for them for now. They fall quiet after a few minutes. This is a car full of men with a lot on their minds.

It's the magic hour when we pass through the grand gate at the entrance to *Jardín del Paraíso,* with the last of daylight casting dusky purple shadows. We look up to see that twinkle lights have been wrapped around the wrought iron railings and potted trees and bushes on Madame's wide veranda. I spot a few of the other tenants holding cocktails under the soft light before the sun sinks down for the night.

Considering that Dean and Jason are modernists, I get a kick out of their reaction to the building.

"It's fantastic . . . yes?" Jason says to Dean, gesturing toward the quaint balconies and tile details.

Dean nods. "Classic, vintage California—so charming."

I turn toward them. "So speaking of vintage . . . you're staying at the Chateau Marmont and you like this place, yet your style is the opposite."

"True," says Jason, "but it's great to have a change once in a while. It keeps everything fresh. As it is, everything about L.A. has a modern vibe, even if it isn't new."

We ascend the stairs and I glance over at Kingsley to make sure he's still good with this. His determined look tells me that he's all in, and my heart beats hard in anticipation of their reunion. I hope to hell it was the right thing for us to do.

When we get to the top level, Charlie turns to Kingsley. "Let's wait a minute while Ramon takes Dean and Jason in first and then we'll follow. Okay?"

He nods and steps into the shadow of the stairwell.

Leading Dean and Jason into Madame's suite, I watch their eyes grow wide. It's a lot to take in with the Mediterranean-inspired splendor of arches and alcoves smoothed over with warm-toned stucco, sparkling Murano chandeliers, hand-painted beams crossing the high ceiling, and rich silks and velvets covering every surface. The seductive beauty of it all is not lost on them.

Gabriella glides over to us, her lithe arms opening wide. She's wearing a dark red dress that flutters around her as she moves. An elaborate ruby necklace curls around her pale, swan-like neck.

She gives me a coy wink. "Darling, you didn't mention that your guests were so stunningly handsome! You must introduce us immediately."

"Madame Fontanoy, these are my friends, Jason Sorentino and Dean Whitley. As I mentioned earlier, they are the architects I went to school with, and they're going to design the club."

"Yes, how absolutely fabulous!" she exclaims as she shakes each of their hands. "Please make yourself at home." She gestures toward the bar set-up. "Marcello makes a mean martini, and the buffet is being set up in the dining room with tables on the patio. I hope you're hungry."

Knowing our plan, they thank Madame, nod, and move toward the bar, while I loop my arm through hers. "Come on, I have someone special I want to you to meet."

"All right, but where's Charlie?"

"You'll see." I pull her forward and linger in the entryway until I see Charlie round the corner with Kingsley. I wait one more long second and then pull her forward.

"Madame, look who we found."

When her eyes lock with Kingsley's she sways and gasps, and I tighten my arm around her waist to steady her. They both stand frozen in place, taking each other in.

Watching Kingsley's gaze soften, I can tell that everything we arranged to make this moment happen was worth it.

Madame places her trembling hand over her heart. "Kingsley, I can't believe it," she whispers. "Is that really you?"

"It is." He takes a step closer. "Gabriella. How can it be? You're even more beautiful now." He shakes his head. "And I thought I'd never see you again."

They gaze at each other silently for a long moment as if unspoken words are passing between them.

"Always my knight in shining armor," she finally whispers, and when I glance up at her I see a tear work its way down her face.

Stepping closer to her, he pulls a handkerchief out of his breast pocket and gently dabs her cheeks. "Please don't cry, Duchess. This is no time to be sad."

She turns to me. "How did you find this glorious man? I tried once several years ago."

I notice Kingsley blink at the revelation, but he stays calm. He projects inner strength and the assurance of protection. There's no question in my mind that he made a great bodyguard.

"It was Charlie, Madame. As you know, he has amazing computer skills."

She turns toward Charlie. "When you found him, did you tell him everything we talked about?"

I glance over at him, remembering that she had disclosed that this was the only man who had ever tempted her heart while she was married.

"No, Gabriella. We didn't."

I can feel her relax, as she leans into me.

She nods at him, gratitude in her expression, before focusing back on Kingsley. "Well thank you, boys, this is most extraordinary."

I can sense she's recovered from the shock and her natural charm sparks up again as she looks up at this handsome man from her past.

"And as for you, Kingsley, will you stay by my side tonight? Now that you're here I want to share every moment with you. We have a lot to catch up on."

He bows his head. "It will be my honor, Gabriella. I'll be by your side as long as you need me."

Her smile is radiant as she looks up at him. "No, dear man, as long as I *want* you, and I suspect that could very well be forever."

He takes her hand in his, and lifts it for a gentle kiss.

"Then forever it is."

Grabbing Charlie, I pull him inside and toward the hallway leading to the dining room and kitchen. "Oh my God. That was epic!"

He appears to be very pleased. "Even better than I'd hoped!"

"I've got to hand it to you. That was the best idea ever. I've never seen her so happy."

"I've been nervous, and now I can relax. Come on, let's grab a drink and find Sasha and Emmett."

We find them at the far end of the veranda trying to sign to each other. Charlie told me that they've been learning ASL together. Sasha laughs at something Emmett signs to her before he leans over and gives her a kiss.

I've never seen him so happy, and Sasha too. The sight of them renews my faith that when all seems lost, there is always a reason to hope.

Our colorful neighbors add to the festive feeling. Francisco, one of the performers in a traveling tour of *Les Miserables,* and who lives on the first floor, is having an animated conversation with Rosalie, a dress designer with a small boutique on Larchmont. They've also been joined by Carly, the actress who lives two doors down from me. The indie film she was set to star in lost its funding, so she's explaining to them her new obsession to find an elusive screenwriter who wrote the part she is sure is her destiny.

At the next table Jason and Dean are having an animated conversation with Nicolas, the older, genteel gentleman on the first floor who owns an eclectic antique store in Los Feliz. He's lived in this building, which had been owned by Madame's husband, Clarence, for many years, and surely has stories to tell.

I'm so happy that Charlie has embraced us working with Jason and Dean on our club. Earlier in the day we joined them in a phone conference with Gene. We were very engaged as they talked about what's important in a club design. My dream for a club is now Charlie's dream, too, and together with our friend's help, we will create something amazing.

I take a deep breath as I notice the moon rising over the terracotta tiles of the roof. The jazz quartet is back from their break and the fine sounds of Charlie Parker are seductive in the evening air. This is a night of magic, of dreams coming true. The warm breeze makes the trees sway and the vines flutter, scattering fuchsia bougainvillea petals everywhere. Everything around us is rendered in silvers and gold from the glowing shine of the lanterns and twinkle lights, to the silver sparkle of the moon. There's an intoxicating feeling in the air of love, hope, and bright new beginnings and I'm drunk with it.

I'm thirsty from all the excitement and I head off to the bar. When I return with two glasses of water I set them down on the table we'd been sitting at, and scan the terrace to find Charlie. Our gazes meet, and he holds his arms open to beckon me. Smiling, I start to walk his way.

When I'm a step away, my beautiful man says, "Dance with me," as he pulls me into his arms. They've just started playing Louis Armstrong's "What a Wonderful World" and we sway together as it occurs to me that dancing is what brought us together, and each time we've danced since brings us closer.

Charlie is my present and my future, and I know without a doubt he was meant to be my destiny. It's amazing to think that if he hadn't been pushed by his co-workers to join them at the club that fated night, none of this would be happening. He is my everything now, and I will spend my days and nights making sure he knows it.

They say home is where the heart is, and I feel the love and support all around me from these friends who've become my second family. My past is now far behind me, and I feel the promise for our happiness in the warmth and love reflected in Charlie's soulful eyes.

We had to find our way, and it's been a long journey to get here, but we're finally home.

Acknowledgements

MY ALEX, MY #1 GIRL . . . thank you for being an awesome daughter. You've encouraged me every step of the way, and your support means everything to me.

To my dear friends who held my hand through my journey with Encore:

Erika, our word-count daily challenges brought a special energy to this book, and your continual unwavering encouragement has been an inspiration going all the way back to my very first fan-fic. Thank you, my wonderful friend.

Jenn, my spitfire partner in crime . . . just being part of your team of authors is an honor for me because I respect you so much. But being your close friend and part of your life is an extraordinary gift. Yes Missy, you are all that!

Flavia, I had no idea that our unlikely meeting all those years ago in Vegas would bring us here. Your belief in me as a writer, and the integrity and kindness in how you conduct your business and your relationships makes you one of the most extraordinary cherished friends of my life.

Kellie, your kindness and loving friendship is a bright light in my life. You've helped me endlessly with your smart book business skills, and made every trip and event we've ventured out on together so much fun.

And much love to early readers and encouragers for Encore: Glorya, Azu and Lisa. To Elli Reid, for her amazing, eagle eye and artful imagery, and Marla Esposito for the final, meticulous polish. Thank you, dear friends from the bottom of my heart.

I love our community of indie bloggers, authors, promoters, designers and readers, and I'm so grateful for your support of my work.

Thank you to my wonderful content editor, Angela Borda. You do a brilliant job keeping me on track, and Encore is better thanks to your thoughtful edits and suggestions.

I mentioned Jenn Watson, from Social Butterfly PR, above. But again I must thank her and her awesome team. What a smart and savvy, hard-working group of ladies that keep things classy and set a high standard for our market. Thank you for all your hard work.

Many thanks to lovely Melissa, of There For You Editing, for being such a pro and easy to work with . . . and to the delightful Christine Borgford of Type A Formatting for making my books look great.

Finally many thanks to you, dear readers. You inspire me, and make me want to always do my best. Whether this is your first MM romance, or you've followed me from the beginning of my journey, I'm so grateful to have your support in this wild and wonderful ro-mance family.

Much love to you all . . . xoxo Ruthy

Also by
RUTH CLAMPETT

Unforgiven
Burn~L.A. Untamed Series Book 2
Wet~L.A. Untamed Series Book 1
Animate Me
Mr. 365

Work of Art~Book 1 The Inspiration
Work of Art~Book 2 The Unveiling
Work of Art~Book 3 The Masterpiece
Work of Art~The Collection

Many thanks to those of you that
take a moment to leave a review
~ it's much appreciated.

About the Author

RUTH CLAMPETT IS A 21ST century woman aspiring to be Wonder Woman . . . now if she could only find her cape and magic lasso. Meanwhile she's juggling motherhood, a full-time job running her own fine art publishing business for Warner Bros., and writing romance late at night. Travel is her second obsession after writing, and it's enabled her to meet reader and writer friends all over the world. She's happily frazzled, and wouldn't change a thing about her crazy life.

The rooms in her home are all painted different colors and her books are equally varied, infusing humor, drama, and passion into the romantic lives of strong heroines and heroes and their worthy and determined counterparts.

Ruth has published eight books: *Animate Me, Mr. 365,* the *Work of Art Trilogy, WET, BURN* and *Unforgiven.* Three of her novels have been translated in German, French and Portuguese. She grew up and still happily resides in Los Angeles, and is heavily supervised by her teenage daughter, lovingly referred to as Snarky, who loves traveling with her mom with a sketchbook in hand.

Connect with Ruth

For book stuff:
https://www.facebook.com/RuthClampettWrites

For a more general stuff:
https://www.facebook.com/RuthClampett
http://instagram.com/Ruth_Clampett
https://twitter.com/RuthyWrites

Printed in Great Britain
by Amazon